THE DREAM

By Edith Williams

Edith Williams

Copyright © 2022 by Edith Williams

All rights reserved.

No part of this book may be reproduced or transmitted in any form or by any means, electronic or mechanical, including photocopying, recording, or by any information storage and retrieval system without the written permission of the author, except for the use of brief quotations in a book review. For permission requests, write to the author at edithwilliamswriting@gmail.com with the subject line: Attention: Permissions Coordinator

This book is a work of fiction. Names of characters, places, and incidents are either products of the author's imagination or are used fictitiously. Any resemblance to actual persons, dead or living, events, or locales is entirely coincidental.

Cover Designer: Barbara Groves

Beta Readers: Tammy Freeman, Misty Dawn, Allie Barley

First printing 2023

edithwilliamswriting@gmail.com

ISBN: 979-8-9874687-1-5

Table of Contents

Chapter 1 1
Chapter 2 9
Chapter 3 23
Chapter 4 35
Chapter 5 43
Chapter 6 57
Chapter 7 77
Chapter 8 97
Chapter 9 113
Chapter 10 131
Chapter 11 147
Chapter 12 167
Chapter 13 183
Chapter 14 201

CHAPTER 1

Walking up the steps to her apartment, Laurel felt Henry's hand slide from her side to cup her butt. She slipped the keys into the door handle as he moved behind her, brushed her hair to the side, and kissed her neck.

"Henry, it's late and we have to work tomorrow."

He nibbled her ear. "I know, sweetheart, but I can't get enough of you. Invite me in. We'll sleep so much better if we're satisfied."

Pushing open the door, she led the way to her bedroom. He locked the door behind him, and she felt his bulge, already hard, press against her as his hand slipped into the front of her pants and through her panties, massaging her clit slowly while he grinded her from behind.

She moaned and let her head fall back to rest on his shoulder. When she was dripping wet, he removed his hand and twisted her around. She lifted her arms as he pulled her shirt off, pausing his passionate kiss when he slipped it off her head.

"God, Laurel, you're so beautiful. I want you so badly." He kissed down her neck, gently sucking each nipple before kneeling as he made his way down her abdomen, unbuttoning her pants and pulling them off with ease. He firmly pushed her onto the bed and began to kiss her thighs, pushing them apart so he could admire her pussy before delving in. He licked and sucked on her clit until she couldn't stand it anymore and climaxed, her legs shaking.

When he was sure she was finished, Henry stood and unbuttoned his pants, letting them drop to the floor as he stood in front of her with his long rod waiting for attention. Laurel took him in her mouth as her hand worked the base of his cock. He grabbed her hair with a groan and pressed himself deeply into her mouth before slowly pulling out and sliding back in, touching the back of her throat. The sounds that came from him turned her on immensely.

"I want you, Laurel," he said huskily. "I want to be inside you."

She licked the precum from the tip of his cock as she pulled away from him. Standing, she pushed him down to the bed and straddled him, slowly easing herself onto his cock. Riding him with intensity, the sound of their skin slapped against each other, and their labored breathing filled the room until they both climaxed and slumped into each other, sweaty and exhausted.

"That was amazing," Henry said softly. "I've always enjoyed being with you, but this last month has been extraordinary. Not that I'm complaining but what's gotten into you?"

She rolled over and stared up at the ceiling for a moment before answering. "I'm not sure."

Laurel had felt the change as well but couldn't explain it. She'd always enjoyed being with him. Henry was an attentive lover. But the past few weeks had been more intense, more driven than before, as if she were trying to fill a space deep within her. And though the sex had been amazing, she still felt something was missing when he got dressed, kissed her on the forehead, and headed back to his condo for the night.

She maneuvers her way through the busy street, barely noticing the faces of the people who brush against her shoulders. It feels like she is moving more slowly than everyone else. She knows that it is in anticipation of someone important. She senses that she is waiting for someone to find her, but it doesn't make any sense to her. Suddenly, her heartbeat quickens. She is standing still, and the bustling crowd eases, almost seeming to move in slow motion. Their figures are blurry and though she struggles to study the faces walking past her, there is nothing perceptible. Her eyes scan the sidewalk, searching for someone, searching for him. Finally, she sees him. He is about thirty feet from her. She cannot clearly distinguish his features, but she knows he is the object of her anticipation. Closer and closer he walks, straight towards her. His profile sharpens as the distance between them lessens. She notices his towering frame, taller than everyone else in the crowd. He has a strong build and broad chest. She is sure that no one has worn a suit as well as this man. Though she still cannot clearly see his face, she knows he is looking at her and purposely seeking her out. It is as if he senses her as well. She stands still, waiting for him as he quickens his pace to her. He is close to her now, slowing. She feels her core tighten and heat up. As he comes to a stop in front of her, she studies his strong jaw, his high cheekbones, and his slightly pouty lips. She breathes in his earthy scent and knows that regular air will never be as satisfying as this. Meeting his eyes, she is lost in a forest of deep green. They seem to know every part of her soul, and she feels herself ache for him. He leans in...

Laurel awoke with a start, sighing in frustration. This is where the dream always ended. Rolling over, she saw the clock and groaned. She must have turned off her alarm while she was dreaming. If she hurried, she could still get to work on time. She'd have to skip makeup today, but it was more important that she be punctual. She had taken the job at the consulting firm when she graduated college with her business degree and had hoped to have made more headway in her career than she had. She was still an administrative assistant, although she'd gotten somewhat of a promotion when one of the big wigs requested her in his department. Still, this was not what she dreamed of when she was in college. It had been the riskiest and most frightening thing she had ever done when she left the comfort and familiarity of her Aunt Lucy's cabin in the woods of Oregon and headed to school in California.

She'd lived with her aunt since she was thirteen, after her parents died in a car accident. Lucy was single and lived about 30 minutes from town. She enjoyed being alone in the woods. "Forest therapy," she called it. But she had welcomed Laurel, loved her, drove her to and from school each day, and never gave Laurel any indication that she wished it were different. Although the loss of her parents never left her,

Lucy taught her how to be content while working through her grief. She also taught Laurel the importance of being able to take care of herself, of taking time to be quiet with Mother Nature, and being accepting of change. She was incredibly grateful to her aunt, which made it even more difficult when she headed off to college a month after her high school graduation.

When she arrived in her new town, the first thing she did was get a job at a local restaurant and find an apartment. On a campus bulletin board, she found a handwritten advertisement on bright pink paper that read, "Looking for a cool and trustworthy WOMAN to share a space with. Must be okay with clutter and loud laughter." And that was how she met Susanna Roberts, or Susu as Laurel called her. They were fast friends and had remained so even after college when Susu moved to New York with Laurel. Susu's parents had divorced when she was young, and she wasn't particularly close to them. Her degree in Philosophy didn't land her any job opportunities so she had moved to NYC with Laurel, saying that she could work at a coffee shop there just as easily as she could in California. Laurel was incredibly relieved. An introvert by nature, she valued the relationships she had and was glad for a friend in the new city. She and Susu had become even closer since making the move to New York, and though their schedules were often conflicting, they spent time together every chance they got.

Laurel pulled on a light blue sweater, zipped up her gray knee-length pencil skirt, and stepped into her favorite nude heels. As she combed her long, wavy hair, she studied herself for a moment. She had been spending a lot of time indoors over the past few years and her freckles had lightened from her years in Oregon and California. She was thankful for her good complexion as she pulled her hair into a low ponytail and grabbed her messenger bag on the way out. She'd never thought too much about her appearance. She chose timeless clothing, easy hairstyles, and wore minimal makeup. A trim, 5'7" frame made buying clothes easy. Her red hair reminded her of her mother, and her brown eyes were precisely the shade of her father's. Although she knew her body and features weren't perfect, she never struggled to make

The Dream

peace with her appearance like other girls she knew. The death of her parents had helped give these things their proper place of importance in her mind.

As she joined the throng of New Yorkers making their way to work, she thought of Henry. They had a standing lunch date on Mondays since that was generally a late work night for him. She'd met him shortly after moving to New York when he accidentally interrupted her interview and then waited by the elevators for her. He was intelligent, confident, and charming. He introduced her to the city, to all the good spots to eat and drink, and where to enjoy a show. She'd found the quiet spaces in the city herself. Those places didn't fit Henry. He was a mover and a shaker and enjoyed being around people and activity.

They had been together for almost three years, and he'd begun hinting they should move in together, but she wasn't ready. Even though she deeply cared for Henry, there was a hesitation in her when it came to taking the next step. Henry was a gentleman, but she often felt like he wasn't listening when she spoke. He was quick to dismiss her frustration that she hadn't progressed beyond a glorified secretary, even though her degree and skills showed she had the competence for a higher-level job. She watched men with similar backgrounds and less time at the corporation advance ahead of her and yet Henry never understood her feeling slighted, saying that "everyone has to climb the ladder."

His suggestions that they take the next step in their relationship were getting more insistent. She sighed as she remembered their conversation the prior weekend when Henry had asked her what was holding her back from moving in. She couldn't give him a satisfactory answer. She just knew she wasn't ready. And then there was the dream that had begun the previous month. Just twice the first week, then three or four times the following weeks. This last week, it had been nightly. She was too practical to put much stock in the meaning of dreams, but its unabating nature began to make her doubt the frivolousness of it. She shook herself free of her thoughts as she came to her office building, a plain 10-story building with two sets of revolving doors, surrounded by other office spaces, all heavily trafficked with individuals orderly filing in to go to work. It was an efficient city. She had always appreciated the way so many people lived in such a relatively small area with so little difficulty.

A familiar feeling rushed over her as a slight opening in the crowd widened. Everything around her slowed down as she anxiously searched for the source of her erratic heartbeat. And then she saw him, the blurry edges of his silhouette sharpening as he came closer. She could feel his eyes on her. Though she couldn't yet make out the features of his face, she knew him. She'd seen him so many times over the past month. She felt unable to move even if she wanted to. And she didn't want to. He was closer now, her brown eyes locked with his dark green ones, an intensity between them that she didn't understand but didn't want to end.

"Laurel? Earth to Laurel?" She felt a hand tighten around her waist and saw a flicker of anger in the forest green eyes before she tore herself away from their gaze, finding Henry beside her. "Are you alright? You look like you've seen a ghost, sweetheart."

She took a deep breath to ground herself. "I'm okay. I guess I'm still tired. I slept in this morning and had to rush to get here on time." She scanned the crowded street as she answered but couldn't find her dream man. She would have noticed him if he were still out here; he was taller than everyone else on the street. She sighed as she stopped looking. Had she imagined him? Was she that tired?

Again, Henry brought her back to reality. "Well, I'll have my secretary bring you over a latte to help perk you up," he said as his lips brushed her forehead.

"No thanks, Henry. I appreciate the thought, but it wouldn't be right for your administrative assistant to bring someone else's administrative assistant a latte." She laughed softly when he responded with a bewildered shrug.

Laurel threw a backwards glance at the busy street as she and Henry stepped into the building but saw no indication that the man from her dream had been real. Henry leaned in to murmur, "I had fun last night. We could have even more fun if you moved in with me." Laurel started to respond but the elevator doors opened, and Henry whispered, "We'll talk later."

The Dream

Laurel got off the elevator before Henry and was immediately met by her boss, Jim Thatcher. He was around the age when men started questioning the meaningfulness of life. Jim was a couple of inches shorter than Laurel, with a soft belly, thinning hair, and a defined line between his eyebrows that clearly showed a history of stress. He had indeed begun to question whether he was proud of his life, where his decisions had brought him- his nice but boring wife, his smart but lazy children…yet he refused to spend much time pondering it, continually bringing himself back to his career- the only thing he felt he had succeeded at. He knew the meaning of life must be found here in the office. So, when Laurel showed up five minutes late on the day of an important meeting with a potential client, he wondered why others couldn't take their careers as seriously as he did.

"Where have you been, Laurel? We have that meeting with Beau Industries today. Do you have copies of the property specs for them?" Jim's face was slightly red, and Laurel tried not to smile at his overreaction.

"Yes, Jim. I have everything prepared. The conference room will be ready by the 10 o'clock meeting, I assure you."

After her first year at the company, she'd got a promotion to Jim's Administrative Assistant. Her previous boss, Harry Levine, was sorry to lose her. They'd had a good working relationship, and it had taken Laurel a few months with Jim to figure out that things in his office would be different. She had stopped apologizing to him even when she was in the wrong, because she noticed that when she took blame, Jim was more condescending. It was in her nature to own up to her mistakes, but that only worked with people who respected you. In Jim's office, where she was treated like a secretary of the 1950's, fetching food and drink orders and choosing gifts for her boss' family- remorseful language made you appear weak. Now, she would only offer a solution to his complaint or assure him that things were taken care of.

By 9:30 that morning, everything was arranged. Coffee and pastries were on a table in the corner, the slide show was ready for the presentation, and booklets with all the necessary information placed in front of each chair at the large conference table. She sat in a chair by the refreshment table with her laptop, where she could take notes and write down any questions that Beau Industries had during the meeting. At first, she hadn't joined the meetings, but she quickly realized that a lot of things were falling through the cracks. Jim would forget to tell her things that needed to be done and then be angry when she didn't do them. She now sat in on the meetings, which ensured that all requests by clients were taken care of.

As she sipped her coffee, her stomach growled. It wasn't even ten o'clock, and she was ready for her lunch date with Henry. She wondered where he'd take her. They had a few regular places, all a quick walk from the office. She knew from break room gossip that Henry was popular with the ladies in the office. And why wouldn't he be? He was handsome, charming, always a gentleman, and a hard worker. Unlike Jim, he managed his own workload, and his department was well-run. Henry was already considered successful and was bound to continue all the way to the top.

However, following in his father's footsteps, where he was sure to be successful, hadn't made him humble. She felt that he didn't understand how difficult it could be for others- of different genders, races, and backgrounds- to have the same success that he enjoyed. It wasn't the reason she didn't want to move in with him, but it did bother her. Certainly, Henry was always encouraging her that she was too smart not to succeed, but she wasn't sure of the sincerity of the words. Her inability to completely trust him when he spoke caused a hesitation in her, and she found that she didn't share her thoughts with him as freely as she should.

CHAPTER 2

The opening of the door interrupted Laurel's thoughts of Henry, and she looked up to find an incredible set of dark green eyes locked onto her. *What was he doing here?* She had been content to imagine that her vision of him on the street had been just that- a vision- stemming from her lack of sleep and encouraged by the nightly dreams. But here he was in the flesh, standing in the conference room. Her heart began to race, and she took a deep breath to calm herself. *What is wrong with you, Laurel? Pull it together!* He had moved completely into the room, not taking his eyes off her.

She noticed that there was another man with him. He was also uncommonly tall, sturdily built, and intensely handsome. His eyes were so unusual- a yellowish brown. She would never have thought that yellow eyes would be beautiful, but here he was proving her wrong. Her eyes lingered on him for a moment too long as she contemplated the odds of two incredibly good-looking, impossibly strong men happening to work together. *They must use the same tailor. They're impeccably dressed.* She thought she heard a low growl and broke her stare, blushing. She hoped that wasn't her stomach! Green-eyes was still boring a hole into her soul, while his associate had a disarming grin on his face.

"I apologize. You caught me off guard," she said as she closed the distance between them and held out her hand. "Laurel Davis, pleased to meet you."

His associate took her hand and gave it a warm squeeze. "Matthias Hart. And this is my boss, Shepherd Ryan."

Laurel struggled to move her eyes and her hand towards Shepherd. Knowing that she dreamed of this man countless times over the past month, and that he was now standing in front of her left her feeling agitated and confused. She didn't know what it meant and not being able to explain it made her nervous. She forced herself to be professional, meeting his eyes with a slight smile.

"Pleasure," she said as she took his outstretched hand. She immediately felt a sensational tingling up her spine and clenched her thighs together in protest against her immediate arousal. Despite her discomfort, she gazed up at his face and was met with a smirk.

"So it would seem," he said as heat rose to Laurel's face. *How could he know? Could this be more embarrassing?* A kindness came to his eyes, and he added his other hand on top of hers, causing more tingling but also a feeling of comfort and said, "I assure you, Ms. Davis, the pleasure is all mine."

Laurel slid her hand from his grasp and felt his grip tighten lightly before releasing her. "Gentleman, please," her arm waved to the table. "Have a seat. You're a little early, but the others will be joining us shortly. Can I offer you any coffee or pastries?"

"I would love some," Matthius said excitedly as he sat down.

Shepherd grabbed his forearm and spoke gruffly, "Then you will get it yourself, Matthius."

"Oh no, I don't mind at all. It's part of my job," Laurel said quickly, but Shepherd's expression was unrelenting.

"You will not serve him his food."

Alrighty, Laurel thought, glancing around awkwardly as she took her seat. *This isn't strange at all. Why would he not want me to get them refreshments? Is he a clean freak? Does he not trust me? Maybe he doesn't want anyone touching their food.*

Matthius stood and good-naturedly said, "You want a coffee, boss?" He was piling pastries on his plate as Shepherd chuckled.

"No thanks, Matty."

Matthius then turned to Laurel with a charming grin, "Can I get *you* anything, Ms. Davis?"

The Dream

"No thank you. I'm drinking my breakfast," Laurel responded while lifting her mostly full coffee cup towards him.

The door to the conference room opened and saved her from any further awkwardness. Her boss, Jim, came in followed by four more suits. The meeting revolved around a site that the firm was selling. The business acumen of both Shepherd and Matthius impressed Laurel. They were intelligent and confident, nimbly turning the conversation to their liking at every point. She was surprised, though, when they disclosed that they had no immediate plans for the facility on site but were more interested in the land as a future investment.

Why would they spend so much money on land? she wondered.

"Although we have no current plans for the building, we own several businesses and would like to tour the location for potential use. Would you be able to set that up, Jim?" Shepherd asked.

"Of course, Mr. Ryan. We can arrange that at your convenience. When would you like it scheduled?"

"As quickly as possible. We'll be in town for a little while." Shepherd glanced at Laurel before continuing, "I'm not sure how long so it would be convenient to schedule it soon."

"Absolutely, we will set up everything as quickly as possible and Laurel can accompany you. She knows the specs of the property well and can answer any questions you may have."

Laurel was flustered. She often managed the needs of their clients, but it was rarely necessary that she had to travel. And now she would find herself alone with dream man for a full day! She couldn't even control herself during a simple introduction. She tried not to show her distress but saw an amused expression cross Shepherd's face as he studied her.

"We've already been introduced to Ms. Davis and would be delighted to have her with us," he said with a twinkle in his eye.

Jim looked between them with suspicion, making Laurel groan inwardly. As everyone rose from the table, she caught Shepherd's eyes and knew by his intense look that he wanted to talk to her more. While Jim was monopolizing Shepherd's time, she slipped past him. It was lunchtime, and Henry would be waiting for her. Letting the conference room door shut behind her, she headed towards the elevator with a sigh of relief. She didn't know what to make of her physical and mental reaction to Shepherd's presence. She had never been "boy crazy" as Aunt Lucy called it, but she'd been in several relationships. None of her love interests, including Henry, had elicited this reaction. It embarrassed her. She was a grown woman! A professional! And in a committed relationship!

As she reached the elevator and was about to push the button, she heard Shepherd's deep voice call her name. His voice brought a delicious sensation all the way down her spine, and she loved the way her name sounded on his lips. It took all of her effort to remain professional.

"Yes, Mr. Ryan?" She hoped her face didn't betray the myriad of emotions that she was having.

"Please, call me Shepherd. I was hoping that you would have lunch with me," he asked softly but confidently as he grabbed one of her hands.

The effect of his touch was immediate. *Why is my body such a traitor?!* she thought as her face reddened. She stopped herself from immediately yelling, "YES!" as if she were some crazed schoolgirl, and the pause was long enough to be rescued by Henry, who slid his left arm around her waist as he stepped beside her. He extended his other hand to Shepherd, whose jaw visibly clenched as he slowly grasped Henry's hand.

"Henry Butler, Laurel's boyfriend. Pleased to meet you. And you are?"

"Shepherd Ryan."

Laurel could tell that Shepherd used more strength than was necessary during the handshake by the way Henry's grasp on her waist tightened.

"I'm afraid that Laurel and I have plans. But I'm sure you can find another lunch partner," Henry said as he turned her towards the elevator, releasing her waist to tuck a loose strand of hair behind her ear.

Laurel heard a low growl, and this time she knew it wasn't her stomach. She couldn't help glancing over her shoulder as she got onto the elevator. Shepherd's face looked furious, and she wasn't sure why it made her chest restrict in concern. She saw Matthius join Shepherd as the elevator door closed.

"Who was that, dear?" Henry asked, trying to keep his voice light.

She could tell that he felt threatened. Henry was good-looking, intelligent, and successful. Feeling threatened was not an emotion that he often experienced.

"Shepherd Ryan. He and his partner, Matthius Hart, are the ones interested in the SkyCorp location. We just finished a business meeting with them. About that, I don't have the details yet but Jim volunteered me to take them to the property soon so they could look around."

"I see." He paused before continuing. "I could ask Jim if there was someone else that could take them if you'd prefer."

Henry had never offered to intervene on her behalf in professional matters before, so she knew that he didn't like the idea of her being alone with the attractive businessman. Her own feelings were so mixed up that she couldn't tell how she felt about Henry's proposal. On the one hand, she didn't like the way she felt out of control when she was around Shepherd. She felt that he knew everything she was thinking and feeling, which made her feel self-conscious. But she also felt an unexplainable need to be around him. Regardless, she couldn't accept Henry's offer to get her out of doing her job. She was a grown woman, and it wouldn't look right for her boyfriend to ask her boss to let her miss the trip.

"No, Henry. I appreciate it, but it's just part of the job. You know that."

Laurel was distracted the rest of the day. Her mind kept returning to Shepherd and wondering how she would control herself around him during the trip. When she found herself daydreaming about his touch on her skin, she blushed and immediately forced Henry into her thoughts. Arriving home that evening, she discovered Susu at the kitchen counter with a cup of coffee. She set her bag down on the table by the door and slipped out of her shoes with a sigh.

"Not even 30 seconds in the door and already a loud sigh?" Susu joked. "Was Jim a bigger ass than usual today?"

Laurel laughed. "No, he was his usual amount of ass."

Laurel sat down beside Susu and told her about the dream she had been having, leaving out her physical response to the dream man. And then she let out a loud, slow sigh and related the details of her day, again leaving out the parts about her response to Shepherd's touch and voice. Susu's eyes slowly got bigger as the story progressed, with a wicked smile on her face during the awkward exchange by the elevator.

"Laurel!! It sounds like he's your soulmate! Why are you telling me this story like it's the worst day of your life?!"

"Well, have you forgotten the little detail of me having a boyfriend for the past 3 years? A pretty great boyfriend who wants me to move in with him and hasn't done anything to deserve me chasing some stranger around?"

"Look, you know Henry isn't my favorite person. He's nice but- I don't know, he's just so haughty sometimes. I don't think he appreciates you, and he definitely doesn't know you as well as he thinks he does. Besides, if he were such a perfect boyfriend, then you wouldn't be avoiding the next step with him…. maybe it's time to admit that just because he's a good guy doesn't mean he's the right guy."

That night, Laurel again had the dream. This time though, Shepherd approached her, and she didn't wake up. He wrapped an arm around her waist and pulled her into his body. His other hand wrapped around the back of her head, weaving through her hair with his fingers, guiding her face upward towards him as his soft lips gently but passionately pressed against hers. She felt herself melt into him. She had never felt so turned on, so safe, so… at home. She awoke the next morning with tingles all over her body and forced herself to shake his face from her mind as she got ready for work.

She was mercifully busy all day. The trip to SkyCorp was set for the following morning. She had called Matthius to arrange the meeting. Her boss, Jim, had pulled her aside early that morning and warned her not to mess up the deal or be too friendly with clients. He was irritatingly smug for someone who let her do all the heavy lifting around the office, but she held her tongue and assured him that she had the situation under

The Dream

control. After work, she stopped by Susu's coffee shop. She wanted to go over the specs for SkyCorp before she went to bed so they'd be fresh in her mind for the trip. And that meant she needed coffee! Susu was leaning over the counter talking to a man with a flirtatious smile on her face when Laurel walked in.

"Well, look what the cat dragged in! You want your usual, Laurel?"

As Susu was speaking, the man at the counter turned around. It was Shepherd. He didn't look surprised to see her at all. Laurel, on the other hand, was completely shocked and not at all prepared to see him. She consciously relaxed the muscles in her face and took a small breath to steady herself.

"Ms. Davis, what a pleasure seeing you! Do you come here often?"

"Please, call me Laurel. Susu here is my roommate, and she makes the best coffee in the northeast."

Laurel hoped her forced calm was convincing. She felt her heartbeat quicken as soon as his eyes fell upon her. Glancing over at Susu, who had a knowing smile on her face, was enough to let her know that she wasn't fooling anyone.

"Would you sit with me for a while?"

"I'm actually heading home. I have some work to look over before our trip tomorrow."

Susu walked back with both of their drinks. "Laurel" was written on her cup, and she inadvertently glanced at Shepherd's cup. "Dream Man" was written on his cup, encircled with a heart. She was going to kill Susu for this.

"I'll walk you home then," he said as he studied his cup curiously. She started to protest but he said, "I insist" with such a charming glint in his eye that she gave in.

As they left the café, he gently guided her to the inside of the sidewalk so that he would be closest to the busy street. His thoughtfulness made her smile. *Stop, Laurel! Do not be charmed! You have a boyfriend. B..O..Y..F..R..I..E..N..D. How was she going to make it through an entire day of this?* She tried to comfort herself that after the trip, she wouldn't see him again, but the thought provided no relief. Her heart constricted at the prospect of Shepherd not being in her life anymore. She marveled that she could feel this way for someone she barely knew. They walked in comfortable silence for a couple of minutes.

"So, Mr. Ryan, —"

"Shepherd," he interrupted.

"Right. Shepherd. I was wondering during the meeting why you would be interested in the company strictly for the land? That's a lot of money to pay for property and SkyCorp could be a profitable business in the right hands."

"We may very well have use for it as a business in the future. But our main operation is always on the hunt for large plots of land close to our current location. It's getting more difficult to find. We're profitable enough that even if we don't have immediate plans for a business, we can maintain the property until such a need arises."

"Hmm. You must be phenomenally successful to buy such a property for a what if."

Shepherd smiled and looked at her sideways, "I am. I've been in business for a long time. Long enough to know when something will be of use to me. I have a lot of people to care for and part of my role is ensuring that no matter what happens in the future, I'll be able to support them. Properties like SkyCorp build our security. I don't like to miss those opportunities." He paused a moment before continuing. "What's your background, Laurel? Have you always lived in the city? Do you have family nearby?"

"No. My parents died when I was young. I grew up with my aunt in Oregon. In a cabin in the middle of woods. About as opposite from New York City as you can get," she chuckled. "I loved it though. I often miss being in the woods. But I appreciate the efficiency of the city too. I moved here after I graduated from Cal State."

"I feel the same. It's important to me to spend time in nature, but I do enjoy my time in the city- if it doesn't last too long. It's part of what I love about being in business. I get the best of both worlds. And of course, I get to mingle with a lot of different people. Although to tell you the truth, I could do without that part."

Laurel laughed at his confession. "Gee, thanks!"

He touched her elbow, and she turned slightly to face him. Her smile faded at the seriousness in his expression. "Of course I don't mean you. I've never met anyone like you, Laurel."

"You don't know me," she gently responded, almost as a question because she was sure that he somehow could know her in a way that no one else ever had.

Shepherd's hands grasped each of hers, gently, yet electrically charged. Everything in her screamed to be his, to be touched by him, kissed by him, fucked by him.

"I want nothing more than to know you, every bit of you. Your dreams, your likes, your dislikes, your everything." She believed him but was using all her energy to remain rational and keep guard against feelings that made no sense. "Laurel?"

She pulled her hands from his. "My apartment is just right up here."

She glanced up the street, where she saw Henry waiting on her stoop with flowers in hand. Her shoulders fell. He was watching them. Laurel felt terrible. Shepherd looked up as well and his posture stiffened.

"Laurel?" he asked again.

"I'm sorry, Shepherd. We should part here. I'll see you in the morning."

"Laurel, please let me see you home. There's more that I need to say to you."

"It's not a good time, Mr. Ryan." She saw Shepherd wince as she addressed him by his last name. "I'll see you at the airport tomorrow morning."

She turned abruptly and forced herself to walk away from him. She wanted to look back at him, to tell him she wanted to hear everything he had to say, that she also felt their connection, but Henry was waiting. Laurel cared for Henry and knew that what he saw between she and Shepherd had hurt him. She didn't know what she was going to say to him. She didn't even understand it herself.

Stopping in front of Henry, she started to explain herself. "Henry, I —"

"Shh." He was still looking behind her at Shepherd as he lifted her chin to gently kiss her. "Let's go inside. These flowers need to be placed in water."

Grabbing her hand, he led her up the steps to her apartment. Laurel felt sick to her stomach. She knew that they would have to talk about what was developing between her and Shepherd, and she didn't know how she felt about it. She had been with Henry for three years and had only met Shepherd a day ago. Granted, she had been dreaming of him for a month. That had to mean something. And she had never felt so connected to someone. Could she give up that chance and live with never knowing where it would have led? Shepherd didn't live in the city and would be returning home soon. How could they start a relationship that way? Yet, even if things didn't work out with Shepherd, could she stay with Henry knowing how she felt about Shepherd? Even if there were no Shepherd, she had still been hesitant to take the next step with Henry. If they weren't moving forward, where did that leave them? Her head was swimming with the barrage of thoughts invading her mind. She felt nauseous and dizzy.

"I need to sit down," she said as she opened the front door of her apartment.

She plopped down on the sofa as Henry made his way into the kitchen to get a vase from the cabinet. She heard him fill the vase with water and put the flowers in, throwing the wrapping in the trash on his way into the living room.

He pulled an ottoman in front of where Laurel sat, his long legs on either side of hers. Grabbing both of her hands, he searched her face.

"What's going on here, Laurel? Should I be concerned?"

She looked into his worried eyes. He had done nothing wrong, and she alone had caused this. What was she supposed to do? She didn't want to hurt Henry. She wasn't a cheater, never had been. Even though she hadn't acted on her feelings for Shepherd, the temptation she felt was undeniable.

"I'm not sure, Henry. I can tell you that nothing has happened between Shepherd...Mr. Ryan and myself. But I do feel attracted to him

The Dream

somehow, and I think he feels the same. I ran into him at the coffee shop, and he wanted to walk me home. I should've said no."

Henry took a deep, slow breath. He looked slightly relieved. "It doesn't surprise me that he's attracted to you, Laurel. He'd be crazy not to be. But it does concern me that you…have some interest in him as well. I can live with that…because my feelings are deeper than a fleeting crush…as long as you aren't planning to act on those feelings. You aren't, right?"

"I wouldn't cheat on you, Henry."

It was as honest as she could be. Her head was a mess. She knew that she had more than a crush on Shepherd. She somehow had already developed very real feelings for him that she needed to sort out. She would have to closely watch herself to ensure that she didn't let whatever this powerful connection was between herself and Shepherd lead her into doing something she would regret.

"Good. Because I won't share you, Laurel. I can't."

Henry leaned over and kissed her gingerly. Pulling her onto his lap, he opened her mouth with his tongue and kissed her more deeply, his hands on her ass as she straddled him. She broke away breathlessly.

"Maybe we shouldn't, Henry. I have an early morning."

Henry studied her warily. "Maybe we should, Laurel. I want you to remember how much I love you." He kissed her neck. "How much I need you," he continued as he kissed her collarbone slowly and sensually. "How good we feel together."

He stood up with Laurel's legs wrapped around his waist and carried her to the bedroom. Continuing to kiss her as he shut the bedroom door behind him, he gently laid her on the bed.

"Tonight, I just want to take my time and enjoy you. Will you let me?"

"Yes," she said softly.

How could she answer any differently? This was the Henry she had cared for the last few years. A flash of Shepherd's face entered her mind, but she pushed it away and focused on Henry's kisses.

He slowly made his way down her body, unbuttoning her shirt, cupping her breasts, and taking his time sucking her nipples while gently pulling her hair as she moaned. He stood up, pulled her skirt off, leaving her high heel shoes on and knelt in front of her pussy. The sensation of his kisses on her thighs caused her core to throb in anticipation.

"Oh god, Henry. I need you. Please," she begged him.

She needed a release from the last couple of days, and Henry knew how to please her. She wanted to stop thinking of Shepherd.

"Patience, Laurel," he cooed.

His fingers separated her lips, and he kissed her nub at the same time as he plunged two fingers in forcefully, causing Laurel to arch her back and cry out. He used his hand to press down on her abdomen, keeping her in place. He continued to lick her arousal and suck on her clit while he worked his fingers in and out until she screamed in ecstasy, bucking against his hand. As soon as she had finished, Henry put an arm around her waist and pulled her further up the bed while bringing her in for a deep kiss so she could taste herself on his lips. He drove into her with one fluid movement, and she moaned in response. Henry kept an agonizingly slow and deep rhythm until she could tell by his breathing that he was getting close. He looked into her eyes and immediately sped up, thrusting hard and deep as he grunted her name. After he finished, he pulled out of her and laid to her side, leaving his arm wrapped around her hips. She had been caught up in the moment but now that it was over, she felt empty and somehow disappointed with herself. She knew that Henry could sense something in the air between them as well and they both lay in silence.

"Let's just stay like this tonight."

Laurel didn't respond and it wasn't long before she heard Henry's breathing change as he fell asleep. She lay awake for a long time before eventually falling into a fitful sleep.

She is in a busy street, so familiar now. She stands still this time, searching for him. Searching for Shepherd. Suddenly, she sees him break through the crowd, and his eyes lock onto her. Her breathing quickens as he nears. She feels so drawn to him. He was closer to her now, slowing. She feels her sex tighten and heat up. He stops in front of her. She breathes

The Dream

in his earthy scent while staring into his deep green eyes. She's been here before. And she knows him now, wishes he would say her name. He leans in...and suddenly his eyes swirl, and she finds herself in the middle of the forest. Shepherd is gone. She looks around and finds herself all alone. She isn't afraid to be in the woods alone. But she is confused. How did she get here? Where is Shepherd? Howls in the distance pierce the silence but she still doesn't feel concerned. She lays on the grass, staring up at the stars that are just starting to show in the night sky. Everything feels calm as she listens to the wolves, still far away. The breeze is light but strong enough to sway the leaves into a lullaby. Laurel breathes in deeply, meditating on the beauty of the colors and the sounds of nature. A twig breaks nearby, and she looks toward the direction she heard the sound. She can't see anything in the tree line but knows that something is there watching her. She stands slowly, keeping her eyes toward the trees. Eyes, deep green and black, come into focus as they move closer to the clearing. Slowly, a large wolf steps out of the forest. The owner of the beautiful and soulful eyes. He is a magnificent and powerful beast. His top half is mostly silver with a snowy white lower half. His nose is silver, and his ears stand perked up straight. He slowly walks towards her, cautiously. She doesn't even consider running away. She is not afraid. She hears another twig crack and her concentration on the wolf in front of her is broken. She looks toward the sound and notices that all along the tree line are wolves. None of them appear scary. Somehow, she senses that they are not here to hurt her. They respect her. They love her even. She turns her attention back to the regal wolf, who is now standing in front of her. He is so tall that his face is almost equal to hers, and he leans toward her. She meets him halfway, her hand reaching up to run her fingers through his fur. He suddenly steps back and lifts his head as he howls. The wolves in the clearing all join in as Laurel looks around her, smiling and proud.

Light flickered through the curtains in her bedroom. Blinking her eyes, she realized that she must have fallen asleep with Henry, even before having dinner, and slept through the night. Grabbing her phone from the nightstand, her eyes tried to focus on the time. 7 am? She slept for 12 hours! She rolled over, but Henry was gone. He had left sometime in the night. She wouldn't have time to review the specs on the property or eat a good breakfast. Hell, she had just enough time to brush her hair and teeth and throw some things in a bag for the overnight trip.

Fifteen minutes later, she rushed out of the building, hailing a cab to take her to the airport where a private plane would be waiting. Once she was in the car, she felt thankful that she had slept so long. It gave less time for her to be nervous about being alone with Shepherd. Bits of last night's dream filtered through her mind, and she wondered what it meant and why the dream had changed from the one that had played on repeat for the past month.

CHAPTER 3

As the cab arrived at the airstrip, she saw a black sedan parked and waiting. Grabbing her bag from the seat beside her, she observed a tall woman stepping out of the backseat of the car. She was stunningly beautiful, with dark skin and shoulder-length curly black hair. Dressed in a smart gray pants suit and donning big sunglasses, she laughed as she looked behind her. Laurel watched as Shepherd climbed out after her and she felt a pang in her chest. Is that Shepherd's girlfriend? She shook the thought from her mind and turned back to pay the taxi driver. *Get it together, Laurel. You have no right to feel jealous. Remember Henry? Actually, this may make the trip more comfortable. Perhaps you misunderstood Shepherd's intentions.*

She turned back around to the group waiting for her by the sedan. She now saw that Shepherd and the mystery woman were joined by Matthius and another man that she had never met. *Where did these people find each other? A modeling agency?* The man was tall and handsome, strong but not as broad as Matthius and Shepherd. He dressed in a blue suit with a white button-down shirt, the top few buttons left casually open. He didn't look mean but also didn't smile, instead wearing a curious expression as he watched her walk towards them.

Shepherd walked forward to meet her but when he got closer, she noticed his nostrils flare as if he were smelling her. She saw him grow tense- his eyes darker and angry. *What's his deal? I know I didn't have time to shower this morning, but I don't stink,* Laurel thought nervously. He stared intensely at her for a moment as if he were trying to keep control of himself. It must have shown in her face that he was frightening her, because she saw him take a deep breath before reaching for her hand and bringing her the last few steps to the rest of the party. Although his words were cordial, his voice was clipped and gruff, betraying his feelings.

"You already know my associate, Matthius. This is his wife, Charis. And this," he gestured to the serious man beside him, still staring at her with an expression that made her think he was sizing her up for something, "is Beck, my right-hand man."

"It's nice to see you again, Matthius, and to meet you both," Laurel said with a warm smile, genuinely feeling much better now that she knew Charis and Matthius were together.

Charis immediately reached out to hug her, which surprised Laurel. "I'm so glad to have another girl on this trip!" she laughed as she intertwined their arms, leading her towards the plane.

"Oh, I need to grab my bag," Laurel hesitated.

Charis kept walking and glancing behind her, yelled, "Boys, grab our bags, won't you?" She looked back at Laurel with twinkling eyes. "That's what we keep them around for, right?"

Laurel couldn't help but laugh. "Well, I'm not sure it's very professional for me to make a client carry my bag, but I guess it's okay since you issued the order."

"Damn straight! Besides, Shepherd would love to carry your bag...or you"

Charis cast a side glance at Laurel to gauge her reaction, but she pretended not to hear.

As she stepped inside, Laurel was amazed. She had flown once before for the company, but this plane was exceedingly nicer. This would only be her third time to fly. Once with her parents, and then not again until her business trip. She had driven to college and back home for visits. Even when she moved to New York with Susu, they made a monumental road trip of it. This plane looked like one that would be featured in *Lifestyles of the Rich and Famous*. Two tables were across from each other with white leather seats. Further down the plane were two couches facing one another. Laurel continued walking

The Dream

and opened the door at the end of the plane, revealing a small bedroom with a queen-size bed and a bathroom with a shower. She hadn't been asked to oversee the travel accommodations and didn't know why Jim would've splurged on this plane for the trip.

When she made her way back to the seats, she was unnerved to see that Charis and Matthius were on one of the couches, snuggled close to one another, while Beck lay down across from them on the other couch, working on a laptop that rested on his chest. That only left the two tables with chairs on either side of them. Shepherd sat at one with his laptop open on the table. She knew it would be rude to sit at the other table alone, so she took the seat across from Shepherd and pulled out her file of the property to review. Shepherd leaned back and peered at her with a look of satisfaction on his face.

"Always working?"

"Eh, I put in a fair number of hours. But I mostly like what I do."

"Mostly? What do you not like about your job?"

She knew she shouldn't complain to a client about her job, but he made her feel comfortable, as though anything she said was acceptable. "I had hoped to be further in my career at this point. I don't want to be a glorified secretary," she chuckled.

"What *do* you want to be?"

"Well, at the head of the table, of course! But I don't think that will happen anytime soon. I guess everyone has to work from the ground up."

"What do you generally handle at your job?"

"Anything that Jim needs done. I oversee several accounts, organize and prepare for meetings, do research on different projects, consult with teams, and of course anything extra that our clients need," she paused here with a smile. "I usually book hotels and travel for our out-of-town clients. But I didn't have to do that for you…"

"We travel enough to warrant having a plane at our disposal. Sometimes we need to go somewhere quickly, and it's convenient to have a plane and a pilot we trust on the ready. As for hotels, we tend to only go to a handful of places and know the hotels we like in each location." He shrugged.

Even his shrug was charming. Laurel felt her heart rate quicken.

"It's just easier when we handle it ourselves, you know?"

"Yeah, I do." She smiled, pulling the folder closer to her as she started to open it.

The engine of the plane started, making her pause. A man walked from the cockpit and said, "Welcome, Ms. Davis. Boss, we're ready to take off. There may be some turbulence, but nothing to be concerned about."

Shepherd nodded to him and glanced over at Laurel. "You fly much?"

"Very little. Once when I was a child and once on a business trip. It makes me a little nervous but my past experiences in planes have been good."

"Your aunt didn't like to travel?"

Laurel hesitated. With the connection she already felt to Shepherd, she wondered if it was wise to share too much of her past with him. But when she looked up at him, she knew she couldn't deny him an open answer.

"My parents moved around a bit, but we mostly stayed near the west coast. We lived in Washington the most." She paused, stealing a glance at Shepherd, who looked interested. "I mentioned the other day that my parents died when I was 13. We were taking a camping trip and there was an accident. I remember driving down a winding road. We had the windows down and Jim Croce was playing on the radio." She smiled, remembering her parents singing along in the front seat. "It was 'Bad, Bad Leroy Brown'. We made a turn on a hill, and I don't remember anything else."

She couldn't recall the last time she had felt so comfortable talking about this, especially with someone who was essentially a stranger to her. She tended to take her time getting to know someone before divulging much about herself, and even more time before she shared her most guarded memories. She certainly had never told anyone the

The Dream

song that was playing when the accident happened. She couldn't even remember when the last time she thought of it was.

"When I woke up in the hospital, my Aunt Lucy was there in the room with me. I knew then that my folks hadn't made it. She never even had to say it. We didn't talk about it. She went to my parents' apartment and packed up some clothes and pictures while I was still in the hospital, and then we made the trip to her cabin in Oregon. That first year I didn't go back to school. I just spent a lot of time in the woods. Aunt Lucy taught me a lot about living in nature. Then, life just.... resumed."

Laurel shrugged and smiled softly at Shepherd, making eye contact for the first time since she started talking. There was nothing in his gaze that made her feel awkward for having shared something so intimate.

"I stayed in Oregon the rest of the time growing up and didn't leave again until graduation. I needed to push myself, you know? I needed to do something different to prove to myself that I could."

"And do you miss Oregon?"

"Yeah, I sure do. And I really miss my aunt. She doesn't leave the cabin too often, and I work a lot. I don't see her nearly as much as I'd like to. She's the best kind of person. Gentle, carefree, independent, accepting. She taught me so much about life."

"I'd love to meet her sometime."

Laurel didn't know how to respond, so she changed the subject. "Tell me about yourself. I know you own a large corporation and that your employees seem to love and respect you. It's almost as if you're family instead of coworkers."

Shepherd paused as if he wasn't ready to stop talking about her but yielded. "Well, we're all from a tight-knit town. Matthius, Beck, and I have known each other since we were kids. So, we really are more like family." He glanced behind him at his friends and turned back, smiling. "Charis and Matty got together about five years ago, but it feels like she's always been with us. She fits right in. She goes on most of our trips with us. We're together a lot."

"And what about your real family? Your childhood?"

Turbulence caused the plane to bounce, and Laurel tensed before Shepherd smiled reassuringly at her and answered.

"Well, my dad ran the family business before me. My mom helped. We were always invested in it and in the...community...that we live in. I'm an only child, but I was never alone. I had a good life. My parents are hard workers, and I trained young to work in the family business, but I can't complain. It's a lot of responsibility. A lot of our neighbors depend on our success, and I feel grateful to take care of them."

More turbulence. This time it was even rougher. She tried to measure whether she should be concerned by Shepherd's facial expression, but he looked completely relaxed. *He's probably not the type to ever show fear. We could be plummeting to our deaths, and he'd probably look calm and collected.* She glanced behind Shepherd at the others to see if they were nervous. They were still in their same positions.

"Any special ladies in your life?" she asked, trying to sound calmer than she felt.

Shepherd's low voice was sexy as he leaned forward, staring deeply into her eyes. "There is only one lady I want in my life, and I'm looking at her right now."

Laurel noticed Charis glance up at her with smiling eyes from behind Shepherd and she blushed, not realizing until now that the others could hear their conversation.

"You shouldn't say things like that."

"I shouldn't say the truth?" he asked with his eyebrows raised and a slight smirk on his face.

"Not to someone who has a boyfriend. Besides, people may take you seriously."

She knew he was serious. But she wanted to diffuse the situation. Shepherd's expression darkened at the mention of Henry, and his eyes blazed. He leaned back in his seat but maintained eye contact.

"I couldn't be more serious. Do I strike you as a man who would play with a woman's heart?"

She gulped. "No. You don't."

They stared at each other in silence for a moment before the pilot's voice came over the speaker. "Boss, this turbulence is going to be worse than I thought for a few minutes. I'm going a bit higher to try to get us out of it." Laurel visibly tensed.

Shepherd motioned to the seat beside him. "Why don't you come sit by me?"

She paused.

"Do you have any pictures of your Aunt Lucy or where you grew up?"

Again, she paused. *It would be nice to have a distraction.* She picked up her phone and moved to the seat beside him. "Sure, I have a few." After a few moments, the flight became smooth again. The distraction had been helpful. Still, she was thankful when the plane landed.

The rest of the day went without any surprises. An SUV met them at the airport and took them to the location. Laurel was surprised at how little time they spent inside the factory. Much of the time was spent riding around the vast property. They got out several times to walk around, and Laurel was glad that she had worn comfortable shoes. Shepherd, Matthius, and Beck were all business, which Laurel was glad for. There were no more uncomfortable moments between them.

Laurel couldn't help but admire the way Shepherd's mind operated. He was constantly determining what would work for his current business, making plans, and figuring calculations while Beck made notes. They worked well together. Matthius and Charis were the types that made you feel like an instant friend and were both good-hearted troublemakers. Beck was reserved but not unkind. She could see how much he and Shepherd respected one another and how close they were. It felt sometimes like they were reading each other's minds. Laurel found it odd how much Shepherd took his community into account, even considering which of his neighbors may want to make the move to the property if they expanded their business.

By the end of the day, Laurel was getting exhausted. They were headed to one last area of the property when Shepherd glanced at her with concern.

"We've worn you out, haven't we, Laurel?"

"I'm used to walking all day in the city, but the terrain is different here. And the plane ride was mentally taxing," she laughed, "but I assure you I'm fine. Take your time."

"I've seen enough, boys. Let's head back to the hotel." She started to protest when he continued, "This property will work well for us. I have a few things I'd like to discuss with you, but we can head to the hotel to rest for a couple of hours and then talk over dinner?"

"That sounds like a good plan," she acquiesced.

He nodded with a warm smile and turned back to the front.

About an hour later, they arrived. Driving down Main Street, she admired how many families there were enjoying the day. After they pulled into the hotel's circle drive, Shepherd grabbed her bag from the back and walked her inside. He stopped at the desk and the clerk immediately handed him a set of keys.

"Here you go, Mr. Ryan. Please let us know if there's anything you need."

"Will do, Carter. Thank you."

Laurel watched the exchange with confusion. *How does Shepherd know so many people?* When they got to her room, Shepherd used the key to open the door. He put her bag inside the door but didn't enter. Grabbing her hand gently, he gave her the room key.

"Thank you for showing us around today and answering all our questions. You're exceptionally good at your job and I enjoyed your company."

He was standing so close to her that she could feel the warmth from his body. She tensed as she felt the now familiar tingling sensation all along her skin as he touched her, her panties getting wet from his touch. *What in the actual hell is wrong with you, Laurel? It's a handshake. Down, girl.* Shepherd leaned in, his hand still grasping hers. His lips were so close to her ear, she could feel his breath. It was all she could do not to grab him and pull him into an embrace. She wanted his hands on her, wanted his lips caressing her neck and face, wanted to feel his skin on hers. He lingered a second longer while she wondered what would happen next.

The Dream

She doubted she would be able to resist him if he tried to kiss her. She wanted nothing more than to rip his clothes off and straddle him. She wanted to see what his clothes hid. She wanted to taste every part of his delicious body.

"Rest up. Let's say we meet in the lobby at seven o'clock for dinner. That should give us time to shower and rest. There's a nice, quiet place here in town that has decent food."

He stepped back and watched her. His eyes seemed darker, his voice strained, as if he felt all the same things she did.

"See you then," she agreed.

Laurel felt relieved to be alone. She forced herself to calm down and think of Henry, vowing to be true to her sense of right and wrong no matter how strong the temptation. As she ran a bath, she thought about Henry. She cared for him and knew he was a good man. He had done nothing to deserve a rejection from Laurel. But he wanted more than she felt ready to give him. She'd had doubts before, and Susu's remark of "Just because he's a good guy doesn't mean he's the right guy" really resonated with her. But the thought of hurting him twisted her stomach.

After just a few days of knowing Shepherd, she not only had stronger physical responses, but she found it easier to be open with him than with Henry. She suspected that she and Shepherd couldn't work out. She wasn't interested in having a long-distance relationship and knew how invested Shepherd was in his town. But the fact that she could have such strong feelings toward someone else told her that she needed to end it with Henry for both of their sakes. She would need to tell him when she got back into town. She thought of how uncomfortable the conversation would be and how much it would hurt them both. The thought that they may have to revisit those feelings every time they ran into each other at work made her want to find a hole to crawl into.

Laurel turned the water on, adding bubble bath before heading into the room to take her clothes off. Digging around in her bag, she found her toiletries and returned to the bathroom to check the water level. She slipped into the tub and turned on the jets. Sighing, she closed her eyes and relaxed. It wouldn't be easy, and it wouldn't feel good, but she felt relief at admitting something to herself that she had been denying for months. The phone ringing interrupted her thoughts. She dried off her hands and picked it up, her chest tightening when she saw the name. *Speak of the devil and he shall appear.* She thought of not answering, because she was unsure of what to say.

But... "Hey Henry!"

"Hey sweetheart, I was just thinking of you and wondered how your day had gone?"

"It was busy but productive. I think they'll end up buying the property. We're having dinner tonight to discuss some of the details, but I'm fairly sure it's a go. I'm surprised Jim hasn't been blowing up my cell phone, but I only got one text from him today."

There was silence before Henry responded, "A dinner?"

The air felt heavy for a moment. Laurel knew that Henry didn't like her being on the trip with Shepherd.

"Yes, a dinner with everyone once we've rested up. Some local place close to the hotel. And then I'll be heading home in the morning."

"Ah, well I hope it goes smoothly. I knew you'd seal the deal. I can't wait to see you. I've missed you."

Laurel didn't know what to say. With everything that she had been thinking, she knew a difficult talk was coming, but she didn't want to have it over the phone.

"Yeah, it'll be nice to be home."

A long pause. Henry had obviously picked up that she hadn't returned his sentiments.

"I better get off and start getting ready for dinner. I'll see you tomorrow?"

"Of course. I love you, Laurel."

"Have a good night, Henry. I'll see you soon."

Laurel hung up and placed her phone on the edge of the tub. She closed her eyes and slid underneath the water, holding her breath for as long as she could. Coming back up, she pushed her hair back and sighed. Her mind centered on Shepherd and just thinking of him made

The Dream

her aroused. His breath against her ear when he whispered to her. The way he stared straight into her soul. His manner of speaking- so forward and confident about his feelings for her. All the feelings she felt silly to have so soon or too awkward to say aloud, he had no difficulty speaking. She envied him. Typically, if a guy were to say those things to her, it would be a turn off. She would think it was a pick-up line. But with Shepherd, she didn't doubt it. And that's what made it feel too real, too frightening. The dream, the raw physical desire when he touched her in the most innocent of ways, the connection they had. It made Laurel feel confused.

She gave in to the thoughts of Shepherd, her fingers slipping under the surface of the water to find her needy clitoris. She immediately felt relief as she rubbed faster, imagining Shepherd's body pressed against her, his lips on her neck. She arched her back and moaned, hungrily fingering herself until she reached her climax. It didn't take long. Spending the entire day with him had caused built-up frustration in her body. She didn't like the loss of control over her emotions. *At least the others will be at dinner. I can slip back to the hotel after the business talk is over. And then tomorrow, I'll be back home. I'll talk to Henry, Shepherd will leave, and all of this will work itself out one way or another.*

Chapter 4

At seven, Laurel stepped into the lobby and spotted Shepherd at the bar. *Where are the others?* She had a sinking sensation in the pit of her stomach but knew she couldn't run back to her room. Before she reached the bar, Shepherd turned to greet her with a smile. His eyes admired her body without embarrassment, taking his time to study how she looked in her blue dress, her red hair left loose around her face. She had put a little eye makeup on and red lipstick. She wasn't sure what type of restaurant they were going to and tried to pick an outfit that would be appropriate for any environment. Shepherd looked breathtaking in his gray blazer and slacks with a crisp white button-up shirt. His eyes had made it back up to meet hers.

"You look stunning. I love your hair down."

"Thank you. Where are the others?"

"They headed home. There are only a few things that need to be discussed, and I'll update them afterwards."

"Oh."

Shepherd grinned as if he were enjoying her discomfort and stood to join her, placing his hand lightly on the small of her back, which caused an immediate reaction within Laurel.

"Ready?" he asked, his deep, husky voice making it even more difficult for Laurel to keep her mind focused on business.

She wanted to rip that suit off and have him take her right here in the bar, hard and fast. She didn't care that there were others around. His touch made her need him. His touch made her think irrationally. She stepped forward to sever the connection his hand brought.

"Sure, let's go!"

She hoped that her voice didn't reveal how nervous she felt to spend dinner alone with Shepherd but judging by his smirk, he was aware. They walked to the restaurant, Laurel purposely staying just out of his reach. If it bothered him, he didn't show it. After being seated, Shepherd asked if she minded him ordering as he knew the menu well. She agreed and after he ordered dinner and wine for them, he leaned back, a mischievous grin on his face.

"I have a confession to make."

She lifted her eyebrows but didn't respond. *This man is dangerous. He could get away with anything with that face! Lord, help me.*

"I don't have any more questions about the property. I've already let Jim know that I'll be purchasing it. I just wanted to have dinner with you."

"Hmm, I don't know what to say to that, Shepherd. I appreciate your honesty. I'll admit there's something between us, but I'm not a cheater. I'm not sure what you wanted to happen tonight."

Shepherd's jaw tightened and then he sighed, leaning forward. "I know that, Laurel. And I respect it. But I need to have a conversation with you. It's difficult for me to explain this in a way that doesn't make me sound like a creep." He paused for a split second before continuing, "I've always known that there was one person in the world for me. And as soon as I saw you, I knew it was you. This isn't something I take lightly. I understand that you can't move as quickly as I would if I had complete freedom with you, but I need to know where you stand."

"I'm with Henry."

"I know, but that doesn't answer my question. What do you feel between us?"

"I feel what you feel…sort of. I've never thought that soul mates were a real thing, and I definitely never looked for one. But…"

"But what? Talk to me, Laurel."

"About a month ago, I started to have this dream. Almost every night. It was you. Before I ever met you." She stopped for a moment, studying his face, looking for signs that he thought she was crazy, but his

The Dream

face held only surprise, so she continued. "The morning we met, I saw you first on the street. I thought that you saw me too. It was exactly as it was in my dream. But when I looked again, you were gone, and I thought I'd imagined it. Then we met in the conference room and when you touched me, I felt a spark, almost like electricity. I've never experienced anything like that. And I don't know what it means or how it makes sense."

"I knew when I saw you too...on the street outside of your office. I wanted to walk right up to you and hold you and never let you go." His eyes darkened. "But then I saw Henry come up to you and embrace you. And Matthius sensed what was happening and pulled me aside before I frightened you."

"Frightened me?"

"I can't bear to watch him with you. I want to be the only man who touches you," he explained with an intense edge to his voice.

She wasn't one to like possessive men, but the thought of him touching her excited her.

"I see. But that's one of several problems- Henry."

She wanted to tell him that she was planning to break it off with Henry. But it somehow felt wrong that he would know before Henry, so she decided to keep silent on the matter.

"And knowing how we feel about each other, the connection we have... you still plan on staying with him?"

"I'm not sure."

"Hmm." He put his fingertips together in front of his face and took a few slow breaths.

She could tell that he was trying extremely hard to control himself. The waiter brought the wine bottle, two glasses, and the appetizer, leaving quickly as if he could tell that he was interrupting something important. Shepherd opened the bottle and poured them both a glass.

"And what are the other problems?"

"Well, we haven't known each other for very long."

Shepherd easily dismissed that. "People stay together for years and still don't really know each other. When you have a connection like ours, you get to know each other quickly. What else?"

Laurel felt frustrated. "You also live far away from New York. Long distance relationships are hard."

"I won't be away from you," he responded passionately before he paused. "Are you set on living in New York?"

"No, certainly not. But I do have a career. And I've worked hard for it. I don't want to give it up."

"But you're not happy with your current position," he pressed.

"No," she admitted. "But I'm also not ready to throw in the towel. I'm hoping it leads to something else."

"Beau Industries is always looking for leaders."

She rolled her eyes dismissively which made him chuckle.

"You don't believe me? Or do you think I'm offering you a job based on my feelings instead of your merits? I admit I have ulterior motives, but I have also seen your work, Laurel. And I've seen the way that ass Jim treats you. You do his job and yours and make it look easy. But you get no recognition. You managed the meeting, the food, the specs, likely wrote the presentation that he gave us about the property," he paused to see if she would deny it, but she didn't. "And you handled this trip without any difficulty. Explain to me why I wouldn't want to hire you?"

Again, she said nothing. He took a sip from his glass.

"So, here's what I'd like to do. I'd like to accompany you back to New York and spend some time with you. And when you're ready, we can fly back to Silver Moon for a visit. I think you'll love it. It's beautiful, the people are the best you'll ever meet, and you'll still get to travel to cities and do work that you enjoy. What do you say?"

"I don't know, Shepherd. Don't you have to get back?"

"I told you. I don't want to be away from you. I have a trustworthy team. They can manage it for a while."

Still, she hesitated. His plan sounded perfect to her. She wished that she had broken things off with Henry before this trip, before she even met Shepherd- back when he started asking her to move in with him and she knew she didn't want to.

Shepherd reached across the table and took both of her hands. "Laurel, I know this is a lot to take in and not the way relationships

The Dream

usually go. I know you have a lot to think about and I can respect that you have big decisions to make. I'll try not to rush you. But I already care deeply for you and want you by my side. I will do whatever needs to be done for you to be as sure as I am about this. I'm asking you to give me some time with you. We'll go at your pace."

He looked imploringly at her. She wanted to tell him that she had the same desires. But she was afraid. She didn't pull her hands away from him. She didn't want to. She simply nodded at him. He gave her a relieved smile. The rest of the evening they enjoyed their food and had a few glasses of wine. She and Shepherd talked as if they were comfortable friends and shared their life stories with one another. By the time he walked her back to her hotel room, she felt disappointed that they wouldn't be sharing a bed. Somehow, she managed to allow a chaste kiss on the cheek from Shepherd before he walked back to his room.

The plane ride home was quiet. Shepherd seemed to sense that she needed time to think. After a couple of hours, she laid down on one of the couches and drifted off to sleep. When she awoke, she was in the bed at the back of the plane. She knew that Shepherd must have carried her there after she fell asleep. Her impending conversation with Henry felt like a weight on her chest. After a little while, Shepherd opened the door and sat on the edge of the bed.

"We'll be landing soon. How are you feeling?"

"Overwhelmed."

Shepherd nodded. She didn't have to explain. He rested his hand on her ankle. *Is there any way that he could touch me that would feel innocent?* Laurel thought with frustrated pleasure.

"It's all going to work out, Laurel. You'll see. I promised you I would be patient and I will. But we belong together. I'm going to take care of you forever if you'll let me."

She believed him.

As she stepped off the plane, she saw Henry standing by the company limo. Shepherd walked beside her, carrying her bag for her.

Henry's face was hard and angry as he watched them walk towards him. He stepped forward to pull Laurel in closely, kissing her passionately on the lips. Henry wasn't one for public displays of affection, and she was so surprised that she didn't push him away. She heard what could only be described as a low, menacing growl escape from Shepherd. Henry pulled away and grabbed the bag from Shepherd.

"Thanks for carrying my girlfriend's bag, Mr. Ryan. I missed her so much, I decided to come meet her myself so we could have a dinner date. But we'll happily drop you off at your hotel. Where are you staying?"

Shepherd's veins pulsed in his neck as he looked at Laurel, fighting the urge to snatch her away from Henry, but then seemed to regain his composure. "The Shalis Hotel," Shepherd snarled.

The car ride to Shepherd's hotel was incredibly tense. No one said anything. The air was heavy with jealousy and Laurel couldn't imagine a more strained situation. She had expected to have some time to gather her thoughts before meeting Henry. And she didn't have Shepherd's contact information. Henry held her hand the entire ride, caressing it with his thumb. When they stopped in front of the hotel, Shepherd nodded curtly to Henry before taking Laurel's free hand and placing a kiss on the back of it.

"Thank you for all your help with the property, Laurel. I look forward to working with you in the future and I hope to talk soon."

She knew exactly what he meant and blushed in spite of herself. She could only manage a small smile and nod as he exited the car. Henry was seething although he tried, unsuccessfully, to hide it. Almost as soon as the door closed, he turned to face her. He looked as if he wanted to ask her something but seemed to think better of it.

"I've made reservations tonight at Damarco's in an hour. How about we stop by your place so you can change before we go."

"I'm pretty tired, Henry."

"Laurel, please. I've missed you, and I have something important I want to discuss with you."

She couldn't refuse. She should've been able to guess that Henry would want to talk about her moving in with him again, especially after

The Dream

everything that she had admitted about Shepherd. She left Henry waiting in the car while she went to change. Thankfully, Susu was at the kitchen counter watching videos on her phone.

"Hey you," Susu said as she set her phone down.

Laurel tackled her with a hug and didn't let go. She wasn't going to cry, but she could if she let herself. She felt so anxious and heavy.

"Hey, what's the matter, Laurel? Talk to me."

She reluctantly let Susu go and sank onto the bar stool beside her best friend. "I don't know what I'm supposed to do."

"Well first, you spill to your best friend and then we figure this shit out together."

"Henry's been pressuring me to take our relationship to the next step. And you know I've had reservations about it. Then the dream, meeting dream man in person, and I have all these intense feelings about him which isn't like me at all. Then, I take this trip with him and find out that his feelings are just as intense as mine if not more so. Henry is jealous, and I know I need to break it off, but I don't want to hurt him. Shepherd lives on the other side of the United States but says he doesn't want to leave me and he's staying until I feel comfortable moving with him, and I just feel so overwhelmed, Susu!" She let her head drop to the countertop with her arms limply hanging beside her. "What do I do, Susu? Tell me," she wailed.

"Whoa."

Laurel lifted her head. "That's all? Whoa?! What am I supposed to do?"

Susu shrugged, "I think you already know what you have to do. It's just difficult. And there's no way around that. You end it with Henry as honestly as you can, and you allow him to feel whatever he feels. And then you give Shepherd a fair chance because you deserve that, Laurel. You just have to trust yourself." Susu paused and then added with a smirk, "I mean things could be worse. You actually dreamed your dream man into existence! And boy was he created with perfection in mind! That body, that face, and a brain! Girl, you got lucky."

Laurel rolled her eyes. "I didn't dream him into existence. Although it doesn't sound any crazier than what actually happened ... which I can't begin to explain. Ugh. I have to change. Henry's waiting downstairs."

"What?! Start with that, Laurel. Are you going to tell him tonight? I think you should. Just cut the cord. It's been coming for a while. You know that. Don't let this thing with Shepherd murky the waters. This was going to happen regardless, and you know it," Susu said as she followed Laurel into her room and sat down on her bed.

"I know," Laurel replied as she grabbed a black cocktail dress from the closet. "I wish I had done this before because now it just feels even more messy. And Henry is such a good guy. He doesn't deserve this." She slipped off her clothes and threw them across the room into the hamper.

Susu raised her eyebrows, "Well, I don't think he's a bad guy, but you know I've never thought he was the greatest for you. He doesn't see you, Laurel. Doesn't know you even after three years! It's time."

Laurel lifted her hair to let Susu zip up her dress. Stepping into her nude heels, she turned around with a sigh.

"Yep, it's time. Alright, will you be home when I get in tonight?"

"I have to go to work for a bit. Someone has to leave early, and I said I'd cover the rest of their shift. But I'll bring home pastries. We can have Saturday brunch tomorrow. If you need me, call. You know I'm here for you."

"Ok, sounds good. Love you, Susu."

"Love you, too! It's all going to be ok. Trust me."

CHAPTER 5

Henry cupped her face, lightly kissing her on the lips after she climbed into the limo.

"You look beautiful, Laurel."

She smiled, but it didn't reach her eyes. "Thanks, Henry."

The ride to the restaurant was quiet. Henry was trying his best to make small talk, but Laurel wasn't doing a particularly decent job participating. Once they were seated, Henry ordered their usual and waited for the wine to be brought to the table while he studied Laurel with a pensive face. Finally, he broke the silence.

"We've talked about it a lot, and I think it's time, Laurel. I want you to move in with me. If you're worried that I'm not ready, know that I am. We've been together for three years. We're a good team. I would marry you right now if I knew you'd have me, but you've been so skittish about moving in…" Henry paused, waiting for some sign from her. "Laurel, what are your thoughts?"

"It says a lot about our relationship, Henry, that I've been so hesitant to take the next step with you. You're a good man, but I don't think we're right for each other. I think it's time we admit that."

Henry's face darkened. "Is this because of Shepherd Ryan?"

"You know it's not, Henry. We've been talking about this for months. You've been ready for our relationship to progress, and I've had reservations about it." She paused, looking around. "Do you want to leave and go somewhere more private to talk?"

"I think enough has been said. I get it. I'm not the type of guy to push things with a girl who doesn't want me. I deserve better."

"Yes, you do. I'm sorry I couldn't be the one to give that to you."

He stood up and threw a hundred-dollar bill on the table. "Me, too. I'm sure you'll understand that I don't want to stay for dinner. Come on, the car is waiting for us."

She sighed as she stood up. This wasn't how she wanted their relationship to end but knew that there was no easy way to say goodbye. "I'll just walk."

"It's a long way from your apartment, and I don't want to worry about you getting home safely. I'll take you."

Laurel nodded and gathered her things. Once they got in the car, Henry stared straight ahead, refusing to look at her.

"Once you figure out that you've messed up, don't come crawling back. I'm a nice guy, but I'm not that nice."

Laurel knew that although things felt bad right now, this wasn't a mistake. She felt entirely sure of her decision.

"I really am sorry for breaking your heart, Henry."

Henry scowled, and they rode the rest of the way home in silence. Laurel wanted to say something to fix it but knew that nothing could. As they pulled onto her street, Henry sighed, reached over, and gently grabbed her hand. Laurel was thankful. She cared for Henry and didn't want it to end with hurtful words. She gave his hand a squeeze. As they stopped outside her building, Henry suddenly jerked his hand from hers and scrambled out the door, leaving Laurel confused. But as soon as she saw Shepherd standing outside her building, she understood.

Henry rounded on her, "Was this planned? Did he know you were going to break up with me?!"

"No, Henry, I swear. I never discussed this with him. Shepherd, what are you doing here?"

While Shepherd studied her, Henry raised his fist and slugged Shepherd in the face. Shepherd looked like he wanted to retaliate but then he looked at Laurel and his expression calmed. Henry turned and got into the car, slamming the door. Laurel watched the car drive away until it was gone. Only then did she turn around to face Shepherd. She couldn't help but feel angry.

"I'm sorry, Laurel. I didn't know that would happen."

"What are you doing here, Shepherd?"

"Can we go inside and talk?"

"No. Talk now. What are you doing here?"

"We agreed to spend more time together and then you had dinner with Henry. I just wanted to see where we stood. I thought that you'd still be out. I came by to leave my number so that you could call me when you were ready to talk. I put it in your mailbox and was just leaving when you pulled up."

Laurel sighed but didn't say anything.

"I won't lie and say that I'm sorry you're not with Henry anymore. I have no doubt that we belong together, and I won't apologize for that. But I hate that you're hurting."

"I only hurt because I caused Henry pain. I know I did the right thing." She paused and glared at him a little. "I didn't break up with him because of you."

His serious expression slowly turned into a smile. "I wouldn't think that for a moment."

"Good."

She stood for a moment with her arms crossed against her chest. "How's your jaw?"

"I've had much worse." Shepherd grinned and gave her a charming wink before taking a step closer to her. "Do you want to be alone?"

"Not really."

She had been thinking about the Henry situation for a long time and now that it was over, she was relieved. She didn't want to sit and ruminate over their conversation all night.

"Well, did you eat? I could take you out to dinner or we could go inside and order pizza? Or talk…or watch a movie. Whatever you want."

"Pizza sounds good. And a movie. I don't feel much like talking."

Shepherd gestured toward her building with a slight bow, "Lead the way."

Shepherd's hand fell to the small of her back as she passed him and led the way up the steps. The sensation that passed from his touch along her spine excited her, and she took a deep breath. She somehow knew that Shepherd was smiling and enjoying this without turning around to look at his face. She gave him a quick tour of the apartment, and he made himself at home in the kitchen, bringing out his phone to order a pizza. After he hung up, he sat beside her on the couch and asked what they were going to watch.

"I don't know. What types of movies do you like?"

"Anything but period pieces and sci-fi."

"Really? The period pieces I get. I mean you're a big, tough guy but sci-fi?!"

"A big tough guy can't like period pieces?"

"I mean you don't, so…." Laurel laughed.

She loved how comfortable they felt with one another as if they had known each other for years.

"You've got a point there. Although I have a friend who is pretty tough and is a sucker for anything romantic, including period pieces."

"So, what do you have against sci-fi?"

"It just feels a little too out of this world, too unrealistic for me, you know?"

"Not what I expected, Shepherd, but ok. So, you like horror, comedy, and drama then?"

"Maybe skip the drama too."

She laughed. "Alright, so horror or comedy then?"

"Yes, and animated. I love kid movies."

"Another surprise! I do too! How about Beauty and the Beast? It's one of my favorites."

"Sounds good to me."

Before the movie was over, Laurel fell asleep on a pillow on Shepherd's lap. She woke to the door opening and sat up, meeting Shepherd's eyes. They reflected his contentment.

"Sorry I fell asleep."

"You can use me for your pillow anytime you want," he replied with a charming smile.

The Dream

Susu came into the room and fell onto the nearest chair. "Well, well, Laurel. You left with one guy and came back with another. Quite the little minx, aren't you?"

Laurel groaned and leaned forward for the remote to turn the television off as Susu continued with a satisfied grin on her face.

"Nice to see you again, dream man."

"Shepherd. His name is Shepherd. Can you stop now, please?"

"Yes, I can. Actually, I'm really tired so I'm going to head to bed, but I brought pastries for our brunch tomorrow. Don't wake me up too early!"

After she left, Shepherd turned to Laurel with a mischievous glint in his eyes. "Too soon to stay the night?"

"It's tempting, but we said we'd take it slow."

"Well then, I should probably leave. Having you close to me for so long is wearing my restraint down. Your beautiful face...," he caressed her cheek, sparks springing from his touch. "These scrumptious lips," he leaned over to kiss her, gently but with so much passion.

She had wanted his lips on her since they met, and she felt it all the way down to her clitoris. He tugged on her bottom lip before releasing her lips and let his fingertips trace down her neck slowly, leaving her breathless.

"You're not playing fair," she whined.

"I never said that I would. You make me ache with desire, Laurel."

His face lingered dangerously close to hers, and she immediately closed the gap, straddling his lap, her dress coming up around her hips. She quickly met his lips, parting them with her tongue. Suddenly his hands were all over her, and she was grinding him as their tongues met and seemed to fight each other with intense desire. His hands grabbed her thighs, and his touch made her throb with longing. She could feel how hard his penis was as she pressed against him. *God, he feels huge. I want him inside me so badly. He's got me so wet; I'm probably ruining his pants.* She didn't care as she continued rubbing against his large shaft. Shepherd pulled back slightly, his eyes dark with lust.

"I want you so badly. But I don't want you to regret this. Tell me to stop, Laurel, or I'll take you right now."

Her head felt foggy with craving, but the voice in the back of her mind wondered if she'd regret being with him so soon. She would be with him. She had no doubt about it anymore. No one had ever felt so right. But she wanted their first time to be special.

"I want you too," she said breathlessly. "So much that it hurts. But I want our first time to be special. Maybe we should stop."

"Let me help you with your desire. I can control myself."

She trusted him as he lifted her, keeping her legs wrapped around his waist, and carried her to the bedroom. Laurel felt him lower his head to the crook of her neck and inhale deeply, his body relaxing, before setting her on the edge of the bed. Her dress was still around her hips, and he knelt in front of her, looking her in the eyes as he spread her legs. He kissed and sucked on the inside of her thighs as he slowly made his way to her core. Through her wet panties, his teeth gently nipped at her pussy. His warm breath against her already sensitive center created intense pleasure, and she moaned.

"Please, Shepherd."

That was all that he needed to hear. He swiftly pulled her panties off and threw them to the side. He attacked her with hunger, and she almost screamed out in delight. His tongue split her seam and began licking her. Then, concentrating on her bud, he sucked and nipped at it. She had never felt such intense pleasure as this. He held her hips down as she started to buck, not letting up as he moaned into her. When she thought she couldn't take it anymore, he plunged two thick fingers into her vagina roughly and thrust in and out of her until she screamed in ecstasy.

She melted into the bed, her legs shaking, her limbs heavy. Shepherd enjoyed every bit of her release, afterward crawling to lay beside her.

Looking into her eyes, he said one word, "Mine," before kissing her deeply so that she could taste herself on his lips.

She could feel his hard bulge against her thigh and didn't want him to go without his relief. Rolling over onto her side, she unbuttoned

The Dream

his pants and worked her way down to grip his hard, long shaft. She started to massage him as he groaned into her hair.

"Laurel, I won't last long."

She let go and shimmied down to pull his pants off and hovered over him. She had never seen such a large cock. She wondered if she'd be able to open her mouth wide enough to take him but wanted to try. Taking him in her hand, she met his dark gaze and held his eyes as she licked the pre-cum before slowly taking as much of him as she could and moving at a torturously slow pace.

"Oh goddess, that feels so good."

He started to move his hips gently, thrusting into her mouth. She could tell by the way his hands gripped the sheets that he was trying to control himself. She quickened the pace, going deeper until she could feel him touch the back of her throat. He filled every part of her mouth.

"I'm about to cum," Shepherd groaned as he pushed against her shoulders to get her to release him.

Instead, she aggressively tightened her mouth around his cock and went deeper and faster until she tasted his hot semen in her mouth. Pulling up until only the tip of his cock was in her mouth, she used her hand to work his dick while he orgasmed, drinking every bit of his arousal. When he finished, she wiped her mouth and crawled up beside him, draping her arm and leg around him. They both lay in complete contentment and silence for a long time, Shepherd running his fingers through her hair.

"I love you, Laurel. I don't ever want to let you go. Nothing has ever felt as good as it feels when I'm with you."

Laurel didn't respond, but he felt her smile against his chest. Under her leg, she could feel him harden.

She looked up in surprise, "Again?"

"Well, I'm…" Shepherd paused, and his face looked like he was searching for the words to say. Finally, he grinned and said, "I think this may be an issue with you. I'm afraid I'll never be soft when you're wrapped around me." After a moment, he added, "I don't want to leave, but I don't think I can trust myself around you. I would never pressure you to have sex when you're not ready, but I think I better head back to my hotel room and take a long, cold shower."

She nodded, understanding how he felt. Instead of relieving her desires, their act of passion had just intensified her need to have him bury himself deep inside of her.

"When can I see you again?"

She sighed and sat up. "I'm having brunch with Susu mid-morning, but we could meet in the afternoon. And then Monday, I'll have to go back to work."

She thought about how awkward that would be. Henry didn't work on the same floor as her, but she was sure word would get around the building quickly that they had split up and it was only a matter of time before they ran into each other. Shepherd sensed her worry and reminded her with a slight smirk that she never had to return to work if she didn't want to. He had every intention of winning her over- to his town and his bed.

"So, I heard that Shepherd stayed pretty late last night," Susu teased, sipping her coffee the next morning.

Laurel blushed in spite of herself, remembering the night before. The walls in the apartment were paper thin. "Umm hmm."

"Umm hmm? That's all? Spill!"

"Yes, he stayed a little late," Laurel replied coyly.

Susu just stared at her with wide eyes, obviously waiting for more details. "And?"

"And we had a really nice time."

"A really nice time?" Susu repeated sarcastically before her face became serious. "You're in love. Like I've never seen you before. What are you going to do?"

Laurel didn't even try to deny it. "I don't know. He wants me to move with him back to his hometown... Silver Moon, I think he called it."

"And you're going to?"

"I don't know. It seems like a big leap."

The Dream

"Well sometimes love is dangerous. Seriously, Laurel. You're always so composed. I've seen you with guys from college and Henry. But I've never seen you the way you are when Shepherd is in the room. I think this may be the real deal. You lucky bitch." Susu paused. "I like him, Laurel, I really do. He feels right for you."

"And what if I did move? What about you? Would you come?"

Susu winced, "We'll always be best friends. You can't get rid of me. But I don't know about moving to a small town."

Laurel took a bite of her pastry. She really didn't need Susu to tell her this time was different. She could feel it in her bones. But that didn't make it less scary.

"So, what happened last night with Henry? Was it terrible?"

Laurel sighed. She didn't even want to think about it. "It wasn't great. He was really hurt. But once I said that I thought we should end it, he just wanted to leave. I think he knew it was coming. And then when he dropped me off, Shepherd was here. Henry lost it."

"Lost it like how?" Susu's eyes gleamed, waiting for the juicy part.

Laurel couldn't help but laugh. "He punched Shepherd in the jaw."

"What?! Why do I miss all the good stuff?!"

"It wasn't good, Susu! Stop it!"

"I mean, I have no doubt that Shepherd could take him. Did they fight for your love?"

Laurel rolled her eyes. "NO! I thought Shepherd was going to kill him, but he didn't do anything. It really didn't seem to bother him at all." She paused, thinking back over the night. "I really hate that Henry was hurt. But I have no doubt that I did the right thing…for both of us, really. And Henry was a gentleman about it. He really was. Maybe things won't be too awkward around the office if we run into each other."

It was Susu's turn to roll her eyes. "There's no getting around the awkwardness, but I bet Henry will hook up with someone else before you can say overwhelming bravado." She paused before asking "So, what's next?"

"I don't know. Shepherd is supposed to call me later. I don't know how long he's staying. He says he doesn't want to leave without me."

"And what do you think? What's holding you back? I mean you're not happy at your job, and you never wanted to spend your whole life in New York City. So, why not take a risk? He seems worth it, Laurel."

"I don't know. He doesn't even feel like a risk. Between me and you Susu, he's it. I know he's it. But that's a big change. I don't want to be irresponsible."

Susu groaned. "Listen, you know I'm the last one to trust a guy. But falling in love doesn't necessarily mean you're being irresponsible. Especially with a gorgeous, rich, charming, totally head over heels in love with you guy like Shepherd. I know you always plan everything out, Laurel, and if I'm being selfish, I really don't want you to leave me. Can you imagine me living with anyone else? Seriously?! But come on, he really is your dream guy. Don't overthink it. You should dive in headfirst on this one."

Laurel sighed, "I think I already have."

A couple of hours later, Laurel was getting out of the shower when her phone rang. She broke into a grin when she saw the caller ID.

"Hey, Aunt Lucy! How are you?"

"Oh, I'm doing good, Laurel. Just thinking about you. How are things in the Big Apple?"

Laurel could tell something was wrong from her voice. "Things here are…interesting. Why do you sound strange? What's going on?"

"Well, that's what I'm calling about. It's time you knew. I had hoped to work things out on my own, but I don't think I'll be able to."

"What do you mean?" Laurel felt her chest tighten. Aunt Lucy was always solid as a rock. It made her nervous that something had her upset.

"I haven't been able to pay the taxes on the land and the cabin for a while, Laurel. I hate to admit that, but it's gotten to the point where I may have to sell. I know you love this place almost as much as I do. It's only fair that you know. It may all be gone by the end of the month."

Laurel didn't know what to say. She didn't have much in savings and doubted that it would be enough if her aunt was in trouble enough to lose the land. She couldn't imagine her home being gone. And what

The Dream

would Lucy do? Where would she go? She'd been there almost her whole life. That land was her life.

"I'm going to come. We're going to figure this out. Don't do anything until I get there."

"Laurel, you have your own life there in New York. You can't drop everything and come here to save the day. I'm a big girl. I'll make it through this. There's nothing to worry about."

Laurel knew her aunt was putting a brave front on, but there was no way she was okay with this. She had to be falling apart on the inside at the prospect of losing her home.

"Promise me you won't sign anything. I'm coming. You can't talk me out of it. Maybe there's nothing that can be done. But I'll be there tomorrow or the day after and we'll try to figure this out."

There was silence on the other end of the line for a long time. Finally, she heard a sigh. "Okay, Laurel. It really would be good to see you and give you a hug. And you may want to come see the old place before she belongs to someone else."

"I love you, Aunt Lucy. We'll figure this out somehow. I'll let you know when I'm arriving as soon as I know."

"Okay, dear. I'll see you soon."

The call ended and Laurel fell back on her bed, tears releasing themselves onto her pillow. She couldn't imagine not having the Oregon homeplace anymore. Even though she lived in New York, the cabin was always her happy place. And she couldn't imagine Aunt Lucy anywhere else. Where would she go?

She hated that Shepherd had stayed in town to spend time with her and she was leaving, but there was no way around it. She had to go home. He answered on the second ring.

"Hey, Sunshine! Are you ready for me to come over?"

"About that. I had a family emergency come up, and I'm afraid I'm going to be out of town for a few days. I'm so sorry, Shepherd."

"Is your aunt alright?" Shepherd asked, his voice full of concern.

"Yes, she's fine." She paused but decided there was no reason not to be completely open with him. "She's been having some financial issues that I didn't know about, and it looks like she's about to lose her land." Laurel's voice shook as she tried not to cry.

"I'll be there in 10 minutes. Don't make any plans."

"But—"

Nothing. Shepherd had hung up.

Laurel then decided to call Jim and give him a heads-up that she wouldn't be at work.

"What is it, Davis?"

Laurel suppressed a scream. *Who answers the phone that way?* "Hey Jim. I wanted to let you know that I won't be in the office for a few days. I've had a family situation come up and need to head home to Oregon."

"Something like your boyfriend broke up with you? Come on, Davis. You're going to have to face the music sometime. Get your butt to work tomorrow."

Now she really wanted to scream. *What a jerk! How did he even know? It just happened yesterday.* She took a deep breath to regain her composure. *Focus, Laurel. None of this matters.*

"I'm not sure what you heard, Jim, but it's not pertinent here. My aunt needs me, and I will be out at least a few days if not the whole week. I've used very little of my vacation time, so it shouldn't be an issue," she reminded him.

He's probably only mad because he'll actually have to work with me out of the office.

"Alright, Laurel, I'll approve it this one time. Get back to work as quickly as you can."

"Will do. I'll let you know when that will be. Have a good day."

She hung up before she could give into her temptation to tell Jim what she really thought. Jim already knowing about her breakup aggravated her. There hadn't even been a workday yet and the word had already leaked. Work was going to be miserable when she got back. She'd have loads of work piled on her desk from being off and she'd have to deal with the office gossips. *Great.*

The Dream

She barely had time to dwell on it before she heard a knock on the door. She heard Susu greeting Shepherd as she walked out of her room. As soon as Shepherd saw her, he enveloped her in his strong arms. She instantly felt comforted. He held her for several seconds before reluctantly letting go and stepping back to look at her.

"I have a plane at my disposal. Let me help you. I know this must be difficult for you, and you shouldn't have to plan a trip when I could take you."

"I appreciate it, Shepherd, but that's too much. I can book a flight."

"What's going on here? Why do you need to book a flight?" Susu interjected.

Laurel looked around Shepherd's large frame to answer. "Aunt Lucy is going to lose the cabin…and the land. I need to see if there's a way for us to keep it somehow."

"Wow. I can't even imagine her being anywhere else. What is she going to do?" Susu asked with concern.

"Hopefully stay in her cabin if I can figure this all out. If not…I have no idea, Susu. It's not good. She loves it there. It's her home."

"It's yours, too," Shepherd interjected, stepping forward to grab one of her hands. His touch seemed to give her strength. "Let me take you, Laurel. We could leave within a couple of hours."

"I don't know, Shepherd."

She heard Susu groan out of exasperation, "Laurel, stop being hard-headed! You need to get to your aunt and Shepherd here has a plane. Let. Him. Help. You don't always have to handle everything yourself. Take the help."

"Okay, okay," she relented, knowing that it made sense.

She looked up at Shepherd and squeezed his hand. "Thank you for doing this. I really appreciate it."

"There is absolutely nothing I wouldn't do for you, Laurel. You're my…you're the one I want to love and take care of forever." He let go of her hand. "I'm going to head back to the hotel and pick up a few clothes. I'll arrange the flight and be back here within an hour."

She fisted the back of his shirt as she hugged him tightly. "Thanks again, Shepherd."

He leaned down and kissed her gently on the lips. If her mind had not been so weighed down with worries, she would've led him directly to her room. He smiled coyly as if he had shared her thought.

"See you soon."

Chapter 6

As they stepped onto the plane, the pilot was there to meet them. Laurel wondered if Shepherd always used the same pilot.

"Ms. Davis," he smiled as he nodded his head towards her.

Shepherd stepped forward to grasp the pilot's forearm in greeting. "Thanks for being ready on such short notice, Truett."

"My pleasure, boss. Skies look clear for our flight. We'll be ready to head out in about ten minutes."

"Good." Shepherd put his arm around Laurel's waist and led her to the couch, holding her hand. "It'll be about a six-hour flight. What do you want to do?"

"I'm actually pretty tired. Would you mind if I took a nap?"

"Of course not. Go lay down. There's a television in there too if you want to watch a movie. I've got to check in with Matty and Beck on a few things, but I'll join you in a little while."

She made her way to the back of the plane and laid down. Exhaustion settled in and the next thing she knew, she was waking up to Shepherd cuddling with her. She turned over to face him as she yawned.

"Hello, sleepyhead. We're just about to land."

"I slept the whole time? Wow, I didn't know I was that tired. Did you sleep too?"

"No. I had work to do. I just came to wake you. I have a car waiting for us at the airport. Do you want to text your aunt and let her know we'll be there in about an hour?"

"Yeah, that's a good idea." Laurel slowly sat up in bed, rubbing her eyes to wake up. She dug her phone out from her bag and sent a text to her aunt. She responded right away.

[Lucy] I can't wait to see you and meet Henry. I'd say it's about time!

Laurel groaned. Lucy obviously thought the "friend" she mentioned bringing was Henry. The news about the land had been so shocking to her, she hadn't thought to update her aunt on the situation. She hated to do it over text, but it was the only way.

[Laurel] About that. Henry and I broke up recently. The man I'm bringing is Shepherd Ryan. We haven't been dating long, but I really like him. I think you will too.

There was a long pause in the message. Laurel stared at the screen, waiting for a response. She didn't want to go into detail over text about what happened between her and Henry or how special Shepherd already was to her. She hoped that Aunt Lucy would be open to their relationship. Finally, her phone dinged, and she looked down at the message.

[Lucy] If he's special enough for you to bring home, I'm sure I will like him. I'll be watching for you both! I love you!

[Laurel] Love you too, Aunt Lucy

Relief rushed over her, a welcome feeling in what had been a stressful day. Before she knew it, the plane had landed, and they were in the car on the way to the cabin. Laurel felt nervous. Not only about introducing Shepherd but how they would resolve the situation with the land.

Shepherd saw her furrowed brow and grabbed her hand. "Don't worry. It will all work out, I promise."

The Dream

"How can you say that? What if there's no way to keep the land? I'm so worried for Aunt Lucy. I just can't imagine her anywhere else. She loves her cabin."

Shepherd hesitated before taking a deep breath. "Okay, this may make you upset. But I did some digging on your aunt's property."

"Why would that upset me? We need all the help we can get figuring this out. What did you find out?"

"The fees in addition to the unpaid taxes have made it a difficult amount for you and your aunt to pay."

She knew that wasn't all he wanted to say. "This is like pulling teeth, Shepherd. Out with it."

"Beck has been working on this since I left your apartment earlier. There's an investment firm who is trying to buy the land out from under your aunt. Because of their connections, I doubt your aunt would even be able to take out a loan on the land. So, I bought it."

Laurel interrupted, "YOU bought our land? Shepherd…" Now she felt angry.

He held his hands up. "Wait, let me explain. There's no way you or your aunt would've been able to fix this on your own. Beck is very savvy, and I told him that if there was any way that you could do this, we would take that route. I knew you wouldn't want to accept help. You barely let me use my plane to get you here faster. And since your aunt raised you and lives on her own, it wasn't a stretch for me to assume she would feel the same." He turned towards her, taking both of her hands. "Laurel, trust me when I say that there was no way you wouldn't lose the land unless I bought it. But let me be clear. The land is to be signed over to you and your aunt jointly. The papers are already drawn up and have been sent to the bank. Once you and your aunt sign them, the land is yours free and clear."

She started to argue, but he cut her off. "I know you don't want this, but you also don't want to lose your land. There is no other way, Laurel. I have plenty of money. This does not impact me other than bringing me happiness. I want to help you and your aunt."

"What if things don't work out between us? You'll regret spending this money."

"I have no doubt we will work out. None." He flashed an amused smile her way. "But I'll play your game. Let's say you decide you don't want to be with me. I would never regret doing this for you. If you left me yesterday, I would still do this for you today. I'm a man who knows myself. I wouldn't do something I was unsure of. No matter what happens, this land belongs to you and your aunt."

It was difficult for Laurel to swallow her pride. She never wanted to be in a position where she felt that she was in debt to someone else.

"Thanks for all you've done, Shepherd. Really. I'll have to talk with my aunt before we decide."

Laurel was silent the rest of the ride. She didn't want to be rude or ungrateful, but she also couldn't be excited that someone had to step in to save her and her aunt. She was the type of girl who prided herself on not needing to be rescued. This felt uncomfortable to her, even though she trusted Shepherd and his motives. She had every intention of looking over the numbers herself to make sure there was no other way. Beck may be good at his job, but her motivation for finding another way was stronger.

With all the thoughts running rampant in her head, it didn't take long until they arrived at the cabin. Lucy was sitting on the front porch, a preoccupied but happy look on her face. Laurel understood her feelings completely. It had been so long since they had seen each other, but the circumstances were not ideal. They rushed forward to embrace and held each other for a long time. Lucy let go of her first and turned towards Shepherd.

"Well, you must be pretty great for Laurel to bring you at a time like this."

Laurel felt an odd sense of pride as she watched Shepherd envelop Lucy's small form in a hug. As they parted, Lucy turned to lead them both up the steps to the cabin.

"Well, there's no sense in small talk. I know you'll want to look at the paperwork. I've got it spread out on the table. I can't see a way around it, Laurel. I'm afraid we're in for heartbreak. I've looked at the numbers until they all blur together and still, I can't find a way out."

The Dream

Laurel sat down at the table and started sorting through the papers. She knew that there was, in fact, a way out but also knew that Lucy would feel the same way as she did about it. She'd rather not disclose the information that the land had already been bought until she inspected the paperwork herself. She knew that if she found something Beck had missed, Shepherd would relinquish the land back in whatever form she wanted if that was her wish. Lucy made fast work of brewing tea, and she and Shepherd sat silently and patiently, sipping from their mugs as they allowed her the time she needed to go over the numbers. By the time she finished, it was dark outside, and Lucy had prepared dinner. She reached over Laurel and shuffled the papers into a neat pile before moving them to the counter.

"I know you've got a sharp mind, Laurel, but I'd be surprised if even you found a loophole in all of this. I've been looking over these for weeks and I just can't find a way out. I'm sorry, honey."

Laurel ran her hands through her hair and closed her eyes, sighing deeply and taking a moment to gather her thoughts. "You're right. I don't see a way to dig ourselves out of this." She grabbed the bowl of soup that Aunt Lucy had placed in front of her. "Thanks," she said, barely looking up. "I'm so sorry, Aunt Lucy."

"I know, darling. I let it all get away from me and now we're going to lose it. But we have to keep what's important in front of us. We still have each other. This is just an opportunity for a fresh start."

Laurel winced, knowing that the solution was already in front of them but unsure of whether her aunt would accept it. "Actually, it doesn't have to be."

Lucy looked up at her with her eyebrows raised, waiting for the rest of the revelation.

"The land has already been bought."

Lucy looked confused. "Well, it's as good as bought, I'll agree. But it hasn't happened yet. We have at least another month before I'll have to move out."

Laurel looked across at Shepherd, who gave her an encouraging nod. He had to know that this wouldn't be an easy conversation but his confidence in the decision gave her strength.

"Shepherd has already bought the land." She watched as Lucy's eyes shot Shepherd, giving him a wary look. She quickly continued, "And he's already deeded it back to you and me. Jointly."

There was a long pause as Lucy studied her dish. Finally, she looked up at Shepherd with determination. "I appreciate the offer, Shepherd, I really do. And I can see that you care a lot for Laurel. But this isn't your problem, and I can't accept your help."

He smiled at her compassionately. "I'm afraid that it's already done, Lucy. I acknowledge this is a tricky situation and I know you and Laurel wish that there was another way. You don't know me, but I love Laurel and I can't stand by and watch her or someone she loves lose something that is so important when it's an easy fix for me. This costs me little and gives me great satisfaction. Let me assure you that this will never be mentioned again. There are no strings attached. The land is yours- free and clear. You just have to sign the papers." He paused, looking at the two strong-willed women. "It's done already. This land has always been yours. It should remain yours."

There wasn't much left to say after that. Lucy gathered the dishes and quietly washed up. Laurel could tell that she couldn't allow herself to feel relieved. She knew that she didn't like the feeling of being in debt to someone. Laurel knew this because she felt the same way. It didn't need to be explained. She hoped that things would feel more natural tomorrow between Lucy and Shepherd. Lucy headed to bed, and Laurel couldn't bring herself to make Shepherd a makeshift bed on the couch. She needed him beside her. He settled in next to her in her old room, holding her gently as they drifted off to sleep together.

When Laurel woke in the morning, she rolled over to find Shepherd sleeping peacefully. She watched his chest rise and fall, admiring his chiseled profile and tranquil expression. She lightly caressed his arm until she saw his eyes flutter open and turn sleepily towards her.

"Good morning, Sunshine." His voice was low and gravelly and filled her with warmth.

The Dream

She snuggled closer to him, nestling her head into his neck. "Morning, Shep. Did you sleep well?"

He chuckled at her using his nickname. "Better than ever. I don't think I can ever go back to sleeping by myself. I hope you're okay with that."

She took a deep, contented breath. "I think I am."

They lay there for a while longer until the smell of eggs and bacon wafted in.

"I guess we better join Aunt Lucy for breakfast." As they dressed, Laurel turned to Shepherd. "Hey, I want to say thank you. It's difficult for us to accept help, but it doesn't mean that we don't appreciate it. We just need to get past our pride. What you did was amazing."

He nodded at her in a way that made her sure that he understood what she meant. She got no sense from him that he was offended by their reaction to his purchasing the land, and it made her belief in his benevolence even stronger.

Lucy appeared cheerful during breakfast but to Laurel's trained eye, it was forced. She hoped that Shepherd didn't sense it. He quickly finished breakfast and asked if anyone minded if he went for a jog. They both agreed, a little too quickly, and his smile showed that he knew they needed time alone. He bent to kiss her forehead before returning to the room to change. Laurel and Lucy sat quietly at the table until after he left and then sat for a few more minutes, just staring at each other. It was Lucy that finally spoke.

"Laurel, I like him. I can see that he has a good heart. But I don't like taking his help. Don't get me wrong. I didn't want to lose the land either. And I'm grateful that I get to stay. But it just kills me that someone had to buy the land and gift it back to me."

"I know, Aunt Lucy. I feel the same way. But that's the way it has to be. You raised me to be independent." She looked into her aunt's eyes with new understanding. "But you also raised me to gather strength from those around me. And that's what we have to do now. I trust Shepherd. And you should too. This is a time when we must accept help. And instead of feeling burdened by it, we should just try to be thankful."

Aunt Lucy reached across the table to grasp Laurel's hands. "When did you get so wise?" She settled back into her chair before studying Laurel. "So, you trust him? I can see that you care a lot for him. But you said in your text that you haven't been dating him for long. That doesn't sound like you, Laurel. To jump into something so quickly."

Her aunt looked concerned. Laurel understood. She tried to think of a way to explain the situation to her aunt in a way that would make sense but telling her that she had dreamed about Shepherd for a month and then he just appeared felt absurd. Still, she wanted to be honest with her aunt.

"You're right, it's not like me. But there's something different about him. We both feel this strong emotional and physical connection. I don't know how else to explain it, but I just know he's the one for me. I don't know how it will work out or even if it will, really. But now that I know him, I can't imagine myself with anyone else."

Something in her aunt's eyes changed as Laurel spoke. "You sound just like your mother. That's almost exactly how she described her relationship with your dad." Her aunt studied her tea for a second before looking up. "And they were incredibly happy together. Happier than any other couple I've ever known. So, what can I say? I trust you, Laurel, and I hope you'll trust yourself. You've got a good head on your shoulders."

Lucy got up and gathered their dishes to wash. Laurel slowly drank her tea and took a minute to look around the home that she grew up in. She loved everything about it. The open concept, the old, creaky floors. The wood paneling on the wall had been painted a light blue many, many years ago, and had worn to a comfortably hue. The open shelves in the kitchen wore curtains that were never closed. Cast iron skillets that had been used to cook meals for a hundred years hung above the butcher block island. They had been Lucy's grandmothers. One day they would be Laurel's.

On the opposite sides of the main room were the two bedrooms, each with their own bathroom. Laurel's room hadn't changed much since she'd moved in at thirteen. There were a few paintings on the wall,

all of them done by her mother, and a quilt made when Laurel was born, shortly before her grandmother had died, lay on the bed. A few pictures lined the dresser. One of her parents on their wedding day, a couple of them with Laurel, and several of her and Lucy, in the woods or in the cabin, all taken by timer. Her aunt loved taking pictures. A few times a year, she would set up a dark room in her bathroom and develop the rolls of pictures she had taken, mostly of nature, angles of light hitting objects in the cabin in a beautiful way, or of Laurel.

Lucy taped them all over her room- a wallpaper of memories. Laurel had studied them for hours. She had even found a few of her mother scattered around, but mostly they were nature shots. The majority of the animals were birds, but there was a red fox, and a couple of a wolf that Laurel loved because it seemed to be staring right at the camera. She knew that the wolf must've been a visitor to their property for a while, because it looked exactly like the wolf in one of her mother's paintings. The painting was of a forest scene with a beautiful, proud-looking wolf standing beside a tree, with yellow eyes staring straight into your soul.

The worn couch and two comfortable chairs in the living room, angled around the wood-burning fireplace, were just a few steps from the kitchen table. A large built-in bookshelf was directly behind the couch, filled with all of Laurel's favorites. Laurel had read and re-read the books on that shelf many times over. The familiarity of their words was like an embrace. In the bookshelf were a few more pictures- Lucy with Laurel's mother, Rose, and their mother. She smiled before walking slowly along the shelf, studying the framed photos. Laurel with her parents, Laurel with Lucy, one of her at her high school graduation and a few that Laurel had sent Lucy over the years. In one frame she and Susu, her face contorted in a funny expression, had their arms wrapped around each other's shoulders, each in their graduation gowns.

Another showed her on the steps of her apartment building, dressed up for her first day of work in NYC. Laurel remembered how excited she had been. She had the feeling that she was going to take on the world. That seemed like a long time ago now. Things certainly had not gone as planned. Her eyes fell on a picture of her and Henry in front of the Rockefeller Center Christmas tree their second Christmas together. Laurel had asked a stranger to take their photograph. She grabbed it, turning to Aunt Lucy, who was drying her hands with a dish towel.

"Mind if I put this somewhere else?" she asked with a slight grimace.

Lucy laughed. "Not at all. It's yours to do whatever you like with."

She didn't want to throw it away, so she took it into her room and put it in a drawer, tucked under some clothing.

When Shepherd returned from his run, he chopped firewood. Laurel and Lucy sat on the front porch and watched him while they visited. Laurel couldn't help but admire the ease with which Shepherd worked. He had shed his shirt after a few minutes of working under the heat of the sun and his glistening arms and chest were enough to make anyone drool. After he had cut a large stack of firewood, he asked Laurel if she wanted to take a walk. He'd found a creek on his run and wanted to take a dip before it started to cool off. While Laurel put on her swimsuit under her clothes, Shepherd borrowed a blanket and a couple of towels from Lucy.

When they were ready, Shepherd grabbed her hand, smiling at her as they started down the path. "So, how long do you have off work?"

"I told Jim I wasn't sure how long I'd be, but we should probably head back tomorrow or Wednesday. I don't want to miss the whole week. Jim wasn't happy about me taking off, and I'll have a pile of paperwork as my punishment."

"You don't have to go back at all. Visit Silver Moon with me instead."

"It's tempting. And I do want to go to Silver Moon, but I'm not ready to quit my job just yet, Shepherd. So much has happened this past week. I need some time to process it all."

"I understand. It's an open invitation. You tell me when you're ready, and I'll whisk you away!"

Laurel appreciated not being pressured. She figured that Shepherd knew it was inevitable. She was no longer denying that she had feelings

The Dream

for him or that she wanted to give their relationship a try even if she wasn't quite ready to jump in hook, line, and sinker.

She squeezed his hand before letting it go. "I'll race you!"

She broke off into a run, and Shepherd quickly overtook her. *Ah, so he's competitive!* She knew that he could easily beat her with speed, but he didn't know the woods as well as she did. She raced off the path, weaving in and out of the trees until she reached the clearing just in time to see Shepherd running up the path.

He stopped, laughing. "You didn't play fair."

She gave him a mischievous look and replied, "I never said that I would."

He raised his eyebrows and chuckled, "Using my own words against me, Sunshine?! I'm going to have to watch myself around you!"

Wrapping his arms around her waist, he pulled her closer to him. She leaned into him, feeling arousal awaken within her. His scent was so alluring, it felt like a drug. His hand went to her chin, lifting her face to meet his. Bringing his forehead against hers, he stared at her for a moment before closing his eyes and deeply breathing in. When he opened his eyes again, they were darker and filled with lust. Before he could react, she kissed him passionately. He eagerly returned her intensity. Quickly, she tugged his shirt up but wasn't tall enough. He broke their kiss with a smile as he pulled his shirt over his head and tossed it aside. Her hands trailed down his chest, and unbuttoned his pants, sliding her hand down to grasp his already hard shaft. He groaned but pulled away slightly.

"Wait, Laurel," he breathed in a strained voice.

She frowned at him. "Why? You don't want to?"

He cocked his head to the side. "More than you'll ever know. But I've been doing some thinking and I need to talk to you first."

She nodded, feeling apprehensive. She waited while he laid the blanket out. She wished now that she hadn't taken his shirt off. His body was more than a distraction. He sat down and patted the spot across from him. She joined him on the blanket and looked at him questioningly.

"Don't look so worried, Laurel. I want you. Nothing will change that, but I'm afraid that what I have to tell you may change the way you feel about me, and I don't want to go any farther with you until you know the whole truth."

"Okay, now I'm really worried. Are you married?" she asked, trying to lighten the mood. She trusted him and knew that he wasn't that type of man. But she couldn't think of anything else that would change the way she felt about him.

He raised his eyebrows at her in surprise. "Married?! No, Laurel. It's not that." He looked down at his hands as if he were unsure of where to start.

"Well then, just tell me."

"Promise you'll let me finish what I have to say."

She paused. "Okay," she responded slowly. "I promise."

He glanced up at her again, his eyes silently pleading. "There is something different about the two of us. You already have an idea about this since you dreamed about me before we even met. But you may have wondered why that didn't surprise me or why we both felt so strongly for each other so quickly. I know that is unlike you. But there's a reason for this magnetic pull we feel towards each other, why we can be sure that we are meant for each other." He waited a moment to see if she had anything to say, but she just stared at him silently, wanting him to continue. He sighed. "I knew this would be hard. I've spent so much time wondering how the best way to tell you this is. I'm just going to say it." He took a deep breath. "I'm a werewolf."

Laurel looked at him with disbelief. *Is he playing a joke on me to pay me back for beating him in the race? That seems petty, and a really intricate ruse.*

"You promised you'd hear me out, remember?"

She nodded, but her expression was full of annoyance.

"I'm not just a werewolf. I'm an Alpha. That means I'm the leader of my pack. Beck is my Beta, or second-in-command, and Matthius is my Gamma. Charis is a werewolf as well. Part of being a werewolf is having what we call a fated mate. For an Alpha, it's even more important. His mate is the Luna of the pack. She's the heart of all of it. Without her, the pack is never as strong or unified as it should be. I've been waiting

The Dream

for you for a long time. An awfully long time, Laurel. You're my mate. I could scent you on the street that day. It was the most alluring scent I'd ever smelled in my life- roses and sandalwood. Then I saw you and if there had been any doubt, it would've disappeared that moment." He smiled at her; his eyes full of hope. "You are the most beautiful woman I have ever seen. Everything in me wanted to rush to you, kiss you, mark you, and make you mine. Then I saw Henry touch you. I already told you that Matty had to pull me aside. To see another man touch you made me feel so angry. I wanted to rip his arm off of his body."

Laurel's eyes widened in shock, and he shook his head before continuing.

"I'm sorry. I know that sounds terrible. Once I knew you were human, I knew that I would have to be patient. But you seemed to sense that we were supposed to be together as well, which is more than I could've hoped for. It doesn't usually go that way for werewolves mated to humans. There's nothing I wouldn't do for you, Laurel. I'm meant to be with you forever." He paused. He wanted her to say something. She stood and he did too, looking apprehensive. She started walking and he whispered, "Please don't leave, Laurel. I don't want to lose you."

"I just need to think. Give me a minute."

He forced himself to sit down as she paced, trying to make sense of what he said. It definitely wasn't a trick. He really believed this. Her mind felt like it would explode, and she was using all her mental energy trying to think this through rationally. Suddenly, a scene from her last dream flashed in her mind. The wolf. The proud feeling that she had when the wolves had howled in unison as they surrounded her. She turned to him.

"Let me see."

He looked confused. "What do you mean?"

"I want to see you turn into a wolf. Or can you only do it during a full moon?"

"No, it doesn't really work that way. I can shift whenever I like." He looked at her guardedly. "But I'm not sure I can trust my wolf right now. He wants to make you ours. That's why I went for a run this morning. Patience is not a virtue he possesses."

"Wait, he's different from you? You're talking about him like he's a different person."

"Well, we share the same desires mostly, but I'm more rational than him. He's governed by his passions. You've seen glimpses of him... when my eyes get dark. That's him trying to surface."

She folded her arms across her chest. "I still want to meet him."

After studying her for a moment, Shepherd could see that she wasn't going to change her mind. He started to pull his pants off.

"What are you doing? I don't want to have sex right now, Shepherd!"

He allowed a small smile. "I know that. I don't want to rip my clothes when I shift." He stood before her, completely naked. She kept her gaze trained on his eyes. She would not be distracted by his body right now. "His name is Angus. He will want to get close to you and smell you. Whatever you do, don't run from him." He paused. "Promise me, Laurel."

She looked frightened but agreed. "I promise."

Shepherd's face showed that he didn't think this was a good idea. "Do you want to close your eyes while I shift? It can be unsettling to watch."

"No."

He sighed. "Ok, I'll shift quickly."

He lowered his head and faster than she imagined possible, a wolf about the size of a small horse stood in his place. Laurel gasped. It was the wolf from her dream. She didn't know how any of this could be happening. Her mind felt fuzzy, and she started to sway. Angus rushed to her side, maneuvering himself between her arm and her body to help steady her. Her hand reached out and instinctively grabbed his fur. It was incredibly soft. She ran her fingers through it, and he nestled his head into her hand.

After a moment, he started sniffing at her. He was close to her neck, and she began to feel afraid. *Maybe I should've listened to Shepherd. What if Angus can't control himself and bites me?* As if he could sense her fear, he looked into her eyes and growled low. His black eyes started to flicker, and she closed her eyes tightly, bracing herself for

The Dream

what may happen. She felt hands cupping her face and opened her eyes to see Shepherd standing before her, his eyes full of concern.

"Are you alright? Angus loves you, too. He would never intentionally hurt you."

"I thought he may bite me."

Shepherd tried to hide a smile. "He does want to bite you. He's been pestering me about it since the moment we spotted you."

Laurel was shocked. "How can you say he doesn't want to hurt me if he's been trying to get you to bite me?!"

"He wants to mark you. It is technically a bite. But it's not one to injure you. He wants to put our mark on you so that we're always connected. So that others know that you are ours. And of course, for you to put your mark on me so that everyone knows that I am yours."

She fell back onto the quilt, her arms lying limply beside her. Shepherd lay down beside her but didn't try to touch her.

"I saw Angus in my dream. After I met you, my dream changed, and I saw him."

Shepherd sat up, resting on his elbows. "Are you sure?"

"Of course, I'm sure. That's one reason I wanted to see him."

He sat, obviously waiting for her to continue. When he couldn't stand the wait anymore, he prompted her. "What are you thinking, Laurel?"

She lay in silence for several more seconds before answering. "Tell me more about mates. How did you know? What does it mean?"

He leaned up and looked at her, but she kept her gaze at the sky. Laying back down, he answered, "Werewolves believe that mates are chosen for them by the Moon Goddess. Each wolf typically gets one mate. When mates accept each other, they mark one another, and other wolves can tell that they're mated. Their scents mingle together to become one." He paused, looking over at her. When she didn't say anything, he continued. "Once they're mated, they can feel each other's emotions more strongly and can speak to each other through the mind link. Pack members can already communicate through a mind link but if the mates weren't part of the same pack, they can't use the link until they've completed the bond."

He paused and Laurel could tell he was struggling with what to share with her. After a moment, he continued. "Sometimes, wolves don't find their mate. They can take a chosen mate. Their bond is strong, but rarely as strong as fated mates. When a mate dies, their connection, whether they are fated or chosen, is often so strong that the other wolf will die as well."

"So, if you or I die, the other will die also?"

"Most likely. Some survive but are often incredibly sad and become loners. Others go crazy."

"And we have no choice in this?" She finally rolled over to look at Shepherd and saw from his expression that he was pained by her question.

He turned to his side; his face close to hers. "You have a choice, Laurel. If you decide you don't want to be with me, you can reject me."

"Will you die?"

His anxiety was evident even though she could tell he was trying to hide it. He took a slow breath before answering. "No, not since we haven't completed our mating."

"What would happen then?"

"I really don't want you to think about that, Laurel. I want you to make the decision that's right for you. I already accept you as my mate and I want you to be happy. I believe that you would be happiest with me and I with you, but it must be your decision and you should make it without guilt or pressure. A lot would change for you. But if you choose me, I will always be here for you. Because I love you and because we are connected, your happiness would always be my motivation and desire. Wolves are protective and passionate, they're loyal. I would never cheat on you or intentionally hurt you. You would truly be part of my soul. Hell, you already are. I love you, Laurel. But I want you to be sure of your decision."

"If I…decide I can't be your mate, will you take a chosen mate?"

"No," he said fiercely, and then calmed himself. "You are it for me."

She stayed quiet for many moments, studying the way the clouds moved and listening to the wind in the trees. She didn't completely

The Dream

understand his words, but knew that there was no rejecting Shepherd. She had felt the connection from the beginning, even if she didn't have the background to know what was happening. She could feel Shepherd's stress, and it pained her. She sat up and looked down at him. He was so beautiful. Not just his face and his body; his very soul was beautiful to her. The way their hearts were connected, their fates intertwined before they even met. That was something she absolutely understood and wouldn't deny.

"I don't understand all of this, and I may not know all the details or how it will work with you being a wolf and me being a human. But I do feel our connection. I want to be with you. I just don't know if I'm supposed to be the Luna of a pack of werewolves when I'm a human. And I don't want to agree to anything before I know what it means. But I will try. Is that enough for you?"

He sat up and grasped her hands as she spoke. "It's more than enough. I know the rest will work itself out."

Everything in her wanted to tell him that he was it for her too, but she was afraid. This new information was overwhelming, and she didn't want to make promises she couldn't keep. She needed to know what she was getting herself into even if she knew, deep down, that it already didn't matter what the consequences were. She would be his and he would be hers. Until she could say that aloud to him with complete confidence, she wanted to give him what she could of herself.

This time when she leaned in to kiss him, he didn't stop her. His eyes were dark with lust already, his wolf just below the surface. Their passion was electrifying, the sparks from his touch igniting a wild desire within Laurel's body. Before she knew it, her shirt was off. She wanted to feel his skin against hers, to have him touch her in every way and in every place. He rolled her over onto her back and began kissing her passionately. Their mouths fought each other for dominance and when Shepherd broke the kiss, she gasped for air as his kisses trailed down her neck. She could feel his teeth rake against the bottom of her neck. The sensation was enough to make her moan. His teeth reluctantly released her, and Laurel wondered if he had wanted to mark her. The thought made her throb with desire. He sucked on each of her nipples as his hand slid down to cup her sex. She arched into it and pressed against him.

"I want you now, Shepherd" she moaned.

"I don't want to hurt you, Love. Be patient. I need to make sure you're ready to take me."

He kissed her soft stomach and released her sex as he moved between her legs, his warm breath creating tingles of pleasure within her. She looked down at him and saw that his dark gaze was focused on her face as his fingers opened her slit. He hungrily sucked her clitoris before moaning into her. The vibrations of his voice made her shudder.

"You're so delicious, Laurel. I can never get enough of you."

He licked and sucked at her sensitive bud ravenously, sending jolts of pleasure through her as she quickly orgasmed, calling out his name. He kneeled in front of her, and she stared again at his large cock. She licked her lips as he moved to hover over her.

"I'll be gentle. Tell me if it hurts." He positioned himself in front of her seam and slowly pushed in, not putting his whole weight on her.

She couldn't help but gasp at the feeling. Shepherd looked at her with concern. "I can take you. Don't you dare stop, Shepherd."

That was all the encouragement he needed. He leaned down to kiss her, entering her slowly, letting her stretch to him. She opened her eyes and could see the strain on his face as he willed himself to take his time. Finally, he was completely inside her, and he paused, breathing slowly for a few breaths.

"Oh goddess, Laurel. You're so tight. Are you alright, Love?"

The sense of being completely filled with him made her impatient for him to continue. "I'm more than okay. Please, Shepherd," she begged.

After he had gently moved within her a few times and was sure that his size wasn't causing her any pain, his eyes went completely dark, and he began to penetrate her harder and faster.

She cried out with delight. "Yes!"

He powerfully thrust into her repeatedly until she couldn't take it anymore. She had never felt this level of ecstasy before. Pleasure raced through her body, igniting every nerve, every cell. As her orgasm hit, her channel tightened and pulsed around his shaft. Shepherd's breathing became more erratic as his ecstasy increased until he finally roared her name, simultaneously filling her with his seed. He leaned down to kiss her gingerly on the lips. Reluctantly, he pulled out of her before wiping himself off and lying beside her, reaching over to hold her hand.

"Laurel," he began but then just sighed.

"Exactly," she responded breathlessly.

Chapter 7

They lay in each other's arms for a long time, enjoying the feeling of being close to one another. Laurel was trying not to think about Shepherd's revelations. When she was in his arms, none of it mattered. She knew she'd have to digest it at some point and figure out what it meant for her. But for now, she wanted to enjoy being in his embrace. Her head lay on his chest, listening to his heartbeat and feeling the rise and fall of his chest. For a man made entirely of muscle, he was surprisingly comfortable to rest on. As the sun was setting, Shepherd suggested they go for a swim before they returned to the cabin. Grudgingly, she agreed, and they waded into the cool water and swam around for a bit. Shepherd's hands were always touching her, and she enjoyed the feeling. It was simultaneously comforting and electrifying. She couldn't seem to get enough of him and didn't think she ever would.

After dinner, Shepherd headed to the bedroom to call Beck, and Laurel and Lucy went to the front porch. They sat silently swaying on the porch swing. Laurel knew that her time with her aunt was ending and wanted to talk to her about all of the things that were weighing on her. The concerns about losing the cabin and needing to accept Shepherd's help felt like the distant past now. She couldn't hide Shepherd's confession from her aunt. As her only relative, she would need to know. Laurel felt that her aunt could help her make sense of it but didn't know how to broach the subject. How could her aunt believe something that she wouldn't have believed if she hadn't seen Shepherd turn into a wolf with her own eyes? And yet, she had to try.

"Aunt Lucy? I need to talk to you about something. Something that will seem unbelievable, but I hope you know me well enough to know that I would never lie to you."

"Sounds serious."

"It is and I need you to believe me because you're important to me and I could really use your advice."

"You can trust me with whatever is on your mind, Laurel. What is it, honey? Is it about Shepherd?"

"Yes."

"Well, out with it. What's on your mind?"

Laurel paused. They stopped swinging and her aunt looked at her expectantly. "Maybe it would be best to start at the beginning."

"That's usually a good place to start," her aunt agreed.

"About a month ago, I had a dream. At first just a few times a week and eventually every night. I was dreaming of Shepherd. And then last week, it happened just like the dream, outside of my office. He appeared for a moment in the crowd but then I didn't see him again. I thought I'd imagined the entire thing because it seemed unreal, you know? So unrealistic. I mean things like that just don't happen. But then he ended up at my work, interested in a site that we were brokering. When I saw him, something inside me awakened. The most innocent of gestures, of touches, electrified me. There was a strange connection there. I already knew that things with Henry and I weren't going to work out. He wanted to move our relationship to the next step, and I never felt ready. But when Shepherd appeared, it all made sense. I knew that he was the one for me, that I was somehow waiting for him all my life even though I didn't know it before that moment. We've been spending time together and it feels natural. I feel like he knows me already. More than anyone else, really."

Laurel waited but Lucy didn't say anything. She decided to say the most difficult part, as bluntly as Shepherd had told her. There was no lead up that would make this easier to explain. "Shepherd knew we were meant for each other, too. Not a 'love at first sight' sort of thing. I mean, it was. But it was more than that, you know?" Still, Lucy said nothing. She wasn't going to give Laurel any help apparently. "I was confused by

The Dream

it all. But tonight, he told me something that made it make sense even though I still don't understand it all."

"Laurel, just say it."

"He's a werewolf. He says that we're fated mates. It means that we were chosen by the Moon Goddess or something to be together forever. He's an Alpha and that makes me something called a Luna. I know it sounds crazy, but I saw it with my own eyes. I saw him turn into a wolf. His wolf's name is Angus. And the really insane part is that after I met him, I had another dream. Well, it isn't the really insane part. That would be him being a wolf." Laurel knew she was rambling out of nervousness and took a quick breath before continuing. "It started out like the one I'd had for months but then it changed. I was in a field alone and suddenly I saw his wolf. Angus. I was surrounded by wolves, and they all seemed to love and accept me. It felt real. I was connected to all of them but mostly to Shepherd…and Angus." She paused before continuing, desperately needing her aunt to understand and believe her. "It's true, Aunt Lucy. I know it seems unbelievable but it's completely true. And I don't know what any of it means or what I'm supposed to do about it, so I need you to believe me."

Time passed in long moments before Lucy spoke. "I believe you. But I can't tell you what to do."

Laurel felt a huge weight come off her shoulders, and a soothing relief rush over her entire body. Her gratitude for her aunt multiplied. She had always been thankful for everything that Lucy had done for her, stepping in as a mother to her and raising her. But believing a tale like this one? One that Laurel would've scoffed at herself just a short time ago? She felt unbelievably lucky to have Lucy in her life.

"I hope you can forgive me, Laurel."

Everything in Laurel seemed to come to a stop. This was not what she had expected from her aunt. What could she possibly have to forgive her for? "For what, Aunt Lucy? You have no idea how relieved I am that you believe me."

"Because there is a reason that I believe you so readily. I wondered about this as soon as you and Shepherd showed up to the cabin. There was something about him, something about the both of you, that was eerily similar to someone else that I knew once…a long time ago."

If Laurel was confused before, now she was completely dumbfounded. "I have no idea what you mean."

"I'm afraid my story may be more difficult to digest than the one you just told me. I always knew it would come out, but I hoped that it wouldn't."

Lucy's face contorted into a painful expression, and it concerned Laurel. Her aunt had always been so sure of herself that Laurel had come to count on her as a beacon of strength.

"What do you mean?"

"Your parents, Laurel. I told you before that your words reminded me of what Rose told me years ago about James. That's because…"

"Because why, Aunt Lucy?"

"Because James was a wolf. Your dad was a shifter. And he and Rose were mates. They knew right away. Rose and I were the closest of sisters. After they were married, they stayed here in the cabin for several months. Rose told James they could trust me, and I kept their secret all these years. Rose wondered whether you would take after James. She was so excited for your eighteenth birthday to see if you would shift. She hoped that you would. And then the accident happened, and everything changed. I was going to tell you if I saw any signs that you had a wolf, but it didn't happen and then life just kept going. I never knew how to tell you."

Laurel didn't know what to say. She kept waiting to wake up from this crazy dream to find that none of this was real and life was what she thought it was before. Instead, they both continued to sit on the swing, the crickets chirping around them like everything that Laurel thought she knew hadn't just come to a halting stop.

"My dad was a wolf?" It seemed like such an absurd response to everything that she had just learned but she couldn't wrap her head around it.

"Yes. He was a beautiful wolf. And a beautiful man. He loved my sister with everything in him. And I saw that same look that he used to

The Dream

give your mother when I saw Shepherd look at you. Somehow, I knew. Or I guessed. That everything had come full circle."

"How did I never know?"

"They wanted you to have a normal childhood. When James met Rose, he was what he called a rogue. He didn't have a family or a pack. He was orphaned when he was young. And he built his whole life around her, and around you. And then, when Rose died, he just—"

Laurel's whirling thoughts abruptly stopped. "What do you mean when my mom died? He died as well. They both died. In the accident."

Lucy's face turned into a grimace. "Essentially."

"What does that mean- essentially?! Either it happened that way or it didn't, Aunt Lucy. I woke up in the hospital and both my parents were dead. Are you telling me that isn't true?"

"No, that is true. It's just that they didn't both die in the accident." Laurel waited while Lucy seemed to search for the right words. "Your mom died in the accident. James was stronger, physically, as a werewolf. He healed faster. But he just couldn't live without her. Within days, he was dead. By the time you were recovered, they were both gone, and it was easier to pretend that they had both died in the accident. I didn't know how to explain it and so I just didn't say anything. I'm so sorry, Laurel. I always meant to tell you, but we never spoke of it, and I didn't know how." She paused a moment before continuing, "Your dad loved you. Both your parents loved you so much and I just couldn't explain why he would lose his will to live when you were still here without telling you that he was a wolf."

The pictures of the wolf on Lucy's bedroom wall drifted into Laurel's mind, and she had to know if that was her dad. Something inside her knew the answer without asking. "The brown wolf…in the pictures?"

"Yes. That was your dad."

Laurel got up without saying anything. She had to be with Shepherd. She needed him right now. As her hand reached for the doorknob, Lucy spoke again.

"Laurel, I love you. I have always loved you. I'm sorry that I didn't tell you the truth before."

She couldn't respond. She didn't know what to say. She just nodded and went inside, feeling numb as she made her way to the bedroom. Shepherd lay on the bed with his laptop in front of him. He met her eyes as she entered, closing the door behind her. Immediately, he shut his computer and laid it beside him on the nightstand, a look of concern on his face.

"Laurel? Are you alright?"

"No."

She climbed onto the bed, curling into him as she began to cry. She couldn't hold it in anymore. It felt like everything had changed so quickly. He held her snugly, gently stroking her back. She cried until she didn't have any tears left to shed and finally, he spoke.

"Talk to me, Laurel. Whatever it is, we can figure it out together."

She lay for a few minutes more, resting against his chest and breathing in his comforting, earthy scent. "I told my aunt about you. And about Angus." She felt him tense beneath her. "Are you mad that I told her?"

"No, my Love. I'm worried that her response hurt you. It's difficult for people to believe that we exist."

"Well, she believed me. She believed me because my dad was a wolf and she never told me." The tears threatened to start again but she took a deep breath to steady herself. "He didn't die in the accident. He died because my mom died. He left me. I wasn't enough to keep him here." The tears started to trickle down her nose onto his chest. She couldn't stop them.

Shepherd's hand rubbed circles on her back as he tried to comfort her. "Oh Laurel, it wasn't that you weren't enough. That's just the way the mate bond works. If I lost you, I don't know what I would do. I don't want to ever be without you. As mates, our souls are intertwined. It's sometimes just too much to be torn apart by death. He had no choice. Your parents are with each other, I promise. They're watching out for you from the other world, proud of everything you've accomplished and

The Dream

of who you are. I imagine they're happy we found each other. The mate bond is a special, coveted thing, Laurel. We are the lucky ones."

He held her until she fell asleep, whispering comforting words to her and pouring all his strength into her through their growing bond. He hated to see her suffer but felt overwhelmingly thankful that he was the one to comfort her. With the news of her father being a wolf, he had so many questions, but knew that none of them really mattered. It only mattered that he had found Laurel and she was in his arms, where she belonged.

Breakfast the next morning was uncomfortably quiet. Laurel and Lucy both knew that they would move past this. Their relationship was too close not to. But Laurel felt betrayed by her aunt's secrecy. She didn't want to say anything hurtful, so she remained silent. For Lucy's part, she felt that nothing she could say would explain her actions. She knew that she had been wrong to withhold the information from Laurel, but she couldn't take it back now. She could only hope that Laurel would forgive her in time. Shepherd, meanwhile, reasoned that the best course of action for him would be to stay out of it. He respected Lucy, but Laurel was his main concern. He believed in her ability to handle the situation in the way that was best.

After breakfast, Laurel broke the silence. She and Shepherd had decided when they awoke that they would return to New York. But they needed to go into town to sign the documents before they left. Lucy nodded, understanding that some time apart was needed for Laurel to move past this. From what she knew of Rose and James' mate bond, she trusted Shepherd to give Laurel all the care that she would need in the coming days.

Laurel sent Jim a message that she'd be returning to the office the following day. "It's about damn time," he had responded. It made going to Silver Moon even more tempting. Before leaving the cabin, Laurel took the painting of her father's wolf from the wall and put it with her things. Lucy followed them to town in her truck so that Laurel and Shepherd could head to the airport afterwards. Once they were at the bank and seated with the paperwork in front of them, Lucy took another look at Laurel and Shepherd, who both nodded at her to sign.

The pen hovered over the paper only for a second before Lucy scribbled her signature on each of the dotted lines and passed the documents to Laurel, who signed them without any hesitation. She leaned over to kiss Shepherd as a gesture of her gratitude. Losing the land was one less thing she would have to worry about, and she was grateful that he had taken care of it. Everything had changed in the last twenty-four hours and any awkwardness she had felt about accepting his help was gone.

"Thank you," she whispered softly to him.

"Worth it," he smiled in return.

They walked Lucy to her truck and embraced.

"I'll text you when I'm home. We won't leave for a couple of hours, so it'll be late when we get back to New York."

Lucy nodded, "Thank you. I love you, Laurel."

"I love you, too."

Lucy then pulled Shepherd into a hug as well. "I wish I could repay you for everything you've done here."

He smiled at her. "You helped raise Laurel. It is I who should be repaying you."

Lucy nodded and stepped into the truck. Just before she shut the door, Laurel suddenly asked, "What was his name?" A flicker of perplexity showed on her aunt's face. "My dad's wolf. What was his name?"

The look of heartbreak that had been on Lucy's face the night before reappeared. "Morpheus," Lucy said softly and closed the door of the truck. A moment passed before the engine turned and she began the trip back to the cabin.

They watched until the truck was no longer visible and then Shepherd turned to Laurel, cupping her cheek. "You alright?"

She stood on her tippy toes to give him a quick kiss. "I will be."

"Well, Sunshine. We have a couple of hours to kill before we meet Truett. What should we do? You care to show me around your old stomping grounds?"

The Dream

Laurel laughed. "There was hardly any stomping going on. Aside from going to the diner after school my senior year and a handful of high school parties, I mostly stayed at the cabin the entire time I grew up. But the diner is just around the corner. They serve good burgers. Want to have lunch?"

"I could eat," Shep grinned boyishly.

The bell on the door of the diner announced their entrance and every head turned to gawk at Shepherd. He didn't seem bothered by it and walked towards a corner booth as the eyes followed him across the room. Once they were seated, everyone returned to minding their own business. After a quick look around, Laurel made an embarrassed face at Shepherd.

"Perks of living in a small town," she joked apologetically.

"I don't mind. I know I'm eye candy," he replied with a wink.

"Mr. Humility over here," Laurel rolled her eyes, which made Shepherd reach across the table to tickle her. "Hey! None of that!" she protested.

"Well, look who's here! Laurel Davis! It's been years since I've seen you."

Shepherd and Laurel both stopped laughing to look at their server, who laid their menus in front of them while smiling at Laurel. Laurel recognized her from school.

"Hey, Jane! How are you?"

She and Jane hadn't been close during school, but she was always friendly. Laurel had heard that she had married Seth a couple of years after graduation. Seth had been Laurel's only serious boyfriend in high school. She had known even then that she was going to move away for college and was happy when her aunt told her that he'd gotten married.

"I'm doing great! Seth and I are expecting our first baby in December," she said as she rubbed her belly.

"That's great, Jane! You look radiant! It looks like Seth is treating you well. Tell him I said hello, please."

"Well, he usually comes by for lunch at noon. You can tell him yourself. He'll be glad to see you, Laurel."

Jane's smile reached her bright blue eyes and Laurel could tell that there were no ill feelings because she and Seth had dated. The same couldn't be said for Shepherd, who was eyeing her suspiciously. She shot him a "don't be ridiculous" glare before returning to Jane.

"That'll be great!"

"I better stop chatting and get back to work. Do you know what you'd like to order?"

After Jane walked away, Laurel pretended to read the dessert menu. She knew it would frustrate Shepherd and wanted to tease him. Finally, he growled low and pulled the menu from her hands, setting it to the side. "Who is Seth?" His voice was low. There was a roughness to it that made her look up to meet his scowl. Hmm, maybe teasing wasn't the best idea. She was surprised that he would react this way. After all, he knew that she was with Henry before. He couldn't imagine her to be a virgin before she met him.

"Seth was my high school boyfriend," she said with exasperation. "Come on, Shep. Am I the only girl you've been with? Don't be this way." She knew he was trying to calm himself, or perhaps trying to calm Angus as she could see his eyes were flickering between green and black. She reached across the table to grab his hand and gave it a squeeze. "Hey. I only want you. I haven't even seen Seth since graduation."

Shepherd's eyes darkened when she mentioned Seth's name but returned to green when she started to rub his hand with her thumb soothingly.

"Did you guys ever…?"

She cocked her head to one side. "You sure that's a smart line of questioning?"

"I know it's not, but I need to know."

Laurel sighed, knowing she should just refuse to answer. But she wasn't ashamed of it and didn't think that either of them had to hide their exes. She couldn't imagine acting jealous of any of Shepherd's exes.

"Seth was my first."

The Dream

Shepherd's jaw clenched and he winced. They sat in silence for a while. By the time Jane brought their drinks and burgers, everything had returned to normal. But Laurel was still bothered by Shepherd's extreme jealousy.

"Will it always be this way?"

Shepherd sighed and ran his hand over his face. "I know I'm overreacting, Laurel. I'm doing my best to control it. Angus is on edge, because we've bonded but you're not marked, so it's definitely worse than usual. But I'll be upfront, I am never going to like the thought of you with another man. I will always be overly protective of you and want to keep men or unmated wolves away. That's just the way it is. But it's worse before you're marked, right afterwards, and when you're pregnant." Her eyes widened as he spoke. "I just want to be upfront with you."

"That seems extreme. Don't you trust me?" Laurel's hurt expression made Shepherd's heart ache. "I mean even when I met you and the feelings were there, I wouldn't cheat on Henry with you. And I wouldn't cheat on you either. It's not who I am, Shep. You don't have to worry about that with me."

Seth and now Henry. His wolf was really getting worked up at the mention of all these males with connections to his Laurel. Shepherd had to take a few calming breaths to stay in control.

"It's not that I don't trust you, Laurel. We're connected. It's our nature to protect you and the bond. But another reason we don't like unmated males touching our mate is because our sense of smell is so sensitive. It's very upsetting to smell someone else on our mate, and it drives our wolves crazy. At first, when I smelled Henry on you, it angered me. The more time I spend with you and without us being properly mated, it just gets worse. When I smelled Henry on you during that business trip, it nearly made me insane. It took so much energy to control my wolf."

Laurel grimaced as she thought back to how Shepherd had sniffed her at the airport and the look on his face. Now she understood why. And when she remembered what she and Henry did the night before and that she hadn't been able to take a shower that morning, her face blanched.

"How good is your smell?"

Her face revealed her horror. Shepherd's face darkened threateningly. She didn't feel afraid. She knew he was just remembering the same thing she was.

"Really damn good, Laurel," he growled. He shook his head as if to rid himself of the memory. "Unfortunately, it may get worse before it gets better. Now that we've been together physically, Angus is even more determined to mark you. I would never rush you, Laurel. But I want you to be aware of why I respond to certain situations the way that I do."

Laurel ate quickly. She wanted to be gone by noon. Feeling relieved as they reached the door to leave the diner with still no sighting of Seth, she stepped into the street and ran directly into a tall man. She let out a scream of surprise and before she could react, Shepherd roughly pushed the man from her and stood in front of her, menacingly staring the man down.

"Whoa," she could hear the guy saying. "My apologies. I wasn't watching where I was going. Is your friend alright?" She leaned around Shepherd to see the man. Of course, it was Seth. "Laurel, is that you?" Seth's face showed his shock. He stepped towards her, but Shepherd mirrored his movement and Laurel could tell that his body was tense, and his breathing heavier. Seth stopped and looked from Shepherd to Laurel with concern. "Are you alright, Laurel? I'm sorry for running into you. Did I hurt you?" He glanced warily at Shepherd again.

She stepped beside Shepherd, simultaneously grabbing his arm so he didn't step in front of her again. She knew he'd explained why he was protective and jealous, but this was ridiculous. She'd clearly been the one to run into Seth, and he was the one apologizing.

"I'm alright, Seth! I'm the one that plowed into you. I should be asking if you're alright!"

Seth laughed good-naturedly. "Oh, that's no big deal. I'm just so surprised to see you. When did you get into town? And do you want

The Dream

to introduce me to your bodyguard?" He smiled at Shepherd, but Shepherd's expression remained stony.

"I came into town yesterday to visit Lucy. This is my boyfriend, Shepherd. We were just grabbing a burger before we head back to New York. We already saw Jane. Congratulations, Seth. I'm so happy for you."

"Yeah, we're having a baby in December. Did she tell you?"

"She did. It's so exciting!"

They stood awkwardly for a moment. Shepherd didn't relax his stance.

"So, what are you doing in New York? Last I heard you had graduated from Cal State."

"Oh yeah, I moved there after graduation. I'm an administrative assistant at a firm there. What are you up to?"

"I work at the factory. Like most everyone around here, you know. It's a job," he laughed. "Well, it was good to see you again, Laurel. Next time you're in town, let's grab a drink." Shepherd let out a disgruntled sound before Seth quickly added, "All of us, of course."

"Sure, that would be great. We need to be going, but it was so good to see you again."

"You too, Laurel. I'm glad you're doing well." He held out his hand. "And it was good to meet you, Shepherd. Take care of this one."

Shepherd paused before Laurel nudged him. He begrudgingly took Seth's hand. "I plan to," he ground out.

Seth nodded to them both before ducking into the diner. Shepherd let out the growl that he had been holding in and grabbed Laurel's hand, walking towards the car.

"Shepherd, that was ridiculous back there. Seth is an old friend!"

"An old boyfriend," Shepherd replied with a scowl.

"An old boyfriend who is married with a baby on the way!" she reminded him.

Shepherd's face relaxed but he kept a firm grip on Laurel's hand. He didn't say anything else though and guided her to the car, opening the door for her before walking around to the driver's side. They rode in silence to the airport, Shepherd calming himself and Laurel looking out the window in frustration. She didn't like jealousy. She saw no reason for it. She'd already explained that she wanted no one but him and that she wasn't the cheating type. She didn't think she'd feel jealous with him around other women. It was a trust issue for her. And she trusted Shepherd completely.

Truett was waiting for them in the plane when they arrived. Once the flight was underway, Shepherd worked on his laptop and made multiple calls to Beck. There seemed to be an issue in Silver Moon, but Laurel couldn't tell much from Shepherd's side of the conversation. She made her way to the bedroom and put a movie on. Halfway into her second movie, Shepherd came in and lay beside her, draping his arm around her waist and breathing in her scent. She felt all the anxiety leave her body and was amazed anew that he could have that effect on her.

"Is everything okay? Things sounded tense on the phone."

"There are some concerns. There's been an uptick in rogue activity and Beck isn't sure why."

She turned into him. "What does that mean?"

"Rogues are troublemakers. A lot of them have been kicked out of their packs for unruly behavior. Not all of them, of course," he added quickly, thinking of her dad. "Sometimes they're orphaned when they're young and their pack either doesn't want them or doesn't find them. Sometimes wolves leave because of harsh leadership within a pack. We sometimes catch rogue scents around our borders but in the past few days there have been more. One tried to cross our boundaries last night. It's probably nothing but Beck is concerned. I'm afraid I'm going to have to go back, at least for a couple of days. I really don't want to leave you with everything that has just happened. Is there any way you could come with me?"

Laurel felt torn. "I don't want to be away from you either, but I need to get back to work."

"I can't imagine not sleeping by your side. Why don't you call in and come with me?" Shepherd's voice sounded apprehensive.

The Dream

"I really can't, Shepherd. I've already missed a couple of days and my work will be piled high when I get back." She paused. "How long will you be gone?"

"I'll leave in the morning, but I can probably be back on Saturday."

Two nights without Shepherd. She wondered at the pang of sadness that calculation brought. She knew the mate bond was real because she had been with Henry for three years and never once felt depressed at the thought of being away from him. She enjoyed her alone time and never pictured herself as the clingy girlfriend type. But here she was, contemplating whether she really needed her job just so she wouldn't have to spend two nights away from Shepherd. She shook her head. *You are not this girl, Laurel. Get a grip on yourself. You need to get back to your job. You can spend two days without Shepherd. It won't kill you.* She wasn't sure she believed her own words, but she willed herself to remain strong.

"Saturday. We can do that. Right?"

Shepherd sighed and gripped her tighter. "I guess we'll have to, Sunshine. I'll come back sooner if I can."

Laurel stayed snug in his embrace, trying to fight off the already looming feeling of loneliness. There was a little turbulence on the flight, but she felt safe with Shepherd. It didn't bother her as much as it had the first time. When they arrived in New York, her stomach was rumbling.

Shepherd looked at her as they descended from the plane. "Are you hungry?"

Laurel smiled, amused that he could hear her stomach growling. "I could eat," she responded, grinning at him mischievously.

"There you go again, repeating back my words," he laughed. "Let's get something to eat before we head back to your apartment."

After dinner, they arrived at the apartment to find Susu on the couch. She sat up to greet them.

"Hey you two! How did everything go in Oregon? Were you able to figure anything out?"

Laurel settled on the couch beside Susu and Shepherd joined her, resting his hand on her knee. "Yes, it all worked out fine. It was a big trip. Lots of surprises." She smiled at Shepherd. "But overall, it was good. Lucy will keep the land."

Susu let out a sigh of relief. "Great! I was really worried about you."

"Thanks, Susu. I'm pretty beat. We're going to head to bed. Do you work tomorrow?"

"Yep! As always! Are you heading back to work tomorrow or....?" She looked from Laurel to Shepherd and back again to Laurel with a wicked grin.

Laurel laughed. "Yeah, somebody has to straighten out Jim's bossy ass. And Shepherd has to go to Silver Moon for a couple of days."

"Coming back for more after that, dream man?"

Shepherd grinned as he stood up, taking Laurel's hand and pulling her up from the couch. "Nothing could stop me."

When the door to the bedroom closed behind them, Shepherd pulled Laurel into a tight embrace. "I love you, Laurel. I'm so thankful to have found you. You know that, right?"

She smiled against his chest. "I think I may have an idea."

Pulling back slightly, he kissed her gently upon the lips. "Good, then I've made my intentions clear."

She kissed him back, more passionately. "Crystal clear."

Shepherd led her to the bed and laid her down, slowly crawling so that he hovered above her. He leaned down and kissed her again, parting her lips as she willingly gave him access to her. Their kisses became more heated, and he growled as he released her, ripping her shirt from her body.

"Hey," she laughed. "I liked that shirt!"

His voice was low and thick with desire. "I'll buy you another."

He kissed her neck, working his way down to her breasts. He sucked and gently bit at her nipples as they hardened, and she moaned out in pleasure. He kissed all along her stomach, making his way to her already pulsating pussy. Kneeling in front of her open legs, he watched her movements as he rubbed her sex, the feeling of his calloused fingertips exciting her. She gyrated her hips against his hand until he

The Dream

plunged a thick finger in and out of her and then added another, kissing her thighs.

"Don't make me wait, Shepherd. I want you now."

He stood and she watched him pull off his shirt and slowly take his pants off. Her mouth watered at the sight of his beautiful body. "Hurry," she breathed. He flipped her over onto her stomach and pulled her to the edge of the bed. Shepherd used his foot to kick her legs wider apart and then lined himself up with the seam of her slit before slowly pressing the crown of his huge cock into her opening. She moaned against the comforter, trying to muffle the sound. Suddenly, he thrust all of the way in, and she screamed out in delight. She was sure that everyone in the apartment building heard her, but she couldn't contain herself.

He groaned and gripped her hips tightly. "You're so tight. You feel so good." Shepherd pulled out all the way and thrust into her again with a low growl. She felt like she was being split in two but had never felt such euphoria. Shepherd paused, buried deep inside of her and she looked back at him, her eyes alive with hunger and arousal. His black eyes met hers. He was breathing heavily, and she knew that he was trying to calm himself, not wanting to be too rough with her.

"Don't hold back on me, Shep. I want all of you."

"Goddess," he moaned.

Before she knew what was happening, he was pummeling into her, exciting every nerve in her body. She grasped onto the comforter for some sense of control but knew that it was useless. He owned her body. He grabbed her hair, pulling her head back, and rode her with such intensity, that her pleasure came out in short squeals in sync with his thrusts. The sound of his thighs slamming against her ass seemed to resonate in the space around them. The intensity was too much for her, and she yelled out his name as she orgasmed, her body shaking. He let go of her hair, one of his hands resting on the bed beside her waist and the other reaching around to rub her already sensitive bud as he slowed his pace but stayed deep inside of her.

"It's too much, Shepherd! I can't take anymore."

"Come for me again, Love," he whispered into her hair as he continued manipulating her clit in rhythm with his deep, hard strokes.

His thick voice rasped out that he couldn't hold back much longer and as if she were given permission, her body responded with a second orgasm. Shepherd came at the same time, a roar escaping his lips, so loud that Laurel knew she should be embarrassed. She was sure that everyone had heard it. Certainly, Susu had. But she couldn't bring herself to concentrate on that. Her body melted into the bed. She had no more energy left. Shepherd leaned against her back, his cock throbbing inside of her. He kissed her gingerly on the neck, creating tingles up and down her spine. Finally, he withdrew from her body and laid beside her.

When he got up, she let out a sound of disapproval. "Where are you going?"

"I'm going to run you a bath. I was a bit rough with you and I don't want you to be sore tomorrow."

"You were perfect," she said, rolling over to study him.

He smiled at her and leaned over to kiss her forehead before heading into the bathroom. She heard the water turn on and closed her eyes. She could have succumbed to sleep right then. When she was about to nod off, she felt Shepherd's hand on her hip.

"The bath is ready."

"Hmm," she replied.

She didn't think she could move. She felt Shepherd's arms wrap around her as he picked her up carefully and walked her into the bathroom, lowering her into the bath with him. She had never had a man take such loving care of her and although she never would have imagined it, she enjoyed it. She savored the feel of his body against hers in the warm water. He took the washcloth and bathed her before massaging shampoo into her hair and rinsing it out.

"Let me wash you," she said sleepily.

"You're too tired. I'm going to help you to bed and then take a cold shower."

"A cold shower? After that?! Why?"

The Dream

"I'm a werewolf, Laurel. My appetite is bigger than yours. But I don't want to make you sore."

Even as sexy as she found him, she couldn't imagine wanting more after an experience like the one they just had. After he toweled her off, he laid her on the bed. She fell asleep quickly and didn't remember him leaving her to return to the shower.

CHAPTER 8

It was difficult to leave for work the next morning, knowing that Shepherd wouldn't be there when she returned. He cooked breakfast before she left for work and they tried to enjoy their morning together, both wanting to pretend that they weren't going to be apart the next couple of days. When they kissed before she left, she could tell that Angus was trying to force his way through. It was endearing. She wanted to spend more time with Shepherd's wolf, but Shepherd thought it was a bad idea until they were ready to complete the mating process.

Jim met Laurel as soon as she stepped foot into the office. "Davis, I hope you brought your running shoes. You've got a hell of a lot to catch up on!"

When she walked into her office and saw the stacks of papers littering her desk, she had to fight the urge to turn around and walk out. She slumped into her chair and rested her chin in her hands. *Why did I even come back? I could be with Shepherd right now, on my way to Silver Moon.* She threw herself into her work, and it distracted her from missing Shepherd. Before she knew it, her co-worker was sticking her head into Laurel's office to remind her it was lunchtime. Laurel surveyed the still-cluttered desk. She considered working through lunch, but she was hungry, and a break would be good.

She was surprised to see Henry in the lobby. She had been so busy, she hadn't even had time to worry about running into him. She wondered why he was waiting for her. True, Mondays were their running lunch date, but they weren't together anymore, and Laurel thought that he would have wanted to avoid any post break-up awkwardness as much as she did. She strongly considered turning around to get back into the elevator but knew that would be immature.

"Hey, Henry," she said quietly, coming to a stop in front of him.

"Laurel," he replied with a strained smile.

She waited a moment for him to explain why he was waiting for her, shooting glances around the room so that she wasn't staring at him. He shuffled his feet a bit, which was very unlike him.

"Look, I let my emotions get the best of me the other night. You were right when you said that we should go somewhere quiet to talk. Can we do that now?"

"I don't know, Henry. I'm really not sure what else there is to say."

He stared at her for a moment before continuing, "Please, Laurel. I have more to say. There are things that I want to make sure you know."

"I don't think this is a good idea. And it won't change anything," she tried again.

"One more Monday lunch?"

He shot her a charming smile, which no longer did anything for her. On the other hand, after three years, Henry did deserve the chance to say whatever was on his mind.

"Alright. As long as you know that it's just lunch."

"Just lunch. Got it." Henry tried to sound upbeat, but she could tell that he was unhappy with her response.

They went to one of their favorite spots, and Henry led the way to a corner booth. Once the server left to put their orders in, an uneasy silence settled over them. Laurel was determined that Henry should speak first since he'd requested this. Finally, when it was clear that Laurel would not speak, he started.

"I know I said in the car that there would be no getting back together after you realized breaking up was a mistake. But after I calmed down and thought about it, about us, I knew that wasn't true. It was a shit thing to say. The thing is, Laurel, that I thought I had made it clear how much you mean to me by asking you to move in with me but the more I thought about it over the past few days, I realized that I could have done more to let you know how I feel."

The Dream

He paused and Laurel didn't know if she should stop him or if it would be better to let him finish. While she tried to make up her mind, he continued.

"I told you I loved you, but I didn't tell you why. It's not just that you're beautiful and intelligent, which you are. There is a strength and a grace in you that I admire. I respect your strong work ethic and how loyal you are to your friends and family. I appreciate that while other girls are rushing around, spending a lot of time and money to make themselves look good, you are effortlessly confident." He took a hurried breath, as if he feared she would interrupt. "I know we're different in a lot of ways. You've had to work hard, while my family basically set me up for the life I live. I love the city and the activity while you often go to the park and find a quiet place to relax. I don't notice things around me, but you are always interested in everything. You may see this as a weakness in our relationship, that we aren't well-suited for one another. But I think that we complement each other perfectly, Laurel. I've been thinking about all this ever since the ride home that night. I was so jealous of the idea of you with Shepherd that I tried to push you into moving in with me instead of just talking to you about how I was feeling. If you're not ready to move in, we don't have to talk about that right now. I just want you, Laurel. Whatever way I can still have you in my life is what I want."

Laurel's chest was tight. Henry had surprised her. The things he said made her realize that he had noticed a lot more about her than she previously thought. If these things had been said before she had met Shepherd, Laurel may have been swayed. A lot of her previous concern with Henry was that she didn't believe he truly knew her and that he only viewed them as a great team. But she *had* met Shepherd, and everything had changed. There was nothing Henry could say now that would change their situation. The raw emotion on his face made her heart ache. She didn't like hurting him but there was no way around it. While they watched each other cautiously, the server set down their plates quickly and left. Neither of them touched their food.

"Eat, Laurel. It's almost time to head back. I don't want you to say anything right now. I want you to think about what I've said, what I should've said a long time ago."

"Henry, it won't—" but he quickly interrupted her.

"Please, Laurel, don't say anything now. Just think for a day or two and then if you still feel the same way, I'll leave you alone." He reached across to grab her hand, but she instinctively pulled it back, which surprised Henry.

After they ate, they walked back to the office in silence. He tried again to touch her hand before the elevator arrived at her floor, but she pulled her arms into her chest. Laurel felt angry that Henry hadn't let her respond and that he was dragging the situation out when there was no reason for it. She would not change her mind. She missed Shepherd more than ever. Before the end of the workday, there was no doubt in her mind that she would leave with Shepherd when he returned. She didn't like being apart from him. She knew that it was likely the mate bond, but the reason didn't matter. Moon Goddess, mate bond, true love, whatever it was- she was Shepherd's, and he was hers.

She called Shepherd on the walk home. He immediately answered and began asking how she was. She knew that he felt torn about leaving her, especially when she was still trying to process what she had learned. His voice was strained, and she wondered what was happening. He sounded busy and assured her that he was trying to finish his business there as quickly as possible. She could tell by his voice that he was feeling the same way as her about their separation. She hated that he was facing so much stress and she wasn't there to comfort him. By the end of the call, she decided to tell Jim that she quit tomorrow. She knew it was unprofessional not to give notice. But she couldn't ask Shepherd to be away from his pack for a month, especially with the security risks they were facing. And if this was how one day apart felt, she wouldn't make it a month. Tomorrow, she'd clear out her desk.

Laurel hoped that Susu would be home, but the apartment was empty. After scrambling some eggs for dinner and watching a few reruns,

The Dream

she began to feel anxious. She went to her room and pulled down her suitcase from the top of her closet. She began randomly opening drawers and pulling clothes off hangers, throwing them all on her bed. It made her feel better to be working on something. About an hour later, when the mound on her bed had started to feel overwhelming, Susu came in.

"Did someone break in and trash just your room? What the hell is all of this?" Susu joked with a look of concern.

"I'm packing. When Shepherd returns, he's not leaving again without me. I want to be ready when he comes."

Susu let out a long breath and fell on top of the heap of clothes on the bed.

"Susu, what are you thinking?"

Susu sat back up and faced Laurel. "I think I'm gonna miss you. But I'm so proud of you. You're doing the right thing. You're usually the calculated one between us, but here you are jumping in the deep end without floaties on. I love it!" She laughed before turning serious. "I really do think you're making the right decision, Laurel."

"Thanks, Susu. Your approval means a lot to me. I'll pay another three months' rent so you have plenty of time to find another roommate. Or you could always come with me to Silver Moon…"

"I can't just follow you around your whole life, Laurel." Susu said with a sad expression before regaining her spirits. "Alright, what are we waiting for? Let's get you ready to go!"

They turned the music up loud and half-worked, half-played until Laurel's two suitcases were full and the bed was clear. It was two am when they finally finished, and they were both exhausted.

"We're not planning on packing up the whole apartment tonight, are we?"

"No way. I'm beat. I've got to get up in a few hours."

"You're still going to work tomorrow?! Why are you so good, Laurel?"

Laurel laughed. "I'm not sure I'd call leaving with no notice good, but I can't miss seeing Jim's face when I quit. Besides, I don't want to leave my desk a mess for the next assistant."

"Sleepover?" Susu asked with a small grin.

"Absolutely!"

They brushed their teeth and changed into their pajamas before collapsing in Laurel's bed. Even though they were both drained, they knew that their time as roomies was ending, and they wanted to savor their time together. They stayed up another hour, talking in bed about all the changes in Laurel's life, how hot Shepherd was, the awkward lunch with Henry, and how funny Jim's face would be when she quit before finally falling asleep.

Laurel's stomach was in knots the next morning. All joking aside, she dreaded the awkward talk she would have with Jim. Shepherd called while she was getting ready, but they hadn't gotten to talk for long. He sounded tired but told her that he planned to come back that evening and could stay at least through the weekend. She hadn't told him about her plans of quitting her job. She wanted to surprise him in person. The stress she could feel from him in their conversation only solidified her resolve to quit her job so they could be together.

When she entered the office, she made her way to Jim's office and knocked.

"What is it, Davis?" he asked without looking up.

She sat in the chair across from his desk and took a deep breath. "Today is going to be my last day, Jim."

"What?!" His face contorted into a furious expression. "Is this a joke? Are you looking for a raise?"

She explained to him that things had changed for her recently and apologized for the short notice, promising to finish the work on her desk before the end of the day. Jim was understandably angry and tried to get her to stay but no amount of guilt could make her change her mind. Shepherd needed her more than Jim did. And she needed Shepherd. She felt secure in her decision. She worked through lunch and several of her coworkers came in to wish her the best. She was thankful that the people she had worked closely with the past few years understood her decision even if they didn't know the real reasoning behind her sudden move. By

The Dream

the end of the day, she'd caught up on all her work. Grabbing the box of her personal belongings, she made her way back to her apartment.

After her lunch with Henry yesterday, she felt thankful that her notice had been short. Prolonging it would surely have brought more uncomfortable situations, which she wanted to avoid. Even though he had asked her to think about what he had said, there was nothing to consider. Her mind was made up. She knew eventually Henry would move on and be better off. There was only one man for her and that was Shepherd. She hoped that he would be waiting for her back at the apartment but hadn't heard anything from him since that morning.

She stopped by the cafe on the way home to see Susu. She was the saddest part of leaving New York, and Laurel had selfishly hoped that she would agree to make the trip to Silver Moon with her. It was Friday night, and the coffee house was busy. She took her coffee to go and slowly made her way to their apartment. She had half expected that Shepherd would be waiting on the steps when she returned home but when she rounded the corner, she was disappointed again. She felt the weight of all the sudden changes in her life as she entered her empty apartment. She sat on the couch and tried to calm the storm of thoughts that plagued her.

The past few days had been so busy and so much had changed that when she sat still for a moment, a tsunami of fear blindsided her. What if she was making a mistake? Before two days ago, she had thought the world existed only of humans. And now she knew that her father and the man she loved, as well as countless others, were werewolves. She wondered what other beings existed, moved around her every day without her knowing anything about them. Before a couple of months ago, her career had been the most important thing to her before a dream had changed everything. A dream about her soul mate. Something she had always scoffed about. She'd never been a romantic. Which, at this moment, struck her as such an odd thing.

She remembered now just how in love her parents had been. She had rarely seen them upset with one another and when she had, they had quickly made up. They always seemed to be touching one another and anticipating the other's needs before they even arose. Only now could she remember these things about her parents and realize how special their love had been. It all made sense. Her dad had been a wolf. They had been fated by a higher power to love each other for all time. And now she had the same gift with Shepherd. It excited and terrified her. Her dad had been unable to exist when her mother died and had left Laurel alone in the world. Is that what she wanted for herself? For her future children?

Lucy's face flashed across her mind. Laurel had always thought she chose to be alone. She viewed Lucy as independent and strong and assumed she just hadn't needed or wanted a partner. But remembering Lucy's face when she spoke of what Rose and James had, the way she whispered Morpheus' name, made her question that assumption. Shepherd was right. When you knew what the mate bond was, when you witnessed it, when you felt it- it was a beautiful thing. Perhaps Lucy had seen what true love was, and it had ruined her for anything else. There was so much that Laurel didn't know.

She realized that tears had begun to fall down her cheeks as her thoughts were interrupted by the buzz of the doorbell. Shepherd. She knew it was him before she opened the door. She rushed into his arms, and he embraced her tightly, kissing the tears from her face. Shepherd made quick work of getting Laurel's clothes off. Neither seemed able to get close enough to the other. His hands were on her body and running through her hair, pulling her face even closer to his, which made her wet with desire. When Shepherd's hand slid down to her sex, he hummed with approval.

"I'm ready for you too, Love," he said as he picked her up and carried her to the bed.

They made slow, passionate love. Their lips never leaving the other's body, savoring the taste. Their hands always on each other's face, chest, ass. He seemed to have every nerve ending on her body sizzling and alive with his measured movements. Even as her ecstasy neared, he kept his slow pace, thrusting into her channel, filling her completely, stimulating every part of her. She moaned against his tongue and then

The Dream

arched her back as her climax hit, crying out his name. The feeling of intense pleasure bordered on delirium and Shepherd gave into his release as Laurel's spasming muscles milked the last bit of his essence from him. They lay limply in each other's arms for several moments, Shepherd draped over the side of her. The feeling was comforting, like a weighted blanket. He feathered kisses along her jawline as they both enjoyed being in each other's arms again.

"I know I said I'd give you time. But I don't think I can do this. I need you with me. Always. It almost drove me and Angus crazy being away from you. I want you to come home to Silver Moon with me." He looked at her intensely. "I'm hoping I can talk you into it, but I've even started having irrational thoughts of kidnapping you and forcing you to come with me. I know it's not the right way, but Angus thought it was a great idea." He chuckled and looked expectantly at her. "What do you say, Laurel?"

She smiled widely and he followed her gaze to the corner, where her two suitcases were. "I quit my job today."

He sat up and pulled her onto his lap, cupping her face and kissing her passionately. "Thank the goddess I didn't have to result to torture to change your mind."

She pulled back, her face in mock surprise. "You'd torture me, Shepherd Ryan?"

"Yes, I'd torture you, Ms. Davis."

She leaned into him, their foreheads and noses touching, their lips just barely out of reach of the other's. "How would you torture me?"

"With desire. I'd bring your body almost to the peak of pleasure and stop…and then start again until you agreed to come with me."

"Hmm, that's truly cruel. Well, since I agreed to come with you willingly, and foiled your nefarious plan, what happens now?" His touch was igniting a heated frenzy within her again.

"The grumblings from your stomach would suggest you're hungry," he teased, his hands around her ass slowly moving her to grind against his already hard shaft. "Maybe we should get something to eat."

"After," she moaned. "Right now, I just want you."

He leaned her back on the bed and stood up, bringing her calves to rest on his shoulders. Supporting her ass with one hand, he used the other hand to work his cock into her opening before quickly taking possession of her. She gripped his forearms as she cried out in pleasure. If their previous session was an act of love, this was an act of passion. Shepherd hammered into her ambitiously, sending jolts of fire throughout her body. Her nails raked against his arms, leaving pink marks and she was sure that his tight grip on her hips would leave marks. She didn't care. One of his hands left her ass and teased her clit as he continued to stimulate every part of her pussy as he pummeled into her with his long, thick dick. She felt the intensity building and begged Shepherd not to stop. A heat spread through her as stars burst into her sight and she screamed out his name several times in a crescendo.

He slowed but continued with short, deep thrusts as her body shook, every part of her sensitive now to his movements, until he groaned out her name and she felt his warm semen coat her walls. He remained in her but unwrapped her legs from his shoulders, kneeling before the bed and leaning forward to rest against her chest until both of their breathing had slowed down. He heard her stomach growl again and leaned up, pulling out of her, and standing.

"Alright, let's go get something to eat, Sunshine."

They were both on cloud nine all the way through dinner. Laurel felt more connected to him than ever now that she had agreed to move with him to Silver Moon and fully accept the mate bond. They finished eating and were on their second glass of wine. Knowing that Laurel had agreed to come with him, Shepherd wanted to talk through everything and prepare her for Silver Moon.

"We can have a few pack members come to pack up the rest of your things. My house is fully furnished, but if there's any furniture you want to bring, we will. Whatever you want."

"I don't want to bring everything right now. Let's just take the suitcases, and we'll worry about the rest later. I told Susu I'd pay the next three months rent, so it's no hurry."

The Dream

His gaze shot up to her questioningly. She knew immediately what he was thinking and was quick to reassure him.

"It's not that, Shep. I'm in this with you. I'm moving to Silver Moon. But like you said, your house is furnished, and this is enough change for now."

He reached over to grab her hands. "I understand that. This is a lot. Whatever makes it easier for you, we'll do. What are your concerns about the move? Maybe we can talk through it."

There was something that had been bothering her. She had assumed that Shepherd would mark her as soon as she agreed to move to Silver Moon.

"Why didn't you mark me tonight? I figured you would once I agreed to move in with you."

"I wanted to. It was pretty difficult to fight the urge. But I don't want to rush you. I want you to be certain."

"I am!"

"It'll happen soon. Let's get you to Silver Moon first. I've let Truett know we'll be heading there in the morning."

"So, if I'm not marked, am I still the Luna?"

"Yes, everyone knows that I've met my mate and that I'll bring you home as soon as you're ready. They're all excited to meet you, Laurel. It's not just me that has waited for you. They've all been hoping for you to be found. A pack is stronger and happier with a Luna."

She sighed, feeling the weight of his words. She didn't want to let anyone down. "Alright, walk me through this again. I don't want to mess up and make the pack concerned about having a human Luna."

"A half human Luna."

She laughed softly, "That's right. It's still hard to wrap my mind around."

They talked about the pack more, Shepherd patiently going over who the leaders of the pack were, telling her about their personalities, their lives, and their responsibilities. He listed the duties of the Alpha and Luna, taking time to answer all her questions and concerns. He knew it would be a huge transition for her and, while he had no doubt that she was up for the challenge, he wanted to make sure she knew that too.

After they finished their third glass of wine, Shepherd paid the bill, and they walked back to her apartment, both excited about what tomorrow would bring. When they got to her street, she could see that someone was waiting on the steps of her building but couldn't make out who it was. *Please don't let it be Henry. Please don't let it be Henry,* she thought to herself although she had a sinking suspicion that was exactly who it was. He stood as they neared the building, and she could see that it was indeed Henry. He looked awful. His clothing was disheveled, his eyes were red as if he had been crying, and she could see that he had repeatedly ran his hands through his hair. *I guess he heard the news that I quit today,* she thought darkly as she worried what would happen between Shepherd and Henry.

Henry's eyes narrowed at the sight of Shepherd, and he rushed towards her.

"Laurel, I need to talk to you right now. You quit your job today? What is going on with you?"

Shepherd stepped in front of Laurel, pushing Henry back. "Do not touch her," he growled.

Henry raised his eyebrows at Shepherd. "I'm the only one who should be touching her. And you won't stand in my way. Laurel and I have three years together. What do you have? A few days? That's nothing. Get out of my way so my girlfriend and I can talk."

He stepped towards Laurel again and Shepherd's hand reached out to block him, but he didn't say anything. He just stood there, effortlessly blocking Henry from moving any closer to Laurel. Henry tried again.

"You quit your job, Laurel? What is happening? I thought after we talked yesterday that you would take a few days to think over what I said. And now you're leaving?"

Shepherd's body tensed. She hadn't told him about the lunch with Henry. She hadn't purposely kept it from him. But when she saw Shepherd's reaction, she knew that she'd made a mistake. She tried to

The Dream

step around him so she could talk to Henry and get him to leave but Shepherd pushed her behind him protectively.

"You're going to let him dictate where you go, Laurel? This isn't you. Talk to me. Come somewhere with me where we can talk."

Shepherd pushed Henry backwards. "You're not taking her anywhere."

She could tell by his voice that Angus was trying to surface. She reached in front of her and touched his back, trying to calm him.

"Henry, you need to leave."

"I'm not leaving until you talk to me." He must've stepped forward because she could tell that Shepherd had pushed him back again. Henry fell and Laurel could hear the fury in his voice. "You really want this Neanderthal, Laurel? This is so ridiculous." He stood up and sighed, losing the anger in his voice. "I love you. Please."

She caressed Shepherd's back and whispered quietly, knowing that he could still hear her. "Shepherd, I need to see his face so that he'll believe me that it's over."

She heard a low growl. "No."

"Shepherd, please. He's not going to hurt me." She saw his fists clench beside him, but he took one small step to the side. "Henry, I tried to tell you yesterday, but you wouldn't listen to me. It's over between us. I appreciated everything you said, and it may have mattered before, but it doesn't now. I know that we're both going to be happier this way. You will get over this and find the person that's right for you. But I'm not her. I quit today because I'm moving."

"You're moving with him?"

"Yes."

"After everything we had? After three years of loving you. After repeatedly asking you to move in with me…you're moving to an entirely different state to move in with a guy you just met?!"

She paused. She could try to explain this to Henry, but she didn't want to. She didn't have to. So, she just spoke the truth. "Yes."

Henry ran his hands through his hair and let out a yell of frustration, which made Shepherd step in front of Laurel again. Henry's eyes darted over to his action. "You think I would hurt her? Ever? I love her. Something you know nothing about if you're just going to swoop in here, trick her, and take her away from everything she's worked so hard for. I should be protecting her from you!"

The suggestion that he was hurting Laurel sent Shepherd over the edge. He lunged forward, grabbing Henry by the shirt and shoving him against the building. Henry's face showed his shock, but he quickly recovered his wits and swung a punch at Shepherd's face, which Shepherd easily avoided. Laurel screamed for them to stop but they were both too angry to hear her. Henry lunged again at Shepherd, and she could see that Henry's attempts to fight Shepherd were actually calming his wolf. He wanted Henry away from Laurel. He was no match for an Alpha wolf. It was like a game. Shepherd let Henry take another shot and then pushed him against the building again, their faces close. In a low, menacing voice that sent shivers down Laurel's spine, he warned Henry.

"She has made her choice and you need to respect it. It's what is best for her. And it's what's best for you. Because if you ever, EVER, come near her again, I will make sure there's not a next time. Do you understand?" Henry glared at him but didn't answer. "I said, do you understand?" Shepherd repeated slowly.

Henry couldn't make himself speak but nodded before looking behind Shepherd at Laurel, as if he wanted to say something. He looked so disappointed.

"Do not look at her. Do not speak to her. Get out of here now."

He gave Henry another push into the wall before releasing his shirt and returning to Laurel, wrapping his arm protectively around her shoulder as he glared at Henry. Henry paused for a moment. Laurel could see that he was struggling with whether or not to walk away. Shepherd growled out, "Don't come back" as he guided Laurel up the steps and opened the door for her, neither of them looking behind them to see if Henry was still there.

When the apartment door closed behind them, Shepherd pulled Laurel into him and buried his head in her neck, breathing deeply.

The Dream

"I'm sorry I didn't tell you about the lunch. I wasn't trying to deceive you. I just sort of forgot about it. It didn't mean anything to me."

Shepherd pulled away. "You think having lunch with your ex doesn't mean anything?"

She could tell he was frustrated, and she understood why. She was surprised when he picked her up and carried her to the couch, sitting down and leaving her on his lap. This wasn't generally how she had arguments. She suppressed a giggle at just how different their relationship was. They were about to argue while cuddling.

"Explain this to me, Laurel. I want to understand. You know how I feel about you being around unmated males and you know why. And then you agree to have lunch with Henry of all people?"

"It sounds bad when you say it like that. I didn't plan it, Shep. He ambushed me in the lobby and basically demanded a private audience. I told him it wasn't a good idea and that it wouldn't change anything, but he wouldn't listen. I thought I owed him a chance to speak his mind after three years together, so I agreed."

Shepherd was silent for a minute and then gripped her waist tighter. "So, what happened?"

"Well, we went to the restaurant, and he told me what was on his mind—"

Shepherd interrupted, "What did he tell you?"

"I don't think that's important."

"I want to know what he said," Shepherd said gruffly.

Laurel narrowed her eyes at him. "Don't try to boss me, Alpha. He spoke to me in confidence. Things he felt he should've told me during our relationship but didn't. And I won't repeat them." She sighed before continuing. "I tried to tell him that it didn't change anything, but he was insistent that I think about it for a couple of days. I was never going to reconsider my decision. But it wasn't worth having a fight at a restaurant."

"Did he touch you?"

"No."

"Did he try?"

She let out an exasperated groan. "Why does it matter? I said he didn't touch me, Angus!" She turned to look pointedly at him and as she suspected, his eyes were swirling green and black.

Shepherd took a deep sigh and stood up, keeping his grip on her. "Well, that's that then. Let's go to bed."

"That's that, huh? You have nothing to say about getting in a fight outside of my building?"

He shrugged. "No. Henry was asking for it. If I wanted to hurt him, he'd be very hurt right now."

Laurel couldn't deny the truth of the statement. They snuggled into bed together, Shepherd holding her almost too tightly. His body heat was so warm, she kicked the covers off them before drifting off to sleep.

The next morning, Susu was up and waiting for them. She and Laurel hugged several times. They both cried. And Susu promised that she would visit as soon as she could.

Before they left, Susu gave Shepherd a playful push, "If you don't take the best care of her, I'll kick your ass myself."

"I'd expect nothing less," he chuckled.

Susu stood on the steps and watched as they got into the car. Once Laurel was inside, she continued to wave goodbye to Susu until they turned from the street. Shepherd pulled her onto his lap and rubbed her back, his thumb making soft circles.

After a moment, she started to scoot off of Shepherd's lap. "I'm better now."

He tightened his grip. "Stay here."

"This isn't very safe. I'm not even wearing a seatbelt!"

"You will never be safer than when you're with me. I won't let any harm come to you," Shepherd replied earnestly.

Laurel scoffed. "Well, I don't think the lawmakers of New York would agree with you, but we'll let it slide this time."

CHAPTER 9

On the ride from the airport to Silver Moon, Laurel tried to distract herself so she wouldn't dwell on how nervous she was. She played twenty questions with Shep, who didn't know there was a game in session but patiently answered all her questions. She counted trees, looked for shapes in the clouds, and briefly tried to read a book. The longer they drove, the more remote the area became. Laurel was used to living in the woods, but this was even more isolated than Lucy's cabin. Finally, they began to see signs of life. There was a smattering of houses but the further they drove, the houses began to get closer together. Shepherd explained that mated wolves and their families lived in their own dwellings outside of the pack house.

Fairly quickly, they came upon a familiar street. Laurel was surprised to recognize it from their trip. A variety of businesses and restaurants were there, and people were out, enjoying the day. It was daytime still and she took in more than she had on their previous visit. She looked over to Shepherd, who was watching her slyly to see if she recognized it. A grocery store, school, and library were located on side streets. Shepherd told the driver to slow down and pointed out what each building was.

"And there's the hotel. You had a nice stay there, no?"

"Why would you not tell me we'd already been to Silver Moon?"

He smirked. "Because I wanted to see your reaction. That's why we wanted that land. It increases our borders. It's still pretty far away from town but if we needed to expand, it's worth it. We've been waiting for that plot of land to hit the market for years."

It all made sense to Laurel now. "How do you keep humans out?"

"We don't. Several wolves in my pack have human mates. But we don't have any humans living here who aren't aware of our existence. Because we've owned the land for a long time, we also control the housing. We only build a house when a pack member needs it. Occasionally, we'll have humans wander into town to explore. We don't shift when we're in town just in case. But they usually don't stay long- just do some shopping and eat and then continue on their way. I mean, we're pretty remote out here but sometimes people look for small towns to visit so the hotel is convenient. It also helps when our human population has family or friends to visit. If they end up wanting to move here, we just tell them we'll let them know when a house goes up for sale." He looked at her coyly. "Our houses never go up for sale."

Laurel found it fascinating that they had created this oasis for themselves. She didn't know what she'd expected but it wasn't this.

"What about your school and library? Aren't they government funded?"

"No. The pack pays for everything. There's no real salary here. Everyone has a job to do, and they do it. They're all cared for. If they need something extra or need to take a trip, we provide for them. We have gardens and enough land to hunt responsibly. And Beau Industries brings in the money we need."

They drove in silence for a few more seconds while Laurel took it all in.

"So, everyone doesn't work for Beau Industries?"

"No, just a small portion of the pack. We have a list of occupations that are open or will be needed within a few years and every year, we talk to the high schoolers about their options. The ones who choose jobs that need more education are sent to the college of their choice and return to the pack when they've completed their degrees."

"And that works?"

Shepherd shrugged. "It works pretty well, yeah. Occasionally, someone will want to do something that isn't on the list. We do everything we can to make it happen and incorporate it into the pack. There's been

The Dream

a lot of growth through those new ideas, you know? Sometimes, a member will go off to college and not want to come back. It's rare but it happens. Usually, it's because they meet their mate, and their partner doesn't want to move here."

"What do you do?"

"We wish them the best, of course. We aren't holding anyone hostage here, Laurel!" he laughed.

"I know, I know. This is just all so new to me!"

Shepherd seemed to sense that Laurel was nervous about going to the pack house. He asked if she wanted to get something to eat in town, but she knew she was delaying the inevitable. Heading away from the town center, they travelled down a long drive that brought them to a massive residence. It was old but in good condition. Laurel was amazed by the size of the estate. There were four stories to the main building and several buildings encircling it, all with landscaped walkways leading from the main residence. She could see multiple gardens, some with fruit trees and vegetable gardens and others with beautiful flowers. Tables and chairs were scattered about the grounds. It was more beautiful than she could have imagined.

She stood outside of the car studying the property until she noticed that several people had come out of the main entrance and were waiting for her and Shepherd. She recognized a few of them. Beck was there, his face more welcoming, and there was a girl holding his hand. Laurel had never met her before, but she knew from Shepherd's stories who she was. Violet. She had been orphaned as a child and was raised by a couple in the pack who couldn't have children. Shepherd said she and Beck had loved each other since they were children, had started dating in high school, but that when they turned eighteen, they'd found out they weren't mates. Beck had wanted to become chosen mates, but she never agreed. Years passed, though, and neither had found their fated mates.

She was tall with straight, blonde hair and bright blue eyes. Laurel could tell right away that she would like her. She wore a sundress with a bright floral pattern and had a pleasant countenance. Laurel smiled at her as she began walking towards the house and she warmly returned the gesture. Matthius and Charis stood beside them, laughing about something between themselves. Laurel amusedly wondered what those two were plotting. Everyone else who waited to greet them was unknown to Laurel, although she could guess who a few of them were from Shepherd's descriptions.

A beast of a man in a black t-shirt and fatigues stood next to Violet. The woman he had his arm around looked tiny in comparison. They seemed so mismatched, but she could see the love between them. Shepherd's accurate representation of them gave her confidence that these two were Rusty and Lilac. Chosen mates and Violet's adopted parents. Rusty was Shepherd's lead warrior, in charge of training new recruits, assigning guard duties, and planning attacks if necessary. He had deep laugh lines in his weathered face and jovial eyes. Lilac exuded strength as well, but hers was of a serene nature. She was the pack healer and Laurel had been curious if that's how she and Rusty had met. Shepherd chuckled at her question, as if it had never occurred to him.

"It seems plausible. Rusty's gotten into a few bad scrapes. You can ask them; they won't mind," he had assured her.

Across from them were another couple that Laurel assumed were Shepherd's parents, Alpha Beaumont and Luna Millie. Beaumont radiated power. Laurel could tell that he would be a frightening enemy to have but when she met his eyes, he smiled and gave her a nod. Shepherd's mother, Millie, stood confident and graceful. Although she didn't smile at Laurel, her eyes were kind. Shepherd had assured her that they both believed strongly in the mate bond and would accept her. She had been doubtful, afraid that they would think her weak since she wasn't a wolf. Now that she was in front of them, she felt more hopeful. Millie took a step forward and embraced Laurel as Shepherd introduced her.

When she pulled away, she said, "My son has waited a long time for you, Laurel. Welcome."

Beaumont stepped forward, called her daughter, and kissed her lightly on the cheek. He smelled comfortingly similar to Shepherd.

The Dream

Shepherd introduced her to the others. There was Charis' father, Rowan. He was on the pack's counsel. Shepherd had warned her that he was moody but assured her that he was loyal to the pack. Laurel could sense that he wasn't pleased to have her as the pack's Luna. His eyes were hard, his mouth drawn into a grim line. He made no attempt to welcome her, only recognizing the introduction with a slight nod. Beck's parents, Noble and Adlai, were also there. They were good friends with Beaumont and Millie as Noble had been Beau's Beta. Noble was still trim and looked like an older version of Beck. The resemblance was uncanny. Adlai was a beautiful woman, her long brown hair pulled back in a braid and her hazel eyes warm and intelligent. She was the pack's historian, having inherited the position from her father.

Shepherd's touch remained on her the whole time, either protectively wrapped around her shoulder, affectionately caressing her back, or holding her hand. She appreciated that he wanted to make it easier for her. Millie stepped forward to tell them that she'd arranged a welcome dinner and it would be ready in two hours. Charis offered a tour of the place, looping her arm into Laurel's and gesturing for Violet to join them. Now that Laurel had met Rowan, she wondered how Charis could ever have come from a man like that. Rowan was distrusting and morose while Charis was full of life. She knew from Shepherd that Rowan's mate had died giving birth to Charis. Laurel wondered how much it had changed Rowan and that gave her empathy for him, remembering that her own father had died from a fractured mate bond.

Violet and Charis treated her like a sister as they gave her the tour. She missed Susu already and was appreciative of their welcome. The contrast in their personalities kept Laurel laughing. Violet was gentle and nurturing while Charis was vibrant and lively, with a sarcastic mouth. They were both loving though, and Laurel bonded with them immediately. As they walked through the main building, she was introduced to more pack members. They seemed excited to meet her and addressed her as Luna, bowing their heads in respect. It felt odd to Laurel, and she wished she could do away with the formalities.

The lower level of the pack house held a conference room and several offices, a kitchen, dining hall, and a smaller dining room that seated around thirty. Off the dining hall were three sets of double doors that led onto a veranda with tables set up. Laurel was impressed at how well everything was designed. On the second and third floor were apartments as well as several common rooms with couches, televisions, pool tables, ping pong tables, and gaming systems. Most of the rooms were in use with people enjoying leisure time.

Three large apartments for the Alpha, Beta, and Gamma made up the fourth floor. No one else was allowed on the floor without permission. Charis wanted to show her Shepherd's quarters, but Violet insisted that Shepherd would want to do that himself. Instead, they showed her the buildings that surrounded the pack house: the training facilities and pool, medical clinic, and an event venue that the pack used for special occasions. Laurel wanted to explore the gardens, but they'd run out of time. Shepherd met them in front of the pack house. Violet squeezed her hand, knowing she was nervous about the dinner.

"Everyone loves you already, Laurel. Just be yourself."

Charis playfully pushed her arm, "You got this, bitch. See you soon!"

Shepherd let out a low growl at Charis' choice of words and Laurel was surprised to see Charis bare her neck to Shepherd in a show of submission, looking ashamed.

"Sorry, Alpha. I meant it as a compliment."

Before Laurel could question the exchange, Shepherd grabbed her hand. "Come on, I'll show you our apartment. I've had your luggage delivered and your clothes put away for you."

There were stairs but Shepherd led her onto the elevator. When the door shut, Laurel turned to Shep.

"What the hell was that?"

He looked at her in bewilderment. "What are you talking about?"

"Why did you growl at Charis for acting like a friend to me? Am I not allowed that as the Luna?"

Shepherd sighed and wrapped his hand around her waist. "You are. But I need to make sure that everyone understands you are Luna and

The Dream

respects you as such. If it were in private, I wouldn't have said anything, but we were in front of the pack house with members around. I don't want them thinking that you can be disrespected."

She scowled at his response but couldn't argue since she didn't yet understand the workings of the pack. Shepherd exited the elevator, turning towards the apartment to the left and scanned his fingerprint, which opened the door.

"We'll get your fingerprint in the system tomorrow. It'll allow you access to all locked facilities."

Laurel nodded as she stepped into their apartment. It was beautifully decorated. Simple yet classy with hues of blue, green, and gray. She was surprised at the size of it. There were three bedrooms, two bathrooms, a large living room, and a spacious kitchen. Two of the bedrooms were bare but the master bedroom had a king-size bed, two dressers, double closets, and the biggest bathroom she had ever been in with a jet tub she was sure she could swim in.

"I had your clothes put into that closet," Shepherd pointed. "You must be tired, but I'm afraid we need to get changed for dinner now."

Laurel wasn't tired at all. She was invigorated by everything she had seen so far and the people she'd met. Everyone truly seemed glad to meet her. Everyone except for Rowan, but she was determined to win him over. Walking into the closet, she saw all her things hung up neatly and spotted the painting of her dad's wolf set carefully on a shelf. From behind her, Shepherd explained that he wanted her to pick where the painting would go. She smiled and then turned to him.

"Alright, get out so I can change, Shep!"

He smirked at her. "I'm not allowed to watch?"

Playfully shoving him out of the closet, she shut the door and sat down on a bench in the middle of the closet before realizing that she didn't know what she should wear to dinner. She opened the door and Shepherd was still standing there, smiling expectantly.

"Wear a dress, something simple. It's casual."

She gave him a light kiss on his cheek before shutting the door again. She slipped on one of her favorite light blue dresses, which she thought looked good against her red hair and pale skin, before slipping on her nude heels and moonstone earrings to top it off. In the bathroom, she dabbed on blush, lipstick, and mascara before walking out where Shepherd sat on a chair by the bed in a smart gray suit.

"You look perfect, Laurel," he said with admiration clear in his voice.

She blushed at his praise. "You clean up pretty well yourself."

As they walked past the dining hall, Laurel could hear conversation and laughter floating through the double doors and snuck a peek inside. The room was full of pack members enjoying each other's company. It made her wish that they were eating in the dining hall instead of the more intimate dinner that Millie had planned. Shepherd squeezed her hand as if he knew what she was thinking.

"We usually eat with the pack. Tonight, mom just wanted to do something special for you that would allow the inner circle to get to know you more."

"Of course. It was really thoughtful of her. I'm just nervous."

"They will all love you. Not as much as me, of course." He stopped outside of the dining room and pulled her in for an embrace, kissing her gently on the lips. "Just be yourself. You are already my mate and the Luna of this pack. Nothing can take that away from you. And I am always on your side. There are perks to being the alpha," he said with a wink. She nodded at him, wishing that she could feel his confidence.

Everyone was already seated, but they stood as she and Shepherd entered. He led her to the table and pulled her chair out for her as he took the seat at the head of the table. It was quiet for a moment as pack members that Laurel hadn't met brought in their salads and drinks. After they left, Millie turned to Laurel.

"So, tell us a little about yourself, dear."

Laurel hesitated. She felt a nervousness that was similar to the first day of school but tried to appear confident. "Sure, what would you like to know?"

Beau glanced at Laurel and then Shepherd before he prompted her. "Tell us about your family. Where did you grow up?"

The Dream

Shepherd squeezed her leg under the table.

"Well, I grew up mostly in Washington with my parents before they died. And then I moved to a small town in Oregon to live with my Aunt Lucy."

Rowan was fast to speak. "Shepherd tells us your dad was a wolf."

"Yes, but I just learned that myself. I didn't know growing up. My mom was human. They were mates. I thought they both died in the car accident until just a few days ago, when Lucy disclosed that it was my mom that died in the accident. My dad died within a few days of her, from heartbreak, while I was still in the hospital recovering."

A look of deep sorrow flashed across Rowan's face before he quickly schooled his expression. "So, your aunt is aware of our existence?"

She calmly regarded him before answering. "Yes."

"And your dad, do you know what pack he came from?"

She tried to hide the anxiety that was creeping up within her. "I know nothing except that he was orphaned when he was young and considered himself a rogue. He was the only wolf my aunt knew. She didn't have any information except what was shared with her by my parents."

"I see."

She could tell that he thought there was more to the story.

"And you've never shifted or heard an inner voice that you thought wasn't your own?"

"No, Rowan, I haven't. Does that concern you?"

She wanted to make a good impression, but she didn't like the way he was speaking to her and thought being direct might be the best approach. If he had a concern, she wanted to address it now.

"Yes, it does."

Shepherd growled low beside her and glared at Rowan.

"My apologies, Luna. I don't mean to offend you, but it concerns me that your dad was a rogue. They're not trustworthy. And as a member of the council, it's my job to ensure the safety and integrity of our pack."

Shepherd pushed his salad plate away from him. "Enough, Rowan. She is my mate. That is sufficient."

Laurel placed her hand on top of his. "It's alright, Shep. I'd rather get this all out on the table now." She paused before continuing, "I wish that I had more information to give you, Rowan, I really do. Until recently, I didn't even know that any of you existed. I didn't know my parents were any different than other parents. I wish they had let me in on their secret, but they wanted me to have a normal upbringing." She smiled at the people at the table. "What I can tell you is that I love Shepherd and that I plan on being part of his life."

Charis grabbed her dad's hand. "And that's enough, isn't it, Dad? We all want Shepherd to be happy. We're so glad you're here, Laurel."

Rowan, however, didn't seem to be done with the conversation. "If you love the Alpha, why haven't you completed the bond? Why haven't you marked her, Shepherd?"

Laurel was curious as well and secretly glad that he had asked.

"Do not question me, Rowan. I will mark her when the time is right."

Rowan had the good grace to let the matter go and the rest of the evening was filled with lighter conversation. Laurel told them about her upbringing, going to college, and moving to New York. She told them about Susu, her job, and how she and Shepherd had met. Violet surprised her by asking about the dream she'd had about Shepherd. By the reaction of those at the table, she surmised that it wasn't a common experience. But it did seem that they were pleased, as if they took it as another sign from the Moon Goddess that their union would be blessed. By the end of the dinner, she felt closer to those at the table with the exception of Rowan. He had been quiet for the remainder of the meal. After the dishes had been cleared from the table, Shepherd stood and took her hand.

"It's been a long day and I think my mate needs her rest. Thank you for the dinner, mother."

Everyone else stood and said their goodbyes as Shepherd led her from the room.

As the elevator doors closed, Shepherd pulled her into an embrace. "How are you feeling?"

The Dream

"Tired," she laughed.

He smiled, "Yes, but I mean, how do you feel about the dinner?"

"I think it went well. Everyone was lovely. And my personal goal of winning Rowan over is even stronger after spending more time with him."

Shepherd chuckled. "You don't have to win him over. Rowan is a good man, but he is distrustful and wary since his mate died. I believe he will come around eventually." He looked Laurel deep in the eyes. "But if he doesn't, Laurel, it changes nothing. You know that, right? No one can take your title from you. No one can take you from me."

"I know, Shep, but thanks for saying it anyway."

As the doors opened onto the fourth floor, Laurel pulled him closer and kissed him deeply. He picked her up quickly and she wrapped her legs around him as he walked them out of the elevator and into their apartment. She didn't feel tired anymore. She just wanted his touch.

"I've been waiting to be alone with you all day," he said gruffly. "It was all I could do to make it through that dinner sitting next to you when all I wanted was to bring you home and make love to you."

She ran her fingers through his hair. "So now that you have me alone, whatever will you do with me, Alpha?"

A rumble in his chest revealed his impatience to get her undressed. Closing the door to their apartment, he pushed her against it, running his hand along her thigh under the dress.

"No panties, Laurel? Very naughty."

She clenched her thighs around his waist. "I had a feeling that choice might come in handy later."

He set her down as she slipped her dress off, watching him remove his clothes. She didn't think she would ever tire of seeing his body. She licked her lips as he closed the gap between them and kissed her passionately. Slowly, his fingers raked down her body, leaving a trail of goosebumps and tingling, until he reached her clitoris. She moved with his hand and leaned her head against the wall with a moan as he lightly bit her neck, not breaking the skin. His touch sent her into an electrifying frenzy. She wanted him inside of her.

"Fuck me, Shepherd."

"Not just yet, Love. I want to taste every part of you."

He knelt before her and brought one of her knees up to rest on his shoulder, opening her pussy to him. As she pressed her hands against the wall in anticipation, Shepherd murmured, "Mine," in a gravelly, satisfied voice. Using his fingers to split her seam even farther, he smiled up at her before thrusting his tongue into her. She didn't expect the sensation that the act gave, and grabbed his head, pushing him farther into her sex.

"Don't stop. That feels so good."

One of his hands gripped her ass while the other massaged her clitoris as his tongue continued to plunge into her pussy. She moved her hips with his movement, riding his face. She could feel the tip of his tongue teasing the magical spot within her that made her entire body flush. He looked up at her, his eyes dark and hungry with desire before taking her other leg to rest on his broad shoulders so that she completely rested on him. His fingers dug into her ass as he pushed his face deeper into her sex. The vibrations from his hum of satisfaction as he devoured her nearly sent her over the edge. All she could do was hold onto his head and press against the wall for support as he took her clitoris into his mouth, sucking and pulling at it until she bucked against him, climaxing hard and fast.

Her moans became soft purrs as he released her clit, gently taking each of her legs from his shoulders and making sure she was steady. Once he was standing, he grabbed under her ass to pick her up. Her arms held onto his shoulders for support as he hooked her legs on his forearms. Slowly, he worked his large sword into her wet and ready sheath. From that position, she could feel his entire length fill her more deeply than ever before. He remained buried inside of her for a moment, driving her crazy as she waited for him to move.

His firm grasp on her legs and back prevented her from riding him like she wanted to. She was completely at his mercy and contracted her vaginal muscles against his shaft to encourage him to fuck her. He groaned, holding her tightly against him, their bodies one, before breathing her scent in deeply. As he released his breath, he pulled her

The Dream

almost completely away from him and drove back in with force. She screamed out and kept a tight grip on his shoulders, the line between pleasure and pain blurred and mingled with her intense need to have every inch of him inside of her.

One of her hands reached around to the back of his head, her fingers digging into his scalp while her other hand grasped his shoulder tightly. He pounded into her already sensitive center.

"Oh my god, Shepherd," she called out in broken breaths.

"You're mine, Laurel. Say it."

He supported her weight easily as he continued to propel into her again and again, the sound of him slapping against her loud and erotic. She was almost delirious.

"I'm yours," she breathed out.

Her declaration seemed to drive him even more. His movements became more intense until all she could do was hold onto him as he owned every bit of her, her mind hazy, her body on fire. She closed her eyes and grabbed him tighter as stars drifted into her vision. "Yes, yes, yes, yes!" Her voice got louder with each wave of explosive pleasure. He slammed into her a final time and held himself deep inside of her with quick, short thrusts as they both erupted in euphoria. She could feel him throbbing inside of her as he leaned against the wall, pulling her closely against his body and breathing into her hair. Her canal walls still pulsed from the intense orgasm as he released her legs from his arms and wrapped them around his waist.

"Goddess, Laurel. You're going to be the death of me!"

After their heart rates had slowed, he walked her to the shower, still reluctant to withdraw from her. Once the water was at a comfortable temperature, they bathed each other- silent, content, and relaxed. As she lay onto the soft mattress, clean and naked, her hands resting on Shepherd's chest, she wondered how she had ever felt happiness before he came into her life.

It had been a little over a week since Laurel had moved to Silver Moon and she was beginning to feel more comfortable. She admired how structured and organized the pack was and loved the town. It had more amenities than your average small town and the surrounding nature was breathtaking. Laurel had explored a little, but since the guards had been scenting an uptick in rogues around the border of their land, Shepherd hadn't wanted her to venture too far. The first few days, Shepherd had taken off work to help her adjust but when the guards reported their growing concerns about the rogues, he'd returned to his duties.

Laurel didn't mind. Charis and Violet seemed intent on being close to Laurel and making her feel part of the pack. They had lunch at different restaurants, enjoyed the gardens or the pool, and hung out with other pack members in the common rooms. She had only seen Rowan a few times in passing since that first night. They ate dinner with the pack, and he always sat at a different table from her. She'd caught him watching her from across the room but could never decipher his expression.

She, Shepherd, Beck, Violet, Matthius, and Charis always sat at the same table but the people that occupied the other seats varied. Matty and Charis kept everyone laughing with their shenanigans. Charis had taken Laurel to a few of the training sessions, and it was difficult to reconcile how vastly different Matty was when he was sparring. He was an authoritative fighter and the only person she had seen get a clear win on him was Shepherd. But as soon as training was over, Matty was back to cracking jokes. He and Charis were constantly teasing each other. Violet, like Beck, was more subdued. Laurel had caught Violet looking at Matty and Charis multiple times with something like sadness, or perhaps longing, in her eyes. It was clear that she loved Beck, but she didn't look at him the same way he looked at her. Laurel could see that Beck worshiped the ground she walked on. She had no doubt that if it were up to him, Violet would already be marked.

Laurel also noticed that pack members instinctively glanced at her neck when she entered a room and knew they were waiting for Shepherd to complete the mate bond. She didn't understand why he hadn't marked her yet and it had begun to hurt her feelings. She was also concerned about marking Shepherd and asked Charis how she would complete the

The Dream

bond if she wasn't a wolf. After she finished laughing, Charis pointed out that as a human, Laurel also had teeth.

"Just press down harder, L! It's the magic of the mate bond that seals the mark anyhow."

There were only a few human mates in the pack and Laurel had never seen marks on them or their partners. Charis explained that marks typically were on the neck, shoulder, or upper chest and that with unions where one of them was a human, they would mark on the chest so that it could be easily hidden from their human family. It made Laurel thankful that the only family she had already knew about werewolves. She wouldn't have to hide it from Lucy. But she would have to tell Susu soon. She was like a sister to Laurel, and she didn't want to hide such a big part of her life.

Laurel wanted to tell her in person when she gathered the rest of her belongings. Moving to Silver Moon had been a substantial change and although she'd known that she was making the right decision, only taking some of her things had seemed like an effective way to make the transition smoother. Now that she was settling in, she wanted the rest. Most of her furniture she would donate but she was ready for her personal belongings so she could make the apartment she and Shepherd shared feel like her home.

When she mentioned it to Shepherd, he'd pulled her into a tight embrace and readily agreed to take her to New York to get her belongings the upcoming weekend. He was only planning on a quick day trip and Laurel decided to call Susu to see if she was off work on Saturday or Sunday. She answered on the second ring.

"Laurel!" she shouted in a high-pitched voice that made Laurel quickly pull the phone away from her ear.

"Susu! Are you trying to give me hearing loss?!"

"I'm just so excited to hear from you! How are things going there?"

They talked for an hour, catching each other up on all the things that had happened in each other's lives. Susu was off on Sunday and offered to pack up Laurel's things for her beforehand, but Laurel wasn't certain of everything she wanted to bring.

"Besides, Susu. If we have to box everything up, it gives us an excuse for a longer visit!"

"Smart thinking! Hey, before you hang up. I should tell you that Henry stopped by here a few days ago trying to get information on where you were. I didn't tell him anything, but it was kind of weird. Not at all what I would have expected from him. Has he called you?"

Laurel sighed. "Actually, I blocked him on my phone. He texted me a few times and I didn't want to have the conversation with him anymore. It's almost like he's more upset that I'm moving in with someone else than that we split up. I don't know. I'm sorry you had to deal with that, though."

"Oh, it wasn't a big deal. I can manage Henry. I just wanted you to know. Text me on Sunday when you're on the plane, okay? I can't wait to see you!"

"Me, too. Love you, Susu."

Leaving New York had not been difficult for Laurel. She'd hardly thought of it, which surprised her. Not seeing Susu everyday was the only thing that she regretted.

By Saturday, Laurel was getting excited about the trip. She had a difficult time focusing on anything else. Violet came by the apartment shortly after Shepherd left to meet with Matty and Beck over the recent rogue concerns. Shepherd had set up a virtual meeting with a neighboring pack to determine if it was a larger issue or isolated to the Silver Moon pack. Laurel had mixed feelings about it. According to Shepherd and the rest of the pack, rogues were trouble, but Laurel knew that her dad was a rogue and was also a loving and trustworthy man. She couldn't reconcile the two opposing descriptions and it troubled her.

Violet suggested they watch a movie since the weather was rainy. They made popcorn and plopped down on the couch. As Laurel was scrolling through their options, Violet looked around.

"I bet you'll be glad to get some of your things in here. Shepherd has good taste but it's kind of bare. It definitely looks like a single man lives here," she chuckled. Her eyes fell on the painting that hung above the fireplace. "That's beautiful though. Is that yours or was it always here?"

"Yeah, that's mine. My mother painted it. It's my dad. I wanted it to be somewhere visible. It reminds me of them."

Violet walked over to it to get a closer look and smiled back at Laurel after studying it for a moment. "He's a beautiful wolf. Tell me about them."

"Well, they met in the city when my mom was in college. She was human but according to my Aunt Lucy, she knew quickly that he was the one for her. Of course, I didn't know about Morpheus until recently, but it makes sense now that I know. Their bond was an unusual one. I didn't realize it as a kid."

Violet cocked her head sideways. "Morpheus?"

"That was his wolf's name." Violet stared at her curiously for a moment. "Why are you looking at me that way?"

Violet looked back at the painting again before taking a seat beside Laurel. "I just find it odd. Morpheus was the god of dreams. And even amongst werewolves, it's not common to have the kind of dream you had about Shepherd or his wolf. It just makes me wonder…"

"What?"

"It makes me wonder if the dream was a gift from your dad."

Laurel laughed softly. "I don't know but it's a comforting thought. I like the idea that my dad would prepare me to meet my mate." She thought for a moment and then nodded. "Yeah, Violet. It really sounds like something he'd do."

Shepherd made it home shortly before dinner, looking exhausted. Laurel got up to meet him, caressing his cheek.

"Is everything alright?"

Shepherd ran his hand through his hair and sighed deeply. "The Perigee pack has also had a few scuffles with rogues. They think it's an organized effort. Beck and I are going to visit their pack tomorrow and map out a plan to squash this thing before it gets bigger."

"Tomorrow?"

"I know, Sunshine, and I'm sorry. But I've already talked to Matty and Charis. They'll go with you to New York to get your things. I trust Matty to keep you safe. Are you angry with me?"

"Of course not! I want you to figure this rogue situation out before anyone in the pack gets hurt. And I trust Matty, of course. Everything in New York will be fine. But, Shepherd, are you sure that the rogues have ill intentions?"

He pulled her in closer. "I know your dad was a good rogue, Laurel. But most of them aren't. And these rogues have already shown a propensity to not just infiltrate our lands but to attack our guards. They aren't like your dad."

Laurel couldn't disagree with that. If they didn't mean harm, then they wouldn't have crossed into Silver Moon territory. But what their intentions were was anyone's guess.

Chapter 10

The next morning, Laurel met everyone downstairs for an early breakfast before they headed to New York. She was pleasantly surprised to find Violet seated at the table, smiling up at her.

"Mind if I join you guys?"

"Of course we don't, bitch. You're family," Charis responded before Laurel could open her mouth. "But it's way too early. L, make sure you get everything because I never want to be awake at this ungodly hour again."

Violet and Laurel chuckled. "You got it, Charis. Matty, get this woman a coffee pronto!"

Matthius hopped up, "You got it, boss!"

Laurel raised her eyebrows before laughing. "I could get used to that!"

After Matty came back with coffees for everyone, they made their way to meet Truett. Shepherd accompanied them to the airstrip, holding her hand as they got out of the car. She started to walk towards the plane, but instead of releasing her, he pulled her into a tight embrace and showered her face with light kisses. She giggled.

"Shep, everyone's waiting for me."

"Let them."

She looked into his dark green eyes and felt the familiar fluttering in her stomach and the tingles down her spine. "You know we can't do anything. You're not being fair."

"I never said I would be, Sunshine."

He reached to the base of her neck and pulled her closer, kissing her deeply, his tongue searching every part of her mouth. Her body was pressed firmly against his hard chest and his free hand grabbed her bottom and squeezed her even closer so that she could feel his rigid member. She moaned against him before using her hands against his chest to push him away. He had an infuriating smirk on his face as he released her.

"That really, really wasn't fair, Shepherd," she glowered at him.

He touched the side of her face and gave her a peck on her lips. "I'll make it up to you tonight. That's a promise."

Matthius howled with laughter when she stepped onto the plane. She knew that they could scent her arousal and it made her even angrier at Shepherd.

"He made damn sure you were coming home to him quickly, didn't he?!"

She narrowed her eyes at him. "Shut it, Matty."

He laughed again before Charis punched his arm, giving him a "behave" face. Once they were in the air, Matty and Charis made their way to the bedroom to get a few hours of sleep while Violet and Laurel stretched out on the couches. Violet quickly fell asleep, but Laurel's mind was racing with excitement. She missed Susu. After a while, her thoughts settled, and she managed a long nap before they landed in New York mid-morning.

Susu was at the kitchen bar when they arrived. She screeched excitedly as they entered, rushing to give Laurel a bear hug. Laurel was filled with warmth to see Violet and Charis immediately embrace Susu upon introduction, as if they were old friends. They knew how important Susu was to her and were determined to love her. It reminded Laurel that Susu needed to know the truth. She didn't want to put it off. It would only get more difficult to find the right time as the day went on.

"We won't be here for long, Susu, and I need to talk to you about something important before we start packing."

Susu cocked her head, confusion on her face. "Okay. Should I sit down? You look so serious."

The Dream

They headed to the couches. The others sent Laurel a look, questioning whether they should leave, but Laurel gestured to the other seats. She wasn't sure how this was going to go and wanted their support in case she needed their help convincing Susu of the veracity of her story. If Laurel hadn't had the dream, she could only imagine how much more difficult it would have been for her to believe in the existence of werewolves. Suddenly, she knew the right way to start the conversation.

"You know how I had the recurring dream of Shepherd before I met him?" Susu nodded. "After I met him, I had another dream that I didn't tell you about."

Recounting briefly the first part of the dream to Susu, she then delved into the deviation- the familiar wolf and the wolves surrounding her and howling in acceptance of her. Susu's face scrunched up in bewilderment.

"That sounds really strange, Laurel. What do you think it means?"

She glanced around at the others to gauge their reaction, but their faces remained impassive. Laurel sighed. It wasn't easy with Aunt Lucy, and it certainly wasn't any easier with Susu. She calmed herself by remembering that Susu was the last person she would have to have this conversation with. She suddenly felt fortunate not to have a large family.

"Well, just like the first dream, it was a premonition."

Susu narrowed her eyes. "So, it's happened? What, you've become a zoologist since you left me?"

Laurel grimaced. "No. Shepherd is a werewolf. So is Matty, Charis, and Violet. In fact, almost the entire population of Silver Moon is."

Susu rolled her eyes. "This is a terrible joke, Laurel. I never thought I'd say this, but can we get to work now? I wanted to have time to get a bite to eat with you before you leave," she said as she started to stand.

Laurel reached out, gesturing for her to sit back down. "I'm not kidding, Susu. I know it's unbelievable but it's an integral part of my life now and you're like a sister to me. I need you to believe me."

Susu searched the faces of Laurel and her friends for signs of deceit. "I'm not sure I can, Laurel. I don't know what's gotten into you. You're worrying me."

"I can prove it to you. But I need you to promise you won't scream or run away."

"Laurel..." Susu began before sighing and leaning back against the couch. "Alright, Laurel. Prove it to me, then."

"You won't scream?"

"You're the one that doesn't like scary movies, not me."

Laurel looked at her friends imploringly. They understood that she needed their help convincing Susu.

Violet stood up. "I'll do it."

Charis and Matty stood as well. "We all will."

Susu's face was full of confusion. Laurel scooted close to her on the couch and grabbed her hand, explaining quickly.

"They're going to shift into their wolves. They won't hurt you, Susu. Do you trust me?"

"Of course, Laurel. But I still don't know what game you're playing at here."

"If you don't want to see them naked, you should close your eyes. I'll tell you when to open."

"Alright. I can't believe I'm doing this," Susu muttered as she squeezed her eyes shut.

Matty, Charis, and Violet quickly shed their clothing and shifted into their wolves. Laurel had seen Matty and Charis' wolves but never Violet's. She was a beautiful blonde wolf with no other markings. Her wolf's eyes were as blue as their human counterpart and had the same kind, reassuring look in them. She nodded at them gratefully before telling Susu to open her eyes. Susu's hand instinctively flew to her mouth to stifle her cry of surprise. Slowly lowering her hand, she sat with her mouth open, trying to make sense of the scene before her. Finally, she looked over at Laurel.

"This is crazy. You know that right?"

Laurel laughed quietly. "Yeah, I know. But what do you think?"

Susu shook her head slowly. "I have no idea."

Violet's wolf tentatively walked towards Susu and laid her head in Susu's lap. Susu looked unsure before resting her hand on the wolf's head.

The Dream

"Wow, they're really beautiful, aren't they?"

Laurel was thankful that Violet had come. She doubted Charis or Matty would want Susu to touch their wolves, but Violet's nature was nurturing and accepting. After a few moments, Susu nodded.

"Okay." She paused before continuing. "Okay, so there are werewolves. What else do I not know about?" A thought suddenly entered her mind. "Wait, are *you* a werewolf also?"

"No, but my dad was. I just recently found out. Aunt Lucy told me after Shepherd revealed himself to me in Oregon."

"You've known since Oregon and didn't tell me?!"

"I didn't know how to. I'm sorry, Susu."

Matty, Charis, and Violet shifted back and put their clothes back on while they were talking, and Susu turned to them. "And you've always been this way?"

Charis smiled and shrugged, "Yep. We were raised in the Silver Moon pack. It's all we've ever known."

"Wicked!" Susu replied excitedly.

Laurel let out a laugh of relief. They made quick work of packing up the rest of Laurel's belongings. Laurel told Susu about the mate bond, how her father had really died, the structure of the wolf pack and her new role in it. Charis and Violet patiently answered all of Susu's questions that Laurel didn't have the answer to. They spent a lot of time talking and laughing. Laurel felt a huge relief that Susu had taken it so well.

"You know you can't tell anyone, right, Susu?"

"Do you think I want to be locked up in an insane asylum, Laurel? Seriously, who would I tell?!"

Matty carried the boxes out as they packed them, and Laurel arranged for a donation company to pick up the furniture. By the time they finished, Susu, Charis, and Violet were getting along like old friends. Charis and Susu were so similar, and Laurel had rolled her eyes multiple times at their sarcastic teasing. After Matty carried the last of the boxes to the moving van, he suggested they get a bite to eat while the driver took the boxes to the airplane to unload.

Susu and Laurel looked at each other and both shouted, "Don Antonio's!"

The others laughed. "Don who?"

"You'll love it, Charis. It's our favorite pizza joint."

Suddenly, Matthius laughed. "By the sound of your stomach, Susu, we should head there now!"

A look of surprise flashed across her face. "You could hear that?"

"Absolutely! We have great hearing."

"Remind me of that when I go to the bathroom. Good grief!"

Everyone chuckled as they gathered their things before heading out. Laurel left last and turned back to take a look at the place she and Susu had shared. She would miss living with Susu but by the way she already missed Shepherd, she knew the right decision was made. Sighing, she turned and closed the door behind her before catching up with the others.

"This place really is delicious," Charis agreed with a mouth full of pizza.

"Um yeah, I think we could tell you liked it when you went for your fifth slice," Susu said sarcastically.

"And I'm about to have my sixth, chipmunk."

Susu looked at her with fake disdain. "Chipmunk?"

Charis leaned in to bump against her shoulder. "Yes, that's what I'm going to call you, my little friend."

Susu rolled her eyes. "Good deflection from your plate. Don't call me that."

"Whatever you say, my little chipmunk."

As they were leaving, Laurel smiled with contentment. At some point, she was sure she would talk Susu into moving to Silver Moon and it helped that she already liked Charis and Violet. There was a coffee shop in town she could work at, or she could have the freedom and support of the pack to try something new. Laurel knew she would love it but didn't want to press her too much.

Just as the bell on the door quieted, Laurel looked up to see Henry on the street outside the pizzeria. She felt her heart sink. She hadn't

The Dream

expected to see Henry on this trip. She certainly had hoped that would be the case. NYC was a big city. What were the odds? For the first time today, she was thankful that Shepherd hadn't been able to come with her. Susu and Matthius were the only ones who understood what was happening, but Charis and Violet could not have missed the shift in the mood. Matthius moved closer to Laurel, standing beside her in a protective stance. Henry glanced over at him, and an expression of confusion flashed across his face before he spoke, breaking the silence between them.

"It's good to see you, Laurel. How are you?" His voice was tense, but he seemed calmer than during their last run-in.

"I'm doing really well. How are you?"

He forced a half smile. "You can imagine."

Laurel glanced at the ground between them, unsure of how to respond. After a brief moment, Henry continued. "I'm glad you're doing well, Laurel. I really am. Has there been…." Here he paused, his face clearly showing that he was gathering his resolve to speak words that cost him his pride to say out loud, especially in front of strangers. "Has there been any change in your feelings?"

"I'm afraid not, Henry."

He sighed deeply. "Well, I suppose that's it then. I want to apologize for how things went down last time we were together. I'm glad I saw you tonight because what I've wished over the past couple of weeks is that I could change my last words. I've loved you for years, Laurel. Maybe I didn't always express it well to you, but I did love you. I do." Laurel felt Matthius stiffen beside her and knew he was getting angry. Henry remained focused on Laurel. "And I just want to tell you that I hope you're happy. Wherever you end up."

He stepped forward to give her a hug, but Matthius reached an arm out to stop him. Henry looked at him, his face showing that he didn't recognize him from their short interaction at the office. "Another boyfriend, Laurel?" He asked, trying to make his voice sound light as he glanced over Matty's build. "Or a bodyguard, perhaps? Good grief, what are they feeding these guys?"

Laurel chuckled but didn't answer. She knew now that Henry would be ok, and she was thankful for it. "I wish the same things for you, Henry. I'm glad we ran into each other."

"Me, too." He looked over at Matty. "I was just going to give her a hug, sport. Is that alright?"

Matty's posture didn't relax. "You're not touching her."

Henry looked at Laurel as if he wanted to point out how strange the situation was but seemed to decide better of it. "Alright," he said, forcing a smile. "In that case, good night. And if we ever run into each other again, Laurel, I hope it can be as friends."

"Me too, Henry."

Laurel watched him walk away and felt unsettled that Matty hadn't let Henry give her a parting hug. She understood his reasoning and his protectiveness of not just her but of Shepherd in his absence, but she knew the hug to be innocent. She wasn't sure she would ever understand that part of werewolf culture. They continued their walk back to the apartment, everyone remaining quiet until Susu broke the silence.

"I must admit. Henry was pretty classy back there. But I still think he's an ass."

Laurel rolled her eyes but laughed along with the rest of the group, grateful once again for Susu.

It was the wee hours of the morning when they arrived back in Silver Moon. Still, Shepherd was waiting for her on the porch when they came up the drive. He stood to meet them as the car stopped and scooped her up as soon as she got out of the car. As he carried her into the house, bridal style, she could hear the others giggling behind her. She didn't care. She snuggled deeper into his embrace as he jogged up the stairs to the fourth floor. Not letting her go, he went straight to the bedroom, tossing Laurel onto the bed and immediately beginning to take off his clothing. Laurel laughed, leaning up on her elbows to watch him.

"So, did you miss me a little, Shep?"

"You know I did, Laurel. And I have a promise to keep."

The Dream

The sensual tone of his voice immediately made her pussy clench in anticipation of the pleasure that was sure to come. Before he could finish taking his pants off, Laurel scooted off the bed. She threw a couple of cushions on the floor and knelt before him, caressing his thighs as she looked up at him. He lifted each foot up as she finished taking off his pants, both looking at each other with intense longing.

"What are you doing, Sunshine?" he asked, his voice low and raspy.

"Showing you how much I missed you first."

With light pressure, she moved up and down his length with her hands while her mouth hummed against the crown of his cock. She worked him deeper into her mouth, moving at a torturously slow pace. Shepherd tried to keep his hands at his side but when she pressed him into her throat, he let out a groan as his fingers wove through her hair, pushing in a little deeper. Laurel increased her rhythm with her mouth and hand until she could tell by Shepherd's moans that he was close to climaxing.

"Laurel, I'm about to come," he warned her.

She tightened her arms around his thighs to signal to him that she wanted every bit of him and pressed him even farther into her mouth, deeper than she'd ever gone before. He gently grabbed each side of her face as she looked up at him with hunger in her gaze. "Fuck," he grunted as he released his load. She pulled away, sucking the tip before leaning back onto her heels. Shepherd caressed her cheek.

"Have I mentioned that you're going to be the death of me?"

Laurel smiled at him as she wiped the corners of her mouth. "Maybe a time or two."

He grabbed her hand and pulled her up into his arms. "I love you, Laurel. I can't imagine life without you."

She leaned in to kiss him passionately in response. He knew she felt the same way about him. Shepherd's hand trailed down to her breast and massaged her nipple while his other hand cupped her ass, pulling her hips into his so she could feel that he was still hard for her. She ached in expectation. Shepherd led her backwards a few steps before breaking their kiss as he maneuvered her onto the edge of the bed, this time kneeling before her. He grinned up at her before delving into her already wet pussy.

"You taste delicious. I can never get enough of you."

He took possession of her slit, making almost animalistic sounds as he devoured her, alternating between quick flicks of his tongue and sucking her bud. She felt the pressure building within her. Her breathing and heart rate increased until she felt like she was losing her mind. When it culminated, all she could do was scream Shepherd's name as her body gave itself up to the intensity, his hand pressing against her abdomen to keep her in place as he continued his siege on her pussy.

She pushed against his head, feeling unable to withstand the barrage of violent pleasure but he growled into her vagina, the vibrations sending an unknown sensation through her as she moaned, arching her back. He tugged at her clit with his mouth as his fingers thrust into her repeatedly, sending her over the edge for the second time. He released her clit and slowly withdrew his fingers, the action causing residual shivers down her shine. Shepherd stood, sucking the last bit of her from his fingers as he watched her, before laying on the bed and rolling her on top of him. They lay together for a long time, Shepherd caressing her back.

"Are you still awake, Laurel?"

She looked up at him, raising her eyebrows in question. His voice sounded serious, and his face mirrored the tone. "What is it, Shepherd? Is everything alright?"

He looked into her eyes for a moment before speaking. She didn't need the mate bond to know that he was weighing his words before speaking them. It was something she loved about him. He wasn't careless when he spoke.

He sat up and took her hands as they faced each other. "I want to mark you, Laurel. I want to complete the bond and know that you're mine forever. But I want to be sure that you understand the implications. I will always be Alpha of my pack and when I mark you, you will always be Luna. It's a blessing from the Moon Goddess but it's also a never-ending responsibility. And one that I can never abandon, Laurel." She smiled at him, letting him know she understood before he continued.

The Dream

"You already know this, but we'll be forever connected, maybe even in death." He paused and she again conveyed her acceptance with a smile, nodding for him to continue. "I want you more than anything. You're already part of my soul. It's not just Angus who has been going crazy to mark you. It's true I've been keeping him in the background but it's me too. Every part of me wants to complete the bond. You are... everything! But I've been waiting to mark you because it's not part of your culture and I want to be sure that you fully understand before we take that step."

She loved him even more for his speech. She'd been wondering why he hadn't marked her yet. There was nothing he could say that could change what she'd already determined within herself. Shepherd was everything to her as well and there was no going back. She climbed onto his lap, straddling him.

"I love you for saying that. But I already know, Shep. There's no decision to be made. You are woven into every piece of my life, my soul, and my heart. I want you. I've never wanted anything more."

He grabbed her and held her tightly for a long while. When he finally pulled away, there were tears in his eyes. Nothing could have surprised Laurel more. She would never have imagined Shepherd- strong, confident, Alpha Shepherd- crying. If there had been any part of her that was unsure, it would've given in at that moment. As it was, his transparency endeared him even more to her. She wiped his tears with her thumb and leaned her forehead against his, closing her eyes and breathing in his earthy scent.

She felt his lips gently caress hers and opened her eyes to find his green eyes swirling with black as he allowed Angus to share the moment. She leaned forward to meet his lips this time, both keeping their eyes on the other. Laurel had never kissed anyone with her eyes open. It always seemed like a strange thing to do. But it felt right. She knew they were going to complete the bond and she wanted to experience it with all five senses. His hand wrapped around the base of her neck as their kiss deepened. Laurel wrapped her arms around his shoulders and into his hair.

Needing him closer, she pressed herself against him, their tongues searching out every part of the other. She could feel him harden beneath her and lifted herself just slightly, pressing her breasts into his chest as she reached down to position him. She eased onto his dick, both moaning into their kiss as he slipped into her wet sheath. When she had fully taken him, she sat for a moment, enjoying the feeling of being one with him. Their hands were searching every part of the others, their bodies connected, their mouths possessing the others. Every part of them was intertwined and connected.

Slowly, she began to grind against him, concentrating on every sensation. The way her hair felt trailing down her naked back as she leaned her head back to give him access to her neck. The sensational tingling from his soft kisses from her ear lobe down her neck and collarbone. The way their stomachs touched as she moved up and down on him, her nipples hard from brushing against his chest. She savored his touch on her lower back and the look of bliss on his face as he watched her ride him.

As the fiery friction built, Laurel quickened her pace, lifting almost entirely off him before impaling herself back down. Shepherd leaned against the headboard, holding onto her hips. His breathing became more erratic, and she could tell from his features that he wasn't going to last much longer.

"Oh goddess, Laurel. You feel so good."

She leaned into him. "Take me, Shepherd. Make me yours."

He needed no further encouragement. He flipped her onto her back and slowed the pace. Laurel started to close her eyes in pleasure.

"Look at me," his low voice demanded.

She forced her eyes open, seeing his eyes swirling between green and black as he kissed her deeply. She moaned against him. His kisses traveled down, concentrating on where neck meets shoulder. Before she could worry about the pain, she felt his teeth sink into her. The intense pleasure mingled with pain sent her into the most powerful orgasm that she had ever experienced. Her tight, convulsing pussy milked every part of Shepherd's release as she instinctively found his neck and bit down with all her force, breaking the skin.

The Dream

"Laurel," Shepherd moaned as she felt the metallic taste of his blood in her mouth.

They collapsed against each other in exhaustion as their ecstasy relaxed. It was the strangest sensation, feeling Shepherd's emotions swirl into her own. She could feel the bond strengthening between them and knew that their very beings were becoming one. When she looked up, it was into black eyes.

"Mate," he said, his deep voice filled with pride.

"Mate," she responded as she reached up to caress his face, breathing him in deeply before he pulled her against him as they stretched out on the bed.

She felt as if she were drugged, drained from everything that had passed between them. When she opened her eyes again, Shepherd's green eyes were watching her with concern.

"Laurel, are you alright?"

She knew he was concerned that their mating had been too much for her, but she had never felt more right. "I'm alright. I'm just so tired."

He rolled her over on the bed and sat up to gather the blankets to cover her. "I'm here, Laurel. Just rest."

Her eyes fluttered for just a moment, and she reached out to pull his arm around her, needing his touch.

She didn't remember falling asleep. But when she woke, she felt that she'd never slept so soundly. Her entire body felt heavy, and it took all her effort to open her eyes. She was surprised to see Shepherd in a chair close to the bed. He was still asleep.

"Shepherd?" Her voice sounded raspy, and her throat was dry.

He woke suddenly and reached out to touch her face. "Laurel? Thank the goddess. I was so worried about you." She tried to sit up but felt solid, as if she were glued to the bed. "You've been sleeping for over twenty-four hours, Laurel. I thought…" Shepherd's voice choked up. "I thought I hurt you when I marked you. I tried to wake you, but I couldn't. I've never been so afraid. How are you feeling? What do you need?" A tingling sensation passed through her body as she tried to rouse herself, her body slowly awakening. "Don't try to sit up just yet." She saw his eyes glaze over and knew he was communicating with someone through the mind link. *Can I do that now that we're mated?* "I'm having some food sent up. Lilac is coming to examine you. Rest easy."

She sat up, this time able to rest on her elbows. "I'm fine, Shepherd. My body just feels weak from sleeping so long."

He moved to the side of the bed and took her hand, insisting that she lay back down. "Humor me. You've been out for a long time. I need to make sure you're okay. Angus has been going wild. We both need Lilac to look you over."

She relented, feeling his anxiety. She could feel everything that he felt, in fact. She knew that the bond would create a pathway between them, but she was still overwhelmed by the experience. It was mere moments before Lilac arrived, rushing in, and quickly taking in the scene.

"Lilac, I've tried to tell him that I'm fine. I was just exhausted."

"Well, let's take a look anyway. It's not often that a human and an Alpha mate. He has reason to be concerned." Lilac examined her thoroughly and then sat on the edge of the bed. "You look perfectly healthy, Laurel. I'm going to take some blood to run a few tests just as a precaution. I would recommend you take it easy today. Listen to your body."

"Thanks, Lilac."

"My pleasure, Luna. Please let me know if you need anything at all. And…congratulations on completing your bond," Lilac placed her hand on top of Laurel's for a moment, giving a gentle squeeze before leaving.

Shepherd and Laurel discussed the Luna Ceremony while they ate breakfast in bed. It was a bigger event than she had anticipated, with multiple packs being invited. Laurel wasn't one who minded large crowds, but she also was never the center of attention. She wished that Susu could be with her, but Shepherd didn't think it was a good idea for

The Dream

Susu to be around that many werewolves so soon after finding out about them. He promised she could come afterwards, and once Laurel thought about it, she knew Susu would have to give a couple of weeks' notice to take off from work anyway.

Charis, Violet, and Luna Millie would help her plan the event and walk her through all the details. Shepherd would oversee the invitations for the event. She had questioned whether it was a suitable time to have a celebration since the pack had experienced an increase in rogue activity, but Shepherd insisted it was non-negotiable.

"It's important that the pack has this. It's a time for you to recognize them as your pack, and they recognize you as their Luna. It's a beautiful ceremony. They've waited a long time for you, Laurel. I won't deny them this. Besides, Rusty is damn good at his job. He'll make sure security is tight. We'll also have the Perigee and Crescent Fang packs here. There's strength in numbers. It's possible that there will be even more. I'll invite all the packs in the Western region, but likely only a few will send representatives."

"How many packs are there?"

"In the Western U.S.? About thirty. There's more in this region than any of the others. There are sixty-three packs in the United States, but some of them are very small."

"Wow, that's a lot. I had no idea."

Shepherd chuckled, "That's the idea. We keep a low profile. Alright, I'm going to send mother, Charis, and Violet in to start the planning. I'll check back in with you in a little bit."

Laurel threw the covers off, which earned her a raised eyebrow from Shepherd. "Actually, can you have them meet me in the gardens in an hour? I'd like a bath and some fresh air."

He leaned in and kissed her forehead. "You got it, Sunshine. But take it easy, alright?"

Laurel smiled and nodded. As Shepherd opened the door, he turned back.

"My mark looks good on you by the way."

Laurel got out of bed and quickly went to look in the bathroom mirror, studying the mark on her neck. It had already started to heal. It was beautiful, appearing more like a tattoo of two crescent moons reaching for each other than a bite mark. She placed her hand over it gently and smiled to herself. Nothing would ever separate Shepherd from her now.

CHAPTER 11

In the garden, Millie stood to give Laurel a hug and admire her mark.

"It's beautiful, dear. Congratulations."

"It's about damn time! Let me get a look at that," Charis squealed with excitement.

Millie and Violet laughed at Charis' reaction before settling into their seats. Violet pointed at the chair with the extra cushions and smiled.

"Shepherd came by and made sure we all knew you were supposed to be resting today."

Charis rolled her eyes. "She makes it sound like he was being sweet. He all but threatened us with death to keep you calm and relaxed today and to feed and water you regularly."

"You make me sound like a pet!"

Millie gave a warning glance to Charis, who quickly sat up straighter. "Sorry, Luna."

"Don't call me Luna anymore, Charis. It's just Millie now. But you shouldn't talk about Shepherd that way. He's your Alpha and he has a new mate. A new mate who isn't familiar with our world yet." She shifted her eyes to Laurel. "They're meant to be protective. It's worse at the beginning but Shepherd will always be protective of you. It's in all wolves' natures but it's strongest in the Alphas."

Laurel smiled at her, "He's tried to explain it to me. I don't mind it so much. What he hasn't fully explained is this Luna Ceremony so I'm going to need a lot of help!"

Violet reached across the table and grabbed her hand. "That's what we're here for!"

A few hours later, Laurel had a much clearer picture of what the ceremony was and how it would work. Really, it seemed like Millie, Charis, and Violet would take care of most everything. They walked her through each step, getting her input on colors, menu options, flowers, and decorations. They made it feel easy. Lunch was delivered to them in the garden as they made the last arrangements.

Millie could sense that Laurel felt uncomfortable that they were doing most of the work. "You'll have plenty to do, don't worry. And you'll slowly start to fall into your role as Luna and take over some of those duties. Plus, after the ceremony is over, Shepherd mentioned you may be taking a position at Beau Industries. You're going to be very busy, very soon; don't worry!"

Laurel gulped. She knew she was capable, but she was also a planner. She liked to do her own research and map out how she should tackle a new job. This was unknown territory for her and besides the expertise of those around her, there was no way to research. The old maxim, "You don't know what you don't know" came to mind.

Millie seemed to read her mind. "Don't worry. We all know that it takes time to figure these things out and we want you to succeed. We'll help you and when you do feel equipped, we'll move out of the way and let you do it your way."

Millie and Beau had been supportive but quiet since she came. Spending the morning with Millie had made her like her even more. "Before you head home, Laurel, I want you to come to my house. There's something I want to show you."

Charis and Violet promised to stop by later in the afternoon to check on her as she and Millie headed to the front of the pack house, where Millie's car was parked.

"I usually walk but I knew that I was going to invite you over and that Shepherd wouldn't want you to exert yourself so soon after the scare you gave us."

The home she and Beau shared was a beautiful cabin surrounded by woods. A set of outdoor furniture sat on the deep front porch and there were lights strung across the pale blue ceiling. It was painted

The Dream

to look like water, with varying shades of blue. Millie noticed her staring.

"Do you like it? I'm from a pack in Louisiana. It's a southern tradition to paint your porch ceiling haint blue. It's supposed to confuse the spirits, so they don't come into your house."

Laurel had noticed Millie's accent but hadn't wanted to be nosy. "How did you and Beau meet?"

Millie gestured to sit down. "He came looking for me," she began with a sly grin.

Laurel raised her eyebrows at her and laughed. "How did he know where to look?"

"Well, he didn't. Beau's a bit older than me. He's calmed as he's aged but I'm sure you can imagine how difficult it would be for him to wait for something once he's decided it was time for it to happen." She chuckled before continuing. "He visited his neighboring packs first and accepted all the invitations from other packs for celebrations and still hadn't found his mate. So, he began to search on his own. He'd leave Noble in charge for a few days at a time and visit the packs that granted him permission. It took a few years of searching but thankfully, he found me in one of the willing packs. He once told me he planned to force his way into the packs that didn't respond to his request! Can you imagine?!"

It was Laurel's turn to chuckle. "Actually, I can. Beau strikes me as a man who gets what he wants. I wonder where Shep got that from."

"Shepherd is much calmer than Beau was. There's no way Beau would've waited this long to mark me."

Laurel knew that her face must have flushed with embarrassment because Millie quickly explained herself. "We understand why he waited, and we support him. It really is a testament to how much he loves you for him to have waited until he knew you wouldn't regret it. We've been amazed to watch your journey. It wasn't the way it was with Beau and me. My father was Alpha of the Roux-Ga-Roux pack. If he hadn't been such a strong believer in the Moon Goddess' plan, he and Beau would've fought. Truly, they were too much alike. I was marked before the end of the first night and moved here the next day."

She laughed when she saw Laurel's shocked expression. "It's not uncommon for wolves. I could have prolonged it if I'd wanted to, but I saw Beau and knew he was my forever. And I was right. We've always loved and supported each other. There were a few times when I had to put my foot down, of course, but Beau usually came around to my way of thinking," she laughed. "We make a good team. But we're proud of Shepherd and happy to let you and him take the reins." She stood and reached out her hand to Laurel, leading her inside. "Which brings me to why we came here. I have my Luna dress that I'd like to show you. If you'd rather pick your own, I won't be offended but I kept it just in case."

There was a large box on her bed, and she sat beside it and lifted the lid. Laurel gasped. It was stunning. She lifted it by the shoulders and held it up. White beads covered the entirety of the dress, with small gold beads that created the appearance of stars dispersed throughout. In the center was a silver crescent moon shape on the chest. It hung off the shoulders and there was a long slit down one of the legs.

"You're about my size. We may have to hem the bottom. Would you like to try it on?"

Laurel could hardly hold her excitement in. It was perfect, and even more special because it belonged to Shepherd's mother. She took it into the bathroom and slipped it on. It had an open back with a low plunge and fit perfectly. She opened the door and lifted her hair so Millie could fasten the hook around her neck.

"We'll have to take it up a few inches on the bottom but otherwise, it looks like it was made for you. Do you like it?"

"I love it. Thank you for loaning it to me. It'll be perfect."

"It's not a loan, dear. It's yours. You can put it away for the next generation to use if you like." Laurel smiled at her in the mirror. "Well, slip it off and I'll put it back in the box until we have it altered." Laurel gave her a quick hug before going.

"Laurel, hurry and come out!" came Millie's anxious voice through the bathroom door. She quickly slipped on her shoes and came out of the bathroom with the dress draped carefully over her arm. Millie grabbed

The Dream

it and carelessly tossed it onto the bed. She grabbed Laurel's hand and rushed towards the door.

"What's happening, Millie? Is everything okay?"

"No, there's been an attack on the southern border. They're close to us. Shepherd wants me to bring you to the pack house."

As they reached the front door, Beau rushed in, and Laurel immediately felt the anger rolling off him. His shirt was torn in multiple places, and he had blood on his arm. Millie moved towards him quickly, but he held out his arm to stop her.

"I'm fine, Millie. The rogues are trying to make it to the pack house. It'll be safer for us here. Shepherd sent me to protect you, Laurel. I want you and Millie in the basement now."

He led them to the back bedroom and lifted a rug which revealed a door going down into the basement. Beau was spraying something in the room when Laurel turned around to see if he was following them. Millie had turned around, too.

"Come with us, Beau. Hurry!"

He caressed her cheek as he kissed her forehead. "No, Cheríe. I don't think we'll get any visitors but if we do, they'll have to go through me. If they happen to make it past me, you protect Laurel."

Before she could protest, he shut the door and she could hear him latch it and pull the rug over the area. Laurel could tell Millie was worried, but she forced a face of calm as she faced Laurel.

"We'll be safe here. Beaumont may be older, but he's strong as a bull. No one will get past him. Shepherd knew that and that's why he sent him." Millie lit the lantern and sat down on one of the chairs across from Laurel.

"Won't they know we're down here? I mean Shepherd can smell my presence from several rooms away."

"Beau sprayed something to hide our scent. We'll be safe."

"Does this happen often?"

"Oh no, dear. We live in relative peace here. We have the occasional rogue and so we keep a watch along our perimeter, but as you know, it's gotten worse lately. The patrollers are tired. I really hope they can figure out what is behind this soon." Millie sighed and Laurel didn't want to add to her stress, so she changed the subject.

"Why does Beau call you Cheríe?"

Millie smiled, "A term of endearment he picked up from my pack. It's French, which we Cajuns still use a bit of. It means 'dear one'"

They sat in silence for a long time, both of them worrying about the pack and their mates. Occasionally, she would see Millie's eyes glaze over and knew that she was getting a message from the pack, but she didn't say anything. Laurel wondered if she would know if something happened to Shepherd. She thought she'd have access to the mind link once she mated with Shepherd, but she hadn't. She assumed it was only for werewolves and felt a heavy dose of disappointment. She wanted to be a full member of the pack and to be able to communicate with them. And right now, it would be beneficial to know what was happening!

"Any news?"

Millie looked at her with surprise. "Oh, my goddess, Laurel, I'm sorry. I thought you were getting the links too." She paused, "You haven't gotten any of them since you mated? I knew that the other human mates didn't have access to it, but I just assumed as the Luna, you would. I'm sorry. You must've been worried sick. They stopped the rogues before they made it to the pack house. There were some injuries to pack members but none of them too serious. They captured a few of the rogues for questioning. Shepherd's doing a perimeter check before we're clear to come out. He wants Beau and I to bring you directly to him as soon as it's safe."

Laurel felt even more disappointed after learning that Millie also thought she'd have the mind link. "Millie? Is it selfish to have the Luna Ceremony with all this going on? Shepherd says it's too important to the pack to prolong but I don't want anyone to get hurt because of my celebration."

Millie reached over and grabbed her hand. "Shepherd is right. Even if this is rare, danger could happen at any time. We must do our best to protect against it but continue to live and celebrate all the good things

The Dream

in life, like finding you!" They both turned as they heard the door to the basement creak open.

Matty smiled down at them, "You guys want to keep going with the girl talk? I can shut this back!"

Laurel laughed but Millie quickly asked where Beau was.

"Shepherd sent me to get Laurel and Alpha Beau asked me to take both of you to the pack house. His wolf was feeling agitated, and he needed to go for a run. But he wanted me to tell you, Luna Millie, not to leave the pack house until he comes to get you."

Millie rolled her eyes. "I already told your mate to stop calling me Luna. We have a new Luna now."

Matty threw his arms up in surrender as they passed him at the door. "Alright, alright! I was just trying to show you respect." He closed the door and moved the rug back. "Millie, I ran over here but Shep doesn't want Laurel walking that far yet. Can we take your car?"

This time it was Laurel who rolled her eyes, making Matty shrug again.

Shepherd stopped in to check on her when Matty brought her and Millie to the pack house but quickly returned to work. Violet came to sit with her and kept her updated on the situation. They hadn't gotten much information from the captured rogues but were organizing a meeting of the Alphas from the neighboring packs to update them and create a structured plan.

"Beck is calling it the Ring of Alphas," Violet said teasingly. "Now that we've had such a blatant attack, the three closest packs will hold a meeting to gather information and strategize an organized effort against the rogues. And with a name like that, how could they fail?" she chuckled.

The fact that Violet could laugh about it eased Laurel's anxiety. As Luna, surely, she should have the same level of confidence in Shepherd's abilities as Violet. Eventually, Violet returned to her apartment to go to sleep. Laurel changed into her pajamas and climbed into bed but was too restless to sleep. She could feel Shepherd's stress through their bond. Throwing the covers off, she headed downstairs to find him. He was in his office, papers scattered on the desk and a glass of bourbon in his hands. The lines on his face showed his anxiety. He usually wore the responsibility of the pack so well that she sometimes forgot what a heavy weight it was on him.

In lesser hands, the happiness and success of the pack may not be as big of a priority but not with Shepherd. Even though no lives had been lost that day, some of his fellow warriors were injured. He didn't take it lightly. And with such a large territory, he needed to ensure that the pack stayed safe. Laurel knew that it would be his top priority to figure out what was causing the rogues to attack. But she also knew that he wouldn't figure it all out tonight. Taking the bourbon and placing it on his desk, she straddled his lap and ran her hands through his hair before lightly running her fingertips along his face, relaxing all of his worry lines.

"Are you ever coming to bed, Alpha?"

He groaned and pulled her hips closer to him, letting his head fall back on the chair. "I don't want you in danger. I don't want my pack in danger. I just need to figure out why the rogues are attacking."

She nestled into his neck. "And you will, Shep. But not tonight. You need a good night's sleep and a clear head."

Shepherd breathed in deeply before tugging at the bottom of her shirt. She leaned up and he pulled it off before tossing it onto the floor and reaching behind her to undo the clasp of her bra.

"This isn't resting, Alpha," she chided, earning her another growl as Shepherd gave his attention to her breasts. She knew he liked it when she called him Alpha and let a chuckle escape her.

Shepherd released her nipple and worked his way up to her neck. "Is something funny, Sunshine?"

His hands wove through her hair, pulling her in for a deep kiss. She moaned into his mouth as she felt his rod lengthen and press into her. Faster than she could register what was happening, Shepherd had stood them both up and leaned her onto the desk before kissing down her abdomen while he unbuttoned her pants. He pulled them

The Dream

down slowly, taking his time to kiss along her thighs, his warm breath hovering over her panties as he gently bit at her, causing her core to ignite as her panties wettened with her desire. He tortured her over her panties as he removed her pants legs one at a time and then stood abruptly, turning her around and bending her over his desk. She could feel his bulge pressing against her ass and moaned out his name. After a day of being away from him and being worried about his safety, his touch and the closeness of his body was enough to arouse all her senses. He reached around to rub her clit and she pressed her ass into him.

"I want to mount you, Laurel. Tell me to stop."

"Why would I do that? I want you too, Shepherd. Take me now."

He groaned and leaned against her, his warm breath against her ear sending shivers all the way down her body. "You feel alright? Are you sure?"

She groaned, this time in exasperation. "Shepherd, the only thing bothering me right now is that you're not giving me what I want. Fuck me already!"

She felt him rip her panties off and throw them aside, using his foot to widen her stance against his desk. Massaging her ass cheeks, he teased her with the head of his cock as he pressed against her opening. She leaned into him, making him enter her. Grabbing her hips, he slowly thrust into her, not stopping until he was fully seated. The pressure within Laurel from his huge shaft made her walls throb and contract, causing him to moan against her.

"Goddess, you're so tight, Laurel."

He stood still as she moved against him, his hand sending shivers of excitement as he traced her spine upward and reached the base of her neck, squeezing firmly but lightly. She was moving at a torturously slow speed, and he groaned as he released her neck and pressed down on her back, holding her securely in place on the desk as he took control. Fast and deep, he hammered into her, penetrating every part, and sending jolts of pleasure throughout her body. Her cries of rapture were in rhythm with his pummeling thrusts and were only interrupted by the sounds of his skin slapping against hers. He shifted his position, moving her legs close together and straddling her on either side with his strong thighs. She wouldn't have thought it were possible for him to feel any bigger but from this position, every nerve fiber in her vagina was awake and screaming with the intensity of feeling him quickly moving in and out of her.

"You feel so good," he growled.

Laurel looked over her shoulder to see that Shepherd's eyes were completely black. She bowed her head onto the desk, gripping the sides for support. She couldn't do anything but rapturously take in his brute strength as he claimed her. He reached around her and flicked her bud in movement with his thrusts until pleasure raced through her body, building until she couldn't stand it anymore, and she screamed his name out again and again. She could feel his warm semen filling her as he sat down on his chair, pulling her on top of him. She leaned forward, holding onto the desk, and slowly moved on and off his lap, allowing him to ride out his orgasm until the very end. Finally, when they were both spent, she leaned her back against his chest, his shaft still buried deep inside her while they enjoyed the feeling of their bodies being connected. After a few moments, Shepherd wrapped his arm around her waist as he leaned forward to grab his bourbon, which he downed before patting her thigh in a sign to stand up.

"Let's get you to bed, Love."

The next week passed quickly. The women worked hard on getting everything ready for the Luna Ceremony while Shepherd put in long hours planning the Ring of Alphas meeting, organizing security, sending invitations to the Western packs, and working extra patrol shifts along with the rest of the warriors. While there was still an increase of rogues in the area, they hadn't suffered another attack. But they also hadn't had any luck breaking the captured rogues. Shepherd had already killed one, but it had done nothing to encourage the other two to talk. Rogues were not known to be loyal, and their behavior had Shepherd feeling particularly anxious.

The Dream

He'd offered pack members who lived farther out on the territory the option to share an apartment or set up temporary housing closer to the pack house until they resolved the rogue issue, but they'd all refused.

"They're so bull-headed," he complained to Laurel multiple times.

"What do you expect, Shep? They're wolves."

He glowered. "I could order them."

Laurel reached out to stroke his cheek. "And they would do it, but that's not who you are. In this, they should have a choice and you know it."

"It would make things easier."

"Easier isn't always better. People need to make their own choices."

He held her tightly. "You're right…again. What would I do without you?"

Laurel snuggled in, "Let's not ever find out."

Saturday arrived and everything was ready. The Perigee and Crescent Fang packs were scheduled to arrive early as they'd agreed to lend warriors for patrol. Everyone wanted a chance to enjoy the festivities and having more patrollers would allow them to take shifts. The hotel was full and large canvas tents were set up around the pack house to hold all the visitors. Throughout the gardens, lights were hung, and tables set. The ceremony was to take place in a grove of Mountain Hemlock trees that Laurel loved.

That evening, when she stepped out and saw Shepherd waiting to perform his Alpha duties underneath those trees, her heart raced. She wished that her aunt and Susu were here to witness this. It felt like everything was falling into place. She thought that she'd be nervous but as soon as she saw him standing under the fairy lights, it was as if she had tunnel vision. She walked straight towards him, oblivious to everyone else. She trusted him. And she was right to. He guided her through the entire ceremony. It was beautiful. She knew then that Shepherd had been correct. This was not something to be skipped.

Traditionally, the pack would go on a run together after the ceremony. But as Laurel was human, it wasn't an option. Instead,

Shepherd told her to go to a place that was special to her. He would have Beck and Matty follow her to keep her safe. And the rest of the pack would go on a run until they found her. He wanted to signify to her that the pack knew her and would seek her out, not just as their leader, but as family. She knew the spot she would go to. She once saw it in her dreams and had found it a couple of weeks ago when exploring with Shepherd. She immediately knew it was the clearing in her dream and when Shepherd mentioned his plan for the Luna celebration, she saw it clearly in her mind.

As the ceremony closed, she slipped off with Beck and Matty, who stayed respectfully at a distance, until she made her way to the clearing. She lay down on the grass, listening to the sounds of the wolves howling in the night as they ran together. Not just any wolves. Her pack. Her family. She breathed in deeply, taking it all in, and staring up at the moon. She said a silent prayer of thanks to the Moon Goddess and to her father for directing her path. She knew that Violet was right, that James and Morpheus had somehow guided her to this very moment. She knew when the others arrived. Sitting up, she saw Angus' eyes staring at her from the tree line. He stepped slowly into the clearing, followed by the pack all around her. They lifted their heads and howled. Laurel stared in wonder at the wolves around her, most of whom she'd only met in human form.

Angus slowly walked towards her and when he reached her, they pressed their foreheads together as she ran her fingers through his fur. When they broke contact, they looked around them as the wolves that encircled them kneeled before her. Even though she'd dreamed a portion of this, she was still taken aback at this show of loyalty. She could do nothing but kneel before them as well. Angus stood proud. She didn't know if what she was doing was appropriate, but it felt right to her, to show that she would serve them as they served her. When the moment was over, the wolves scattered while Angus stayed before her. He nuzzled against her neck, and they stayed alone together until Laurel worried that the pack would be waiting for them. Only then did Angus shift back to Shepherd's form.

The Dream

"Are you happy with the way the ceremony went?"

"It was beautiful, Shep. Did I do it correctly?"

He laughed at this question. "You couldn't have done it incorrectly, Sunshine. It was *your* Luna Ceremony. You made it yours by responding how you felt was right. I'm proud of you. And so is the pack. But they're asking for you. We better get back." She looked at him questioningly. Shepherd tapped his head, "Mind link. They're asking where you are." He pulled her in closely. "You're loved, Laurel." He stopped by a tree where he'd hidden his clothes and quickly changed.

When they returned, the party was in full swing. The food was out, music playing, and people assembled in small groups, talking. Some pack members were already on the dance floor.

Turning to Shepherd, she asked "There's been no disturbances?"

He squeezed her hand. "None. But we have a heightened presence along the borders. The warriors will alternate so everyone gets a chance to enjoy the gathering. Plus, none of the single ones want to lose this chance to meet wolves from other packs…just in case their mate is among them."

Laurel hadn't even considered that. She and Shepherd headed to the bar to grab a drink and then spent the next hour mingling. Shepherd never left her side, and she was grateful he was there to guide her through the evening. There were members of six other packs present and Shepherd was pleased with the large attendance. Most of them had sent their Beta or Gamma along with several warriors and single pack members. The two closest packs, Perigee and Crescent Fang had a stronger presence as they were integrally involved with resolving the rogue issue. The Perigee pack was represented by Alpha Elias, Luna Corinne, Beta Silas and his mate, Gemma. They were broad men, even for werewolves, and quick to laugh and tease. Even Corinne and Gemma looked unusually strong for female werewolves.

The Crescent Fang pack members were solemn. When Shepherd introduced her to them, Laurel wondered if they held something against her for being human. They weren't impolite but also were not friendly. Their Alpha, Japhy, and his mate, Lucia, stood apart from the other packs. They explained they'd brought several pack members who hoped to find their mates, and that their Beta, Whit, had come as well but was currently on patrol.

Laurel smiled, "Hopefully, I'll get to meet him soon. Thank you both for coming."

They inclined their heads but didn't respond.

Shepherd could feel her unease as they walked away. "They're a good pack. Japhy and Lucia are just reserved. They're that way with everyone so don't take it personally. You'll like Whit though."

The Ancient Shadow pack sent several single pack members along with their Beta Barrett and his mate, Cady. Their pack would stay through tomorrow afternoon with Barrett sitting in as a substitute for Alpha Morgan during the Ring of Alpha's meeting. Shepherd had been surprised when Morgan didn't attend because he hadn't found his mate yet. Barrett explained that Morgan had no interest in finding a mate, which shocked everyone within earshot. As he explained that his Alpha felt mates were a weakness, he glanced at his mate.

"He only thinks that because he hasn't found his mate yet. We're all hoping he'll find her soon. It would be good for him…and for the pack." Cady smiled lovingly at him and took his hand.

While Shepherd rubbed shoulders with the other Alphas, Laurel slipped away to get a glass of wine. Someone pinched her ass and she quickly turned around, only to see Charis smiling widely.

"Hey beautiful," she laughed.

Violet rolled her eyes. "Really, Charis, come on. Can you not be serious for one night?"

Charis feigned offense. "Are you saying our Luna isn't beautiful, Vi? How dare you!"

"I give up," Violet sighed as she shifted her gaze to Laurel. "You really do look beautiful, Luna. Tonight was perfect. How do you feel?"

"I feel great! And I'm glad you found me. All night I've been thinking of how perfect the ceremony was and how none of it could've happened without you two and Millie. I'm so thankful to you. I couldn't ask for better friends."

The Dream

Violet hugged her while Charis gleefully shared, "I can't wait to tell Susu you said that."

Laurel laughed as she pulled away from Violet. "Don't you dare!"

A change in Violet's posture caught their attention and they watched as her eyes frantically searched the room. "Violet, are you alright?"

She didn't respond but instead moved quickly past them into the crowd while Laurel and Charis followed in alarm. Violet stopped abruptly and Laurel followed her gaze to a man she'd never seen before. His eyes were on Violet, and he wore the same intense look. They walked slowly towards each other, both looking at each other as if there were no one else in the room.

Charis muttered, "Shit" and Laurel turned to her in confusion.

"What the hell is happening?"

Charis sighed. "Looks like Violet just found her mate."

Laurel had never witnessed fated mates meeting for the first time. It was different for her and Shepherd. Studying the magnetism that pulled Violet and the man together, she wondered if Shepherd had been disappointed with their own meeting. It must've been disheartening not to have someone instantly recognize him as their soulmate. From behind Violet, Beck's face came into focus- full of anguish, his jaw tight, his hand on his heart as though he were concerned that it had stopped beating. As Violet and the man hurriedly walked off together, she saw Beck's face harden and he began to go after them when Shepherd put a hand on his shoulder to stop him. Laurel watched Violet and the mystery man leave out a side door and when she turned to find Shep and Beck again, they were gone.

Her heart was a mixture of emotions. As Violet's friend, she felt happy for her. She knew Violet desperately wanted to find her fated mate, enough to deny a chosen bond with a man she genuinely loved. A part of Violet's heart must be broken to leave Beck. They had known each other since they were kids. But when she recalled the look on Beck's face, her heart broke. How was any of this supposed to make sense? Did choosing to love someone every single day make that choice more beautiful and meaningful than waiting for magic to bond you together?

How could she feel equally happy that Violet had received her heart's desire as she felt broken for Beck losing his heart's desire?

Charis' hand slipped into hers and brought her attention back to the present. When she met Charis' eyes, she knew she felt the same confusing mixture of emotions. Laurel wanted nothing more than Shepherd's comforting presence, but when she scanned the crowd, he was nowhere to be found. She would have to step up as host. Charis leaned over and whispered, "I'll help you," as she squeezed her hand and made them both start moving again, against the will of their bodies. They both knew what this meant. Violet would be lost to them. And Beck would be heartbroken.

But they also understood Laurel's role. Charis would be damned if she didn't help Laurel through this first event as Luna of the pack. Neither of them could change what just happened; neither of them was sure that they would even if were possible. But they both knew that the other packs were watching what kind of Luna Laurel would be. And that made them pull themselves together and get back to the party. Somehow, Laurel and Charis put on a happy face and finished the night out. Shepherd made it back in time to take his place by Laurel as they thanked everyone for coming. Laurel could tell that he was just going through the motions while his mind was still with Beck. She wanted to ask how he was and what she could do. She wanted to check on Violet, but knew they had to focus on the task at hand and finish out the celebration. Tomorrow would hold its own obstacles. The meeting would take place and they were both wondering whether Beck would be able to fulfill his role as Beta.

After the guests left, Charis and Matthius nodded solemnly at them and departed without saying a word. Seeing them so serious made Shepherd and Laurel's hearts even heavier. They silently made their way back to their apartment. As soon as they entered, Shepherd pulled Laurel into a deep embrace, taking in her scent as if his life depended on it.

"Goddess, I'm so thankful for you, Laurel. My life is infinitely better because the Moon Goddess gifted you to me." He paused, and

The Dream

she could sense his struggle. "And yet, Beck has been my friend since childhood. His pain is so deep and so real, I don't know if he'll ever recover. Laurel, it makes me question…everything. Even the Moon Goddess' plan, so help me. Tell me what I'm supposed to do, Laurel. Tell me."

She pulled away and led him by hand to the couch. "You can't fix everything, Shep. You're such a good man. You're always looking out for everyone around you. But there are some things beyond your control, and you have to trust that they'll work out the way they're supposed to. All you can do is continue being a great friend to Violet and Beck. Beck's going to need you to help him through his heartbreak. Be his hope when he doesn't have any. Remind him that even though it hurts like hell right now, he's going to be okay, and that there's a bigger plan."

Shepherd sighed and pulled her onto his lap. "Thank you. You're right. Now if you could just tell me how I'm supposed to manage the Ring of Alphas meeting tomorrow, the world would be right."

Laurel looked at him quizzically, "Are you wondering whether Beck will attend?"

"No, that's the problem. I need Beck and Matthius at that meeting. It's affecting our pack the most and I need all hands on deck to figure out this problem. But Violet's mate is Whit, the Beta of the Crescent Fang pack. He'll be there too. I don't know how either will be able to stand to be in the same room. As Beck's friend, I would release him from his duty but as the Alpha, I need him there. He's put in a lot of work on the rogue situation and knows more than anyone. I can't afford for him to miss it."

Laurel groaned. "Poor Beck. I'm afraid I don't have an answer for that one."

He pulled her in for a tight embrace. "I hate to leave you, Sunshine, but I'm going to check on Beck with Matthius and make sure everything's in place for tomorrow morning. Don't wait up for me, alright?"

Sleep remained elusive for Laurel. She lay awake for a long time thinking of Beck's broken heart and wondering how Violet was feeling now that she'd found her mate. As Violet's friend, she wished she had more time to get to know Whit. How were they supposed to know whether he would make Violet happy if she were in another pack? Eventually, a fitful sleep overtook her. In the wee hours, she felt Shepherd slip into bed. Immediately, she felt calmer and snuggled into his chest.

"I'm sorry I woke you, Love."

"That's alright. It wasn't a good sleep without you anyway. How'd it go?"

"Well, Beck will be at the meeting. Matty's sobering him up right now. That's about all the good news I have." Shepherd leaned over her, kissing her lightly on the lips. "I just want you close to me right now."

She wrapped her arms around his neck and deepened the kiss, wanting the distraction as much as he did. His hand rested on her cheek as they kissed, his thumb gently stroking her face. He slipped his other hand into the back of her pajama pants, grabbing her ass as he slowly moved against her. She moaned into his kiss. Breaking away, he gruffly spoke into her hair, "I need you, Laurel." She reached to the bottom of his shirt and pulled it off, throwing it on the floor. Shepherd stood and unbuttoned his pants, his eyes never leaving hers. After he was naked, he leaned over her, pulling her tank top off and then her pajama pants. He slowly inched back onto the bed, kissing her legs, stomach, breasts, shoulder, and neck as he made his way back to her lips. This time when he lowered himself on top of her, there was nothing between them. He grinded against her with his long, hard shaft. Laurel shifted her hips up to meet his movements.

"Take me, Shep," she murmured.

Groaning, he slowly pushed into her tight channel. "I love you. You're everything I've ever wanted, Laurel."

He grabbed one of her legs around her knee, pulling it up and making it easier to slide into her pussy. He worked his way into her until he was buried deep. Releasing her leg, he leaned down until they were chest to chest and continued his slow pace while he kissed her sensuously. Her fingernails raked down his back, leaving pinkened trails in their wake. It felt good to be completely filled with him. She wished they could stay this way forever. She could feel the pressure

The Dream

from his large size making her walls clench and squeeze his dick as he slowly worked in and out of her. His passionate kisses, the feel of his skin, the angle of his cock as he penetrated into her, hitting just the right spot, made her feel intoxicated from the pleasure. She could feel her orgasm building and moved her hips to meet him in the middle. Reaching down, she grabbed his ass and pulled him in deeper each time their hips met. Shepherd rested his forehead against hers, watching the passion on her face.

"Come for me," he demanded, stirring something within Laurel that made every nerve fiber within her awaken to his voice.

She brought her hands to rest on either side of his face as they watched each other. He kept his slow, deep pace ensuring that his thick shaft touched every sensitive spot in Laurel's pussy. She felt her breathing quicken as the ecstasy within her grew.

"Oh, Shepherd, you feel so good. Fill me up. Now." She closed her eyes as she savored every sensation.

"Open your eyes, Love," he growled as he grabbed the side of her face, his fingers moving into her hair.

She forced her eyes open, and he watched as her passion erupted in an intense orgasm, her vaginal walls pulsating and restricting his movements even more until he hammered into her with short, powerful thrusts. Her rapture came out in short bursts that increased in loudness until he joined her, filling her with warm jets of semen as his eyes completely darkened, never releasing her gaze as their orgasms culminated in a crescendo. Shepherd finally broke their connection, closing his eyes and gently kissing her before they both collapsed limply onto the bed.

He held her tightly as he whispered into her hair, "Don't ever leave me, Laurel."

She pushed herself onto her elbow to look into his eyes. "Never."

Chapter 12

Shepherd slept restlessly, even with Laurel beside him. He worried not only about the meeting, but about Beck. He'd always been strong and dependable. He was the one Shepherd could count on to bring calm and reason into a situation. But the way he'd seen Beck tonight was completely different. He was drunk, reckless, and ready to fight Whit to the death to mark Violet as his. Shepherd knew that Beck wouldn't have acted upon it. He would never hurt Violet in that way. She deserved to make her own decision. Shepherd knew it was mostly likely his wolf, Ulfred's, baser instincts coming out. But that, too, had been surprising. Even in wolf form, Beck was dependably clear-headed. To know that his heart was so broken that he could say such a thing made Matty and Shepherd uneasy. Matthius had been quiet all evening and insisted on staying with Beck while Shepherd returned to Laurel.

It felt like everything Shepherd could depend on, the very foundation of his leadership, was in chaos. Besides Beck being his closest friend, it also meant the pack was less secure at a time when they all needed to be on the top of their game. When he saw the first signs of morning creep through the curtains, he rolled over to brush the hair out of Laurel's face and gently kiss her forehead before getting out of bed. She was still asleep when he finished his shower, so he closed the apartment door quietly behind him and made his way downstairs. He needed to make sure everything was ready for the meeting, and he wanted to check on Beck and Matthius before the other leaders arrived. He hoped that Beck was calm enough to come through for the pack. He could fall apart tomorrow, but today Shepherd needed him to be a strong Beta.

Laurel woke to the sound of someone knocking on the door. She sat up, still groggy, and sighed when she saw that Shepherd's side of the bed was empty. She'd wanted to see him before the meeting. Standing up, she slipped on her robe, tying the straps tightly around her waist and moving quickly to the front door. She'd suspected that Violet would come by during the meeting, especially after she learned that her mate was Crescent Fang's Beta. Her suspicions were confirmed when she opened the door to see Violet, tall and beautiful as ever in a white t-shirt and loose linen pants. Her expression was calm as she smiled softly at Laurel. The only thing that betrayed her anxiety was that her eyes were darker than usual.

"Can I come in?"

Laurel felt a blush rise to her cheeks as she realized she'd been studying Violet for a moment. "Of course, Vi! Come in! I was hoping you'd come by this morning." She shut the door and they made their way to the couch. "Do you mind if I call Charis? She's worried about you."

Violet sat down stiffly, nervously settling her hands in her lap. "She's on her way. I already asked her. I'll be leaving shortly and wanted to see you both. I hope you don't mind."

Laurel tried not to show her disappointment. She knew that she would likely leave with her mate but hearing her say it aloud made it real. She couldn't imagine Silver Moon without Violet. Her thoughts were interrupted when Charis burst through the door without knocking, purposely making her way towards Violet. Before taking a seat, she brushed Violet's hair to the side and gasped. Laurel hadn't even thought to look for a mark. She and Shepherd waited so long to complete their bond that she forgot most werewolves mark each other quickly after meeting.

Charis' shoulders slumped. "I figured. I know you've always wanted your fated mate. But I had to be sure."

Violet shrugged. "Who am I to question the Moon Goddess' plan?" No one responded. "How's Beck?"

Charis' eyes shot up and then softened. "Come on, Violet. Do you need to ask? Why torment yourself with that question?"

The Dream

Violet shrugged with a slight smile, "I know it doesn't make sense. The decision is made. He's heartbroken. I know that. But…how is he?"

Laurel understood her need for a more detailed answer. "Shep says he's never seen him this way. His wolf wanted to mark you no matter what. He's angry and unreasonable. Shepherd wanted to relieve him from coming to the meeting since your mate will be there but since Beck's been the one overseeing the rogue situation, he couldn't."

Charis reached over and grabbed her hand. "Matty spent the last few hours sobering him up and trying to get him in a better mindset. I'm sure everything will be alright…I'm happy for you, Vi, I am. But I'm sure as hell going to miss you." She paused before continuing. "I know it's selfish, but I hope Beck doesn't see you before you go, especially since you're already marked. I just don't know how he'd take it."

Violet looked down at her hands. "It was the only way, especially with Beck being so close. You know how wolves are."

After a moment, Laurel broke the silence. "Do you need any help packing? What are your plans?"

She could see Violet was gathering more courage than she really had to appear unflustered. "No, my mom's packed my clothing for me. She said Beck never came home last night but I didn't want there to be any reason for Whit and Beck to fight. Besides my clothes, there's not anything I need. Whit has a fully furnished cabin at Crescent Fang. We'll leave after the meeting. I thought it best."

"So, what do you think about him?" Charis asked with more excitement than she felt.

Laurel and Violet understood the need to avoid more sensitive topics and gladly joined in. "He's great! He's intelligent, kind-hearted, even-tempered. Even about Beck, he understood. There was jealousy, of course, but he promised me he wouldn't fight Beck unless he was forced. They're actually a lot alike…" Violet trailed off.

Laurel couldn't keep up the charade. "Violet, are you sure? Is there any doubt? You know Charis and I would support you no matter what. Of course, our hearts are broken for Beck, but you're our sister. We're here for you, no matter what. You know that, right?"

Violet smiled, this time sincerely, and reached over to grab Laurel's hands. "You are going to make a perfect Luna." She let go of one of Laurel's hands and reached across to grab Charis' right hand. "I'm sure. I'll love Beck forever. And my heart is breaking right now. But I've always known that if I found my fated mate, I'd accept them. And Beck knew that, too. Whit was planned for me from the beginning of time. How could I deny him? All I can do is hope that Beck finds his mate. It's the only way my heart will truly be happy." Violet squeezed both their hands before standing. "I've got to go. Whit says you can visit whenever you like. You'll always be welcome at our house."

They shared a group hug before Violet left, giving a little wave before she stepped into the elevator. Charis and Laurel sunk onto the couch with a deep synchronized sigh.

"How do you really think it's going to go at the meeting?" Laurel asked.

Charis looked over at her meaningfully. "I think it's going to be a real shit show."

When Shepherd returned home, he poured a few fingers of bourbon, drank it in one gulp, and poured another before joining Laurel on the couch. Sitting down, he leaned against the couch, propped his feet on the ottoman and grabbed Laurel with his other arm, pulling her close to him. After giving him a moment to relax, Laurel couldn't wait any longer.

"So? How did it go?"

Shepherd looked over at her and caressed her hand with his thumb. "Do you want the good news or the bad news first?"

"Good."

"Well, the Perigee pack has a lead on the rogues' headquarters. They're not sure but while they were scouting, they found some tracks that led into the mountains. At the time, there weren't enough wolves to pursue the lead, but we've planned a combined trip to check it out. And there are a few rumors about who may be leading the group that we'll investigate further. It's more than we had to go on before."

The Dream

Laurel nodded. "And the bad? I'm guessing it has to do with Beck?"

Shepherd ran his hand over his face. "Yeah. Matty managed to sober him up before the meeting. I talked to him beforehand and reminded him the safety of the pack had to be top priority. He tried to hold it together, Laurel, he did. But as soon as Whit spoke up, I could see Ulfred trying to surface. Two Beta wolves, both in love with the same woman, in the same room together? You can imagine. It got heated and Beck ended up shifting. To his credit, Whit remained fairly calm. He didn't shift at least. I could see anger in his eyes when Beck railed about Violet being his. It took a lot of restraint. From all accounts, Whit's a good man. That makes me feel better for Violet. But it took Matty, Dad, Rowan, and Noble to get Ulfred out of the room. I had to use my Alpha command on him. Matty came back to the meeting, but it took the others the better part of an hour before they convinced Ulfred to return form to Beck." His face was strained. "Not that it was much better after he shifted. I've never used my Alpha command on Beck. I don't know how to help him, Laurel."

She climbed onto his lap and wrapped her arms around his shoulders. "You continue being his friend, Shep. You're doing the right thing." They sat silently for a moment before she continued. "Violet came by to say goodbye while you were gone. They already completed the mate bond. They're leaving after the meeting."

Shepherd looked grim. "Yeah, I saw Whit's mark. And Rusty met me outside the conference room before it started to let me know that Violet would be leaving with Whit. She wanted to meet with me personally but knew there was a lot going on. She didn't want to risk running into Beck and a fight occurring. It's really a shame, you know? They've been best friends since they were little kids. Once Beck calms down, it's going to be another heartache that he couldn't tell her a proper goodbye." Laurel wondered aloud if they'd ever get to meet again in the future, to which Shepherd shook his head. "It's not likely. For one thing, our packs don't mingle often. But I also don't think Whit would like Beck and Vi to continue their friendship. I may be wrong, but most werewolves are pretty protective of their mate bond."

After a few moments, they reluctantly got up to go downstairs. They were serving lunch not only to their pack but also to the packs that had remained for the meeting. Their guests would leave after they ate and would take Violet with them. Laurel wondered whether Beck would make an appearance and as if he were reading her mind, Shepherd said the elders who were with him had mind linked him that there wasn't enough improvement to trust his judgment. Rowan, Noble, and a couple warriors would stay with him while Matthius and Beau would join Shepherd to pay respects to the departing packs.

After the last of the neighboring pack members were gone, Shepherd and Matty left to check on Beck while Laurel and Charis agreed to an early cocktail in the gardens with Lilac and Millie. Once they were seated, Millie grabbed Laurel's hand.

"I'm proud of the way you've handled all this. It's easy to forget that all this happened at your Luna Celebration and yet you didn't hesitate at all. You immediately put your friends and your pack first. You may be doubting yourself right now but don't. Beau and I are so impressed with you. We've always known the pack was safe with Shepherd, but you balance him out so well. I don't know how he would've managed this situation without you. It's been many years since our borders have been this tense and Violet and Beck…" she paused and glanced over at Lilac. "Well, we've all loved them their entire lives. This is hard."

Lilac leaned forward to pat Millie's knee. "We're all worried about Beck. But he's strong. I know he'll make it through this. And I'm going to miss Violet like crazy. But we all saw her with Whit today at lunch. She's loved Beck since they were children. But there's no denying she's different with Whit. Her eyes light up when she sees him. It's like she's fully alive for the first time. This is what she's always wanted."

Laurel had seen it as well. Just yesterday, she couldn't imagine Violet with anyone other than Beck and yet today, seeing her with Whit had felt right. Laurel had noticed the sadness in Violet when she was around other mated couples. Today, when she left, that deep sadness was gone. But that didn't alleviate Beck of his heartbreak. They had

The Dream

another drink, but it was obvious that they all felt the same way. And it was weighing on all their minds. They ended up repeating themselves until a silence settled over them.

Laurel took a long walk in the gardens afterwards to clear her head. Before she headed back to the apartment, she called Lucy. She told her all about the ceremony and briefly recapped the Beck and Violet situation. She hadn't told Lucy about the rogues. She wasn't sure she'd understand why the pack was worried about rogues when her dad was such a good man. But she also didn't want Lucy to worry about her. Slowly, their relationship had returned to normal. Their conversations no longer felt forced, and the silences were no longer awkward. Lucy didn't like to leave the cabin but agreed to come for Christmas.

Shepherd was getting out of the shower when she returned to the apartment. She stopped to admire him. The man was entirely muscle but not like a bodybuilder. Laurel never liked the idea that anyone would spend that much time at the gym. No, Shepherd's muscles were from years of working and training to be the protector and leader of his pack. A good Alpha had very few weaknesses and judging by Shepherd's bare form, he was an exceptionally good Alpha. Glancing up at her as she leaned against the door, he smiled cheekily at her.

"Like what you see, Sunshine?" He came up to her and pulled her into a hug. His hair was still wet and dripped onto her shoulders, making her shiver.

She laughed and playfully pushed him away. "You're getting me wet, Shep!"

His eyes darkened and he backed her against the door frame. "That's what I like to hear," he growled wickedly. He leaned into her, his mouth sucking at her mark and his other hand massaging her breast. He kneaded her nipple as she arched her back and moaned.

"Shepherd, it's almost dinner time. We have to go downstairs."

He moved from her breast to cup her sex, the heat from his hand arousing her. "You sound half-hearted, Love. Are you sure you don't want me?" He rubbed her pussy from the outside of her pants. "Tell me you want me, Laurel."

She moved her hips to grind against his hand. "I want you, Shep. You know I do. But hurry," she breathed.

He needed no other encouragement. He quickly undressed her, tossing her clothes on the floor. He lifted her and walked them to the dresser where he sat her on the edge. Leaning back slightly, she watched as his mouth closed onto her nipple, sucking and pulling as his fingers made their way to her entry, rubbing along the length of her slit until she was wet. He separated her folds and positioned his large cock at the opening. Laurel wiggled her butt in anticipation, making Shepherd growl.

As he slowly penetrated her, his free hand lightly swirled around her clit. Once he was deep inside her, his hands made their way under her ass to cushion her cheeks against the edge of the dresser as he started to pound into her. His eyes were dark with passion and Laurel grasped the sides of the dresser to keep herself steady as he pummeled into her with fast and deep thrusts. The angle of his advance hit her G-spot and it didn't take long before she was screaming his name. He slowed his pace and used her release to wet his fingers as he stimulated her clitoris. She lay back on the dresser, keeping hold of the edges, and gave herself over fully to the second climax, her body shaking as her already sensitive bud clinched and throbbed at his touch. She felt him cum inside her as he moaned her name.

"I'm going to need a shower after that or the whole pack will know what we did!" she laughed, still out of breath. "You should join me."

He slapped her ass as she walked to the bathroom. "I already took a shower, Sunshine, and I don't care if the whole pack knows."

She shot a glance over her shoulder and gave him a pointed look. "Well, I do. Come on, Shep. I don't want to be late to dinner."

He chuckled and joined her in the shower. "This could be dangerous," he rumbled as he maneuvered behind her to share the water stream.

She felt his still hard rod push on her backside and bucked against him. "Stop that, Alpha. We just had the best quickie ever."

"Quickie," he grunted as if it offended him. "I'll take my time with you tonight."

The Dream

She felt her heartbeat quicken as she forced herself to focus on showering and ignore the snicker she heard behind her.

A few days after Violet left, Beck asked Shepherd for some time off. Matty offered to go with him, but Beck wanted to be alone, and Shepherd couldn't risk having the two of them gone at the same time. Beck agreed that when he was ready, he'd meet up with the teams searching for the rogues' headquarters and then report back to Silver Moon. It had only been a few days since he left but Shepherd and Matthius were sorely missing him. She and Charis had been spending a lot of time together. Charis had spoken to Violet once since she left and was convinced she was happy.

"We'll just have to find Beck's mate. That's all. Then everything will be right in the world!"

Laurel laughed at the simplicity of it. "That's it, huh? How do we go about doing that, Char?"

Charis looked at her mischievously. "Parties. Lots and lots of parties."

Shepherd eventually got a call from Beck. He didn't sound like himself, but they were relieved knowing he was safe. "You've got to call me, brother. Matty and I have been worried sick." There was no answer. "Even if it's just to say, 'I'm alive,' call me once a day." Beck reluctantly agreed. Some days, "I'm alive," was all that was said but Beck was true to his word and called every day. Shep and Matty were still worried. It wasn't like him to run away from anything. He was the strong, steady one that others depended on. It made his absence felt even more since everyone was still on high alert. There'd been a couple of rogue attacks since he'd left. Pack members were injured but no deaths. Mostly, they were exhausted due to the extra patrolling shifts that everyone had to take on.

Laurel eased into her role as Luna. Pack members started coming to her with concerns and she was relieved to find they trusted her advice. She took her role seriously. If she was ever in doubt, Millie always welcomed her at the cabin. She had made a habit of joining her for coffee at least once a week on her porch. Shepherd seemed pleased they were so close. Truthfully, Laurel missed having a mother figure and although Millie was her friend, she was more than that. She was an advisor. After years of being a protector and guide to the pack, she was well-versed. Laurel had been unsure of what her role would entail when she began. The pack was well ran but it was a large pack so there were always issues to resolve and situations that could improve. Laurel seriously considered the job offer at Beau Industries but now that she was here, she felt she could use her expertise just as well in her role as Luna.

The next few weeks went by quickly. The rogue situation died down enough that Rowan returned to his apparent job as nuisance of the pack. He'd begun by asking Laurel during dinner whether she was on birth control, which made her almost spit her drink out. Shepherd quickly tried to diffuse the situation, but Rowan insisted, loudly enough to draw attention, that it was time for the pack to have assurance of its future by the birth of an heir. Laurel was frustrated but didn't respond. In truth, she hadn't considered having children. Not anytime soon. And she also hadn't considered that children would be a pack concern. Shepherd had angrily silenced Rowan.

Laurel glanced around during the exchange and noticed everyone's interest was piqued by the conversation. She saw, even if Shepherd didn't, that Rowan wasn't entirely wrong. His approach had been, per usual, ill-timed, and rough around the edges. But he was right that the pack was eager for the next alpha to be born. Laurel felt a heaviness rest on her. Lucy had given her a wonderful childhood. But losing her parents made her feel vulnerable in the world. She'd never put a lot of thought into being a mother. When she sealed the mate bond with Shepherd, the risks she took on by doing so were only meant to affect her. Could she bring children into a union where they could so easily lose both parents?

The week of Christmas arrived, and still there was no Beck. His Sunday calls continued, and he was planning to join the scouting teams

The Dream

soon. They'd lost two pack members during an attack the previous week. Shepherd blamed himself. The patrols had become a little lax after so long without an attack and it was what the rogues were waiting on. Still, the attack was not large. They were sending a message that they were even now prepared to take down Silver Moon. The Perigee pack had lost five pack members in total since the Luna Ceremony and were more invested than ever to find out what was causing the rogues to band together.

Lucy arrived a few days before Christmas and eagerly joined in the decorating. Laurel was surprised. They'd always celebrated Christmas- cutting down and trimming their own tree, and a few gifts- but it was a simple affair. Silver Moon was a different story. They loved a good party. Lights hung all over the pack house and the gardens. A large tree was decorated beautifully and filled with presents for the children. Lucy settled in quite naturally. Laurel wanted her to stay in the pack house, but she'd insisted on a room at the hotel in town.

Laurel arrived early every morning to pick her up. They went Christmas shopping together and explored the pack house and gardens. She desperately wanted to show Lucy the natural beauty of the surrounding areas but knew it wasn't possible. When Lucy asked, she hadn't wanted to tell her about the rogues. Instead, she'd explained that there wasn't time with so much to do in preparation for Christmas. She could tell from Lucy's expression that she suspected there was more to the story, but she hadn't pressed Laurel. It wasn't a lie. There was a lot to do. But with so many hands, the work went quickly.

Christmas Eve arrived, and Laurel's heart felt full as she handed out a present to each of the children after dinner. Her eyes found Shepherd and they shared a smile. They hadn't spoken about children since the incident with Rowan. After Shepherd silenced Rowan, he'd assured her that the choice would always be hers. He admitted wanting children but insisted she was enough. Laurel continued taking her birth control, but the incident made her think more on becoming a mother.

And then Violet called to share the news that she and Whit were having a baby. Laurel was surprised at the timing, but Charis assured her, with a sad look, that it was common for wolves to start a family quickly. Charis hadn't said so, but Laurel suspected she and Matthius had tried and not been successful. It made her question her own hesitance even more. She wasn't sure she'd be a good mother or if she wanted to bring a child into a world where safety couldn't be guaranteed. But tonight, handing out gifts to the children, she and Shepherd were enjoying the family scene spread before them. When the festivities were over, Lucy headed back to the hotel. Laurel walked to the window to watch her leave and was surprised when she saw someone walking with her. She felt Shepherd join her and nudged him.

"Who is that with Aunt Lucy?"

Shepherd leaned into her as he looked out the window before chuckling. "Damn. That's Rowan. I never would've guessed!"

Laurel gasped, "You're wrong! Look again!"

Squeezing her, Shepherd reminded her that his eyesight was keener than hers. "Besides, Rowan's a good man, even if he is annoying. This will be good for him. I've never seen him show interest in anyone before."

"I'm more worried about my aunt," Laurel muttered.

Christmas morning, Shepherd woke Laurel early with breakfast in bed. He roused her gently by kissing all along her collarbone up to her lips.

"Wake up, Sunshine. I've got a surprise for you."

Laurel sat up groggily, sweeping her hair out of her face into a high bun. "Merry Christmas," she said with a raspy voice.

He set the tray in front of her and climbed onto the opposite side. Mimosas, fried eggs, strawberries, and cinnamon toast lay before her in a mouth-watering spread.

"This looks delicious, Shep. Thank you!"

They talked about how well the Christmas celebration had gone. Neither of them mentioned Lucy and Rowan or what had become of their night. Laurel didn't want to think about it. Of course, she wanted Lucy to be happy, but she couldn't imagine her with stuffy Rowan. Shepherd interrupted her thoughts, wondering if Beck was alone for Christmas.

The Dream

Laurel sighed and grasped his hand, "He's going to come back to us and he's going to make it through this. We have to keep faith, Shep."

"You're right. I know it. I just miss him. Wolves aren't meant to be alone... But I'm not going to be distracted from your surprise!"

Laurel raised her eyebrows, "Didn't I just eat my surprise?"

"No way," Shepherd chuckled. "You should know me better than that." He brought out a small blue box from his pocket and slid it across the breakfast tray. "For you, Laurel. To celebrate our first Christmas together."

"Aw, Shep. You told me we were taking a trip together for our gifts to each other. I didn't get you anything."

He smiled mischievously. "And we will, when Beck gets back, and the rogue issue is resolved. But I bought this for you when we were still in New York. I've been waiting to give it to you."

"But—" Laurel began.

Shepherd cut her off, "You are my gift, and trust me when I say you're more than enough. Now," he pressed his finger against her open lips, "open your gift."

Laurel grabbed the box, sliding the ribbon from around it. "You've had this since New York? You're very good at surprises, Shepherd!" Opening it, she found a silver necklace with a moon pendant encrusted with diamonds. She gasped, fingering it delicately. "It's beautiful," she exclaimed. "I love it."

"Turn it over."

On the back was the date they met outside of her office building. She smiled at him. "I'll wear it forever." She handed it to him, and he brought it around her neck, his big fingers trying to work the clasp.

"These things are not made for men," he grumbled as Laurel laughed.

Her hand rested on top of the pendant as Shepherd moved the tray off the bed and lay down beside her. She looked down at him, filled with appreciation for everything they had together. There was only one thing that could improve such a perfect morning. Climbing on top of his large, strong body, she let her hands travel up his chest as she took time to feel every ripple of his muscles. Cocking an eyebrow, his hands found her hips.

"I lied," she said seductively, releasing his nipple that she had been fingering and lifting her nightgown over her head. "I do have a gift for you, Alpha." She knew he liked it when she called him that, and she was rewarded by an immediate swirling of black into his dark green eyes. "Oh, does Angus want to play?"

"Careful, Love. You may get more than you bargained for," Shepherd growled.

Laurel responded by lowering her breasts onto his chest and bringing her lips crashing down upon his. She grinded against his hard shaft as her nipples hardened from brushing against his chest. Their passion always escalated quickly, his touch sending her into a frenzy of desire. But today, she wanted to savor him. She broke the kiss as he groaned and nibbled on his ear, working her way down his neck, and shimmying down his body, kissing his nipples and all along his cast-iron abs before coming to the object of her yearning. She glanced up at him wickedly as she took it in her hands. He pulled himself up onto his elbows so that he could watch her as she swirled her tongue around his crown.

Shepherd breathed deeply, trying to keep himself controlled. The sight of her sweet face with her lips wrapped around his cock was enough to send him over the edge. She kept their gaze for a moment longer as she sank his cock deeper and deeper into her throat at an agonizing pace. She worked past her gag reflex and slipped into a rhythm of hungrily sucking him off and coming up for air, licking along the top of his head, savoring his taste, before going deep again. She moaned into him as he wove his fingers lightly through her hair and gently raised his hips with her rhythm, fucking her mouth. She watched him as she bobbed up and down on dick, enjoying the look of almost painful satisfaction on his face as he fed her his warm semen. Only when she knew she'd enjoyed every last drop did she release him, wiping the edges of her mouth as she climbed on top of him. Her pussy was dripping wet with desire and as soon as Shepherd felt it, he grabbed her and flipped her underneath him on the bed.

"My turn," he said huskily as he kissed her before almost jumping off the edge of the bed, pulling her hips to the right spot and spreading her legs before him like a banquet. He licked along the slit and growled. "You're so wet for me."

"Always," she moaned breathily as she gyrated her hips against his mouth. "I want you, Shepherd. I ache for you. Please," she begged.

He savagely went at her waiting pussy, alternately licking and sucking at her bud. She kept up the rhythm of her hips against his mouth and felt the pleasure mounting inside of her as he plunged his fingers into her, adding one at a time while his teeth grazed against her clit with just the right amount of pressure. She lost herself, stars in her vision, as she bucked against him and screamed his name. Shepherd sat back with satisfaction and watched her pussy pulsing before him. She leaned up and saw him, his rod still at full attention and knew she could never get enough of him.

Sliding off the bed, she crawled over to him. She could taste herself on his lips and it turned her on even more. Climbing onto him, she lowered her still throbbing sex onto the head of his dick, her hand holding it in place as she teased him by rubbing it against her slit as she hovered above him. He took her nipples in his teeth as she whimpered, his free hand kneading her other nipple. She continued to hold the crown of his cock at her opening, gyrating slowly against him. The movement against her already sensitive clit while Shepherd was stimulating her tits was enough to make her cry out.

"Oh god, Shep."

He released her breasts and grabbed her hips, lifting himself to plunge into her. As he entered her fully, her walls tightening against the intrusion, they both screamed in ecstasy. He lowered his hips back to the ground and she came down upon him, her hands on his shoulders as he leaned back slightly, using his arms to brace them both. He watched her breasts bounce as she rode him hard, short squeals escaping her as she took every bit of his long, thick shaft over and over until her orgasm exploded in a pulsing, molten heat. He grabbed her waist, holding onto her as she wrapped her legs even more tightly around him. Coming onto his knees, he hammered into her as her walls clamped down on him, milking every part of his release until they both collapsed onto the floor together, out of breath, and completely satiated. She looked over at Shepherd as he rolled over to watch her.

"Best. Christmas. Ever.," Laurel said with a huge grin on her face.

Shepherd chuckled, leaning over to kiss her before laying on his back and pulling her into his chest. "The best," he agreed.

Chapter 13

Lucy left the day after Christmas. Laurel wanted to know more about what happened between her and Rowan, but Lucy hadn't brought it up. They'd been seated next to each other during the Christmas dinner, but Laurel hadn't noticed anything out of the ordinary. Rowan had been more quiet than usual. But there was no indication they were anything other than acquaintances. Laurel couldn't imagine Lucy ever permanently leaving her land and also couldn't picture Rowan moving away from the pack. In Laurel's mind, it would be a perfect world if she could get Lucy and Susu to move to Silver Moon. But for now, she'd have to be satisfied with visits.

Susu arrived the day after Lucy left. Unlike Lucy, Susu took a room in Shepherd and Laurel's apartment. Her outgoing personality made her a fast favorite at the pack house and mealtimes were more lively than usual at their table. With Susu there, the vacant seats were a hot commodity. Charis and Susu were like two peas in a pod, and it made Laurel happy to watch them together, but Violet was still missed.

"I never met Beck, but I can't help but be happy for Violet. She has such a good heart, and she deserves this. I'll never forget how gently she introduced me to her wolf. I'm just sorry I didn't get to spend more time with her."

It was a rare moment when Susu was serious, and Laurel reached out to hug her. "I know. She really did seem happy. Now, we just want Beck to find his mate. We're all worried about him."

Susu pulled away and smiled at her. "It'll work out. It always does."

The next few days passed quickly. They packed each day full of activities and spent their down time watching movies and hanging out in the common rooms. When New Year's Eve came, they were feeling disappointed that they only had one more day before Susu returned to New York. At breakfast, they picked at their food and the table was missing its usual liveliness. Shepherd finished his coffee as he looked around at the three girls' glum faces, sighing loudly as he stood up.

"This is the saddest breakfast I've had in a while, ladies. Why don't you just stay, Susu? It's obvious you belong here."

Susu shrugged, "I've got a job and a life back in New York. Can't you all just come back with me?"

He chuckled before leaning down to kiss Laurel on the top of her head. "I'm headed to the office, Sunshine. Try to make the most of her last day."

The girls looked at each other for a moment before Susu leaned forward. "He's right. We can't sit around dejected all day. What are we going to do?"

Charis rested her head on Susu's shoulder. "Yep. Alright, I have a few ideas and I'll let you pick, Susu, but only because I'll be rid of you tomorrow."

She laughed, "Deal."

They spent the day on Main Street, shopping for outfits and eating lunch at the diner. They chose Loco Lupus as their party destination and word got around to all of Susu's new friends. There were only a few bars in town, and they'd already taken Susu to the other two. Loco Lupus was a rustic bar on the outskirts of town with a limited food menu. The dresses they bought were too extravagant for the bar, but the girls didn't care. They wanted to go all out for Susu's last night. Charis called the owner, Carl, so he'd expect a large crowd. He laughed her off, "We're always ready for a party here, Charis. You should know that!"

Shepherd chuckled when he entered the apartment later and saw the girls with face masks on and cotton between their toes.

"Your toenails are all the same color, ladies. How will I tell you apart?"

The Dream

Charis rolled her eyes, "Shep, we're going to need you to make yourself scarce until it's time to leave."

Leaning against the kitchen counter, he raised his eyebrows. "You're kicking me out of my own home? Laurel, are you going to allow this?"

She looked at the others with a mischievous glint in her eye before holding Shepherd's gaze. "I'll allow it."

He grabbed his heart dramatically before heading to the door. "Alright. Well, rumor has it the place to be tonight is Loco Lupus. You want me to meet you there then?"

She hobbled over to him, careful not to let her toes touch, and gave him a kiss before opening the door for him. "Yep, I'll see you there. Dress nice, Alpha," she whispered sensually in his ear.

His low growl rumbled in his chest as he pulled her in for a deeper kiss. "You're not playing fair, Sunshine."

She smiled and pushed him lightly out the door. "I never said I would."

"You guys make me sick," Charis said after Laurel closed the door and leaned against it.

Her heart was racing from his kiss, but she quickly gathered her senses. "Please, Char. You and Matty are the same way when you're not pranking each other."

"I will neither confirm nor deny. Susu, what about you? Any men in your life?"

"Susu hasn't had a serious man in her life in all the time I've known her."

Sitting up, Charis looked Susu up and down. "Why not? You're a hottie. That dark complexion and long brown hair. I'd hit it."

Susu laughed and rolled her eyes. "Shut up, Charis. I date sometimes. I guess my parents' divorce was so messy, I just don't take love lightly. I know it can go wrong."

"Not if you get with a wolf, baby!" Charis teased. "Mating is forever!" Susu laughed but it was forced. "I'm only half joking, Susu. Listen, if you don't want a man- that's different. More power to you!

But if you're only keeping men at arm's length because you're worried it'll turn out the way your parent's relationship did, I think you should take a chance on love. You deserve it the same as everyone. And you've got a good head on her shoulders. You'll know which ones are worth taking a risk for...So, you're welcome. And if you stick around, Auntie Charis will give you more life advice!"

"Tempting," Susu laughed.

Matthius was waiting for them downstairs when they finished getting ready. He whistled as they stepped off the elevator. "You ladies clean up nicely!"

"You too," Charis said as she cheekily slapped his ass. "I like a chauffeur who dresses to impress."

Matty looked back and winked at Laurel. "Looks like I may be getting lucky tonight!"

"Don't get cocky!" Charis shouted over her shoulder.

Matty's mouth opened and then closed. "Nope. Too easy," he laughed as he shook his head.

Laurel and Susu were laughing by the time they climbed into the back of Matty's car.

"Are you guys ever serious?" Susu asked.

"I seriously love her. Does that count?"

Charis turned around from the front seat. "He really is trying to get lucky tonight! Don't encourage him." She lowered her voice. "Or do. I never turn down a compliment."

Matty raised his eyebrow as he side-eyed her. "Blue is your color, Charis. And that slit on your dress," he growled as his finger traced up her thigh.

Charis laughed and brushed his hand aside, "We have guests, lover boy! But I want to hear more about that later."

Laurel laughed. "What was that you were saying earlier? Oh yeah, you guys make me sick!"

It only took a few minutes to get to Loco Lupus. The place was already packed when they arrived. Charis found them a table while

The Dream

Matty ordered their drinks from the bar. Laurel was looking around when he brought the tray over.

"Looking for Shepherd?"

"Yeah, he said he'd meet us here."

"He's going to be late. I was supposed to tell you at the packhouse. Beck came home earlier, and he had news. Shep knew I was supposed to bring you girls to the bar and said he'd catch up later."

Charis leaned in. "How is he? Did you see him?"

Matty nodded. "Yeah, I saw him briefly. He seemed okay. At least, better than before."

"Maybe he'll come with Shep. I know we'd all love to see him."

"Maybe," Matthius responded, although his voice sounded doubtful.

"Well, at least we have him back. Let's toast to dear friends," Charis said as they raised their glasses. "To spending time with new friends and to having old friends back! Cheers!"

"Cheers!"

"Let's go dance!" Susu suggested.

"Let's have one more first," Matty laughed.

A couple of drinks later, one of Susu's favorite songs came on and they all headed to the dance floor. Charis immediately backed into Matty, grinding against him, while winking at Susu and Laurel. "I'm definitely getting lucky," he laughed as he twirled her around. Laurel and Susu made their way to the far end, where the dance floor wasn't as full. It felt like old times in the living room of their apartment, dancing with each other without a care in the world. After a few dances, they headed to the bar to order another round.

"Hey, I'm going to the restroom. Watch my drink?"

"I got you, sister!" Susu agreed.

After Laurel used the restroom, she tried to call Shep, but he didn't answer. Sighing, she headed back to the bar. She laughed when she saw that her seat was now occupied by Jamie. He'd been hitting on Susu all week at the packhouse. He was charming but it wasn't getting anywhere with Susu.

She came up behind him, "Hey Jamie! Having a fun time?"

He looked over at her and smiled. "Luna, please tell your friend I'm a good guy!"

"Jamie, don't call me Luna here. You know the rules. And Susu is her own woman. You'll have to convince her yourself."

"There's no one but wolves here anyway."

"You don't know that. You know what Shepherd says."

He nodded. "Right…Susu, want to dance?"

"I may in a little bit. Laurel and I were going to have a drink or two. But I'll catch up with you later, okay?"

Grabbing her arm, he gently pulled. "Come on, it'll be fun!"

Susu started to look irritated. "Not right now, Jamie," she said, pulling her arm back from his grasp.

Laurel could see that Jamie was tipsy because he'd never been pushy with Susu before. From the look on his face, he was about to try again when he suddenly disappeared from view. Laurel and Susu froze in surprise as they saw Jamie sprawled out on the bar floor. Beck was hovering over him with a look of fury on his face.

Jamie spluttered, "Beta, what was that for?"

"She said no, Jamie. I think you've had enough. Go home." When Jamie didn't move, Beck leaned closer, his face tight with restraint, and spoke in a quiet but fierce voice, "Go home, Jamie. Understood?"

Jamie scrambled up and mumbled, "Yes, Beta," before quickly leaving the bar.

Susu looked at Laurel questioningly before Beck shifted his attention back to her. "Are you alright? Did he hurt you?"

Susu shook her head, her usual humor and quick wit failing her. "I'm fine. Jamie's harmless."

He reached out and took her arm, turning it over in his hand. "Are you sure? Does your arm hurt?"

"Nope, it feels fine. Really. I don't think he meant anything by it."

Beck let go of her arm, his fingers trailing down to linger at her hand. "He shouldn't have touched you."

The Dream

Shepherd stepped into view from behind Beck and grabbed Laurel's hand, leading her away.

"What the hell was that, Shep? Is Beck alright? Should he be in public? It doesn't look like he's regained his composure since leaving…" she worried, looking over her shoulder to watch him with Susu.

"What you're seeing is what I wanted to do the first time I saw Henry touch you. I wanted to rip his arm off his body for touching what was mine."

Laurel scrunched her face up. "But that's because you were my mate, and I didn't know it." Shepherd watched her face with a small smile as the realization dawned upon her.

She quickly looked back over at Beck and Susu to see them heading out the bar, Beck leading her by the hand. "Beck and Susu?!"

A huge smile broke onto Shepherd's face. "Beck and Susu. Could this get any better? Our closest friends are mates. He sensed her as soon as we entered, and once he spotted her, I told him who she was. I could tell he was torn. He's still trying to get over Vi. But when he saw Jamie grab her arm…apparently, that helped him make up his mind." He chuckled before his smile faltered. "You don't think she'll reject him, do you? I don't think he could take it, Laurel."

She glanced towards the door they'd just disappeared through, unsure of the answer herself. After a few minutes, Laurel texted Susu to check on her. She didn't care if Beck was a friend or not. If Susu was scared or not into him, she'd be getting her away from him. Her phone immediately dinged with Susu's response.

[Susu] I'm ok. Beck and I are talking. Don't worry.

[Laurel] Are you sure? Let me know if you want me to rescue you.

[Susu] Don't you dare try to rescue me. And don't wait up.

Susu's response made Laurel raise her eyebrows in surprise. "What did she say?" Shepherd asked apprehensively.

Laurel turned her screen around to show him her response. They shared a knowing smile before Shepherd stood and took her hand, "Care to dance, Mrs. Ryan?"

Laurel's heart fluttered. Luna, mate, wife, Mrs. Ryan. She loved all the terms that linked her to him. "I'd love to, Mr. Ryan."

After the New Year countdown, they left Matty and Charis at the bar and headed home. Laurel paused as she exited the elevator, eyeing Beck's apartment door but Shepherd, as if he were reading her mind, grabbed her hand and led her towards their apartment.

"No being nosy, Sunshine," he snickered.

"I just wanted to see if I could hear Susu's voice in there," Laurel complained.

"You may hear more than you bargained for. Leave them be. You'll see her tomorrow."

Laurel grinned up at Shepherd as he opened the door for her. "I guess this means Susu will be staying in Silver Moon," she said slyly.

Shepherd patted her rear as she walked past. "Sunshine gets her way again," he teased.

"Can you imagine them together? They're so different. And she's nothing like..." Laurel stopped herself.

Shepherd finished her thought. "She's nothing like Violet, you're right. But that doesn't mean they're not right for each other. Violet and Beck were both serious. Maybe Susu will balance him out."

Laurel nodded her head. "Yeah, you're right. Susu's parent's divorce really hurt her. I think she uses her humor as a defense mechanism. Maybe Beck will be good for her, too."

"The Moon Goddess works in mysterious ways."

Laurel didn't want to compare Susu to Violet. She loved them both. But they couldn't be more different. Violet was tall, slender, with pale skin and light features. Susu was short, athletic, with an olive complexion and dark hair. Violet was quiet, thoughtful, and serious. Susu was... none of those things. Laurel couldn't help but laugh when she tried to picture them in a relationship. She'd only ever seen Beck with Violet. This would be interesting. Laurel was too excited to go to sleep and had

The Dream

to resist the urge to text Susu. Once Shepherd snuggled beside her, she slowly relaxed and drifted off to sleep. Knowing that Susu was staying with Beck all night eased her excitement into a deep satisfaction. Silver Moon was always a wonderful place to live but it had just gotten even better.

In the dining hall, Laurel sat at their table with her breakfast and scanned the food line for Susu and Beck. Disappointed, she stuffed her French toast in her mouth and grumbled. Typically, she was a patient person. But she'd known Susu for eight years and had never seen her serious about a man. Her decisive text the previous night surprised Laurel and she desperately wanted to know what made Susu change her stance. Werewolves could be persuasive, certainly, but Susu was a human, not looking for a boyfriend, and typically took some convincing. There was the mystical draw that mates inherently felt. It was weaker for humans, but still felt. That could explain some of it, but even with Laurel's premonition, it had taken her time to accept it.

Susu had no warning and yet she'd left with Beck within minutes of their introduction. A cough disrupted Laurel's musings and she looked up to find Beck and Susu smiling at her from across the table. Beck was a foot taller than Susu. Laurel remembered when Susu told her in college that she liked shorter guys because she didn't want to get a crick in her neck smooching. She laughed under her breath as Beck set his tray down and then pulled a chair out for Susu, who was still watching Laurel's reaction.

"What are you laughing about?" Susu asked warily.

Laurel shook her head, "Nothing important. Sooooo, how are you two?"

Susu smiled up at Beck and he reached over to pull her chair closer to his.

"That good, huh?" Laurel laughed.

Shepherd joined them and after he sat down, nonchalantly commented, "The mark looks good on you, brother. Congratulations."

Laurel almost choked. She hadn't even noticed.

Beck reached over and pulled Susu's hair to the side so the table could see his mark on her. "Susanna's is more beautiful," he said, which made a warm blush rise to her cheeks. Susu wasn't one to blush, but she wore it well.

When Matty and Charis sat down a few moments later, Charis' nose wiggled. "Something is different," she said, suspiciously eyeing everyone at the table until her eyes settled on Susu. "No way." The table was silent for a split second before Charis squealed excitedly. "Didn't I tell you werewolves were better?! This is fantastic!"

Susu smiled shyly and Beck beamed. Laurel sat back in pleasant surprise at the differences she was seeing. She was sure that Susu would quickly become her brazen self again but the fact that love had hit her so fast and hard that she was speechless for the first time since Laurel had met her convinced her they were a good match for one another.

"I guess we'll be making a trip to NYC since we're stealing another resident from them?" Charis teased.

Beck shared a look with Shepherd, who glanced at Laurel before nodding to him. "Actually, that will have to wait. I returned last night because I received intel on the leader of the rogues. His name is Padraig O'Shea. He's a distant cousin of Shepherd's whose family was exiled many years ago, right before Beau became Alpha. He's on an ill-fated journey to regain his family's previous power and prestige. We believe he's trying to get close enough to challenge Shepherd for the position of Alpha and he's involved the other packs as a show of strength. Plus, successfully crossing several pack's borders to attack substantially grew his following. But we have a promising idea of where their hideout is, and we've called a meeting of the Ring of Alphas. They'll be here this afternoon." He looked at Susu with concern. "I'm sorry I didn't tell you last night, Susanna. It wasn't intentional. I was so overwhelmed with finding you, I didn't think of anything else." Susu's face was tense, but she allowed him to take her hand as he continued his update to the rest of the table, "There will have to be a battle. But with the help of the Perigee and Crescent Fang packs, Padraig doesn't stand a chance."

The Dream

Charis' eyes blazed with anger as she turned to Matthius. "You knew this was happening and didn't tell me?!"

Raising his hands in surrender, he assured her he'd just found out and reminded her that he'd left early to take them to the bar. Laurel didn't need to ask. Shepherd had known there would be a dangerous battle and had kept it from her. Her chair scraped loudly across the floor as she stood abruptly to leave. "Laurel, don't go," Shepherd said softly as he reached for her hand. She pulled it away from him and quickly made her way to the double doors to leave. She needed to clear her head.

It was Susu who found her in the garden.

"Hey there," she said as she joined Laurel at her table. "I won't ask what you're thinking about. I'm worried, too."

Laurel looked up at her. "I am worried but it's not just that. I know being in a pack means there are occasional dangers involved. But Shepherd didn't tell me. He had plenty of opportunities last night and he chose not to confide in me. We're supposed to be a team, Susu. He's repeatedly told me that I'm an integral part of this pack's leadership and yet my mate and my pack are going to be involved in a dangerous battle and he doesn't deem it necessary to include me in the decision making?"

Susu nodded in agreement. "Well, if I know you, you'll make your voice heard. He's been the Alpha of the pack for a long time and maybe he did what he's always done without even thinking about it. But you're right. That has to change now that you're together. You need to talk to him about it. He tried to come after you, but I told him to let me find you first. I needed to talk to my best friend."

Laurel smiled across the table at her. "I know. And I will talk to him. All those years I spent qualified to be in a higher position but I wasn't allowed to progress. That's not going to happen here. I'm a leader of this pack, too, and you know I'll remind Shep of that." Susu chuckled before Laurel continued, "There's another aspect of this, Susu. And I don't know if you remember me telling you about how my dad really died?"

"I remember. And Beck made sure I understood last night before he marked me. I know the risk."

"I hope you don't think I'm not happy for you and Beck. I really am. He's a great guy and now I get to have you here in Silver Moon with me. But I was really surprised you let him mark you so quickly. What happened last night?"

Susu crossed her legs in her chair and ran her fingers through her hair. "I know it was sudden. After what happened with my folks, I never wanted to be in a committed relationship. I couldn't trust that it would last and didn't want my heart broken. But when you got together with Shepherd, I'll admit I felt a yearning for that kind of love. For love, period, really. I've actually gone on quite a few dates since you left. You know, just putting myself out there more. When Beck told me that we were mates, that he felt an instant connection and love for me and never wanted to be separated from me, I decided to trust him. I've seen how Shepherd treats you. And although I've never thought much about god, the idea that someone…something… chose to connect Beck and I, maybe even before we were born just feels…beautiful to me. I'm willing to risk it. I'm all in, Laurel. I'm not going to let fear ruin this. As crazy as it sounds, he feels like home to me already."

Laurel's eyes sparkled with pride, "I'm happy for you, Susu."

There was a cough behind them, and they turned to see Beck and Shepherd. Beck held his hand out to Susu, who grinned at Laurel before standing. "Give him hell," she laughed before taking Beck's hand and walking back towards the pack house. Shepherd hesitated before joining her at the table. He sat silently for a moment, gauging her emotions, before he spoke.

"I'm sorry, Laurel. I was wrong."

She didn't relax or lower her gaze. "Strong start, Shepherd. But not good enough."

Running his hand over his face, he exhaled loudly. "I'm not sure what you want me to say, Laurel. I had to move quickly on this, so we contacted the other Alphas last night before we met up with you at the bar. And you know what happened then. I didn't want to ruin the night. It just became harder to say anything."

The Dream

She stared at him for a moment. She understood that it was a difficult situation but wanted to make sure he understood her expectations. "You said that as Luna, I was an important part of the pack. But you made a huge decision without me and then didn't even tell me about it. Felt a bit like you were Jim Thatcher in there."

Shepherd gulped at the comparison. "I didn't really think of it like that. I'm sorry, Laurel. I didn't mean to hurt you or exclude you. I'll do better next time. Sometimes split decisions have to be made but you have my word that, when at all possible, you'll be part of all future decisions. Will you join me for the Ring of Alphas meeting?"

Laurel didn't want to continue to fight, especially with danger coming so soon. And there was really nothing else that Shepherd could do at the moment. She reached across the table and took his hand. "Yes, I'll be there. I forgive you, Shep. But don't do it again. I'm part of this pack now and part of the leadership. I want to be treated as such. I may not be able to fight alongside you on the battlefield, but I have a good mind. Let me use it."

He stood and pulled her into an embrace, breathing in her scent. "I promise."

Tension was thick in the air as the leaders of the Silver Moon, Perigee, and Crescent Fang packs gathered in the conference room. When Whit entered, all eyes were on the two men who had previously fought. A couple of the men shifted towards Whit in order to step in if needed as Beck approached him. Whit's face showed no emotion as he maintained eye contact with Beck. When Beck reached him, he greeted him in a clear, strong voice that the entire room could hear.

"I owe you an apology for my actions at the last meeting. I've loved Violet since we were children, and my heart was broken. Violet always wanted to find her fated mate and I'd just like to say that, as usual, she was right. I've since found my mate as well and she's healed my heart. Please accept my belated congratulations. I wish you and Violet the absolute best," he finished as he extended his hand to Whit, who nodded with a smile as he gripped Beck's forearm.

"I accept your apology and hold no ill will. I understood your actions. But Violet will be very relieved to hear that you're well and wish us happiness."

There was a visible relief that washed over the room as everyone took their seats. Shepherd made eye contact with Beck and gave him a nod of appreciation. They needed everyone to focus on the issue at hand.

Following the meeting, everyone returned to their respective packs. The plan was a fast-moving one. Each pack would leave enough warriors to protect their pack in case of a rogue attack. But the majority of their warriors would participate in the battle so they could end it swiftly. They would meet at a location close to the rogue headquarters in two days' time and attack from all angles. Each team was assembled and knew the route they'd take. The distance would be longer for certain warriors and the fastest wolves were put into those groups. When the farthest group reached their spot, a howl would alert the other groups and they would attack at once, surrounding the rogues and attacking without hesitation or mercy.

Laurel wasn't happy with the situation but knew she was out of her element. She appreciated Shepherd inviting her. There were no other Lunas present but if any of the other Alphas were surprised or offended at her presence, they didn't make it known. The unanimous agreement that battle was necessary relieved her uncertainty and their confidence in the plan gave her some comfort.

It was evident at dinner the following evening that everyone shared Laurel's anxiety over the upcoming battle. It had been a long time since the pack had anything other than remote skirmishes. But they were trained well and had remained strong and prepared. They were ready for this. After everyone settled in with their food, Shepherd stood and motioned for Laurel to join him. All eyes were on him.

"Silver Moon, tomorrow we will gather our warriors and join the Perigee and Crescent Fang packs to end our common enemy. Your Luna and I don't take this decision lightly. We would never put any of you in harm if it weren't absolutely necessary. But we will not live in

The Dream

fear. Tomorrow, we will show any who may be watching what happens when you mess with the Silver Moon pack. Our warriors are fierce and determined. We will return to you with victory." Everyone beat their fists on their tables in unison to show their support until Shepherd raised his hands and spoke again. "Tomorrow, we meet in front of the pack house at dawn. Because there will be limited guards here, we ask that all remaining pack members come to the pack house at dawn and remain until we can ensure your safety. It's not an order but if you remain in your homes, it's at your own risk. Tonight, eat well, laugh with your friends, read to your children, and make love to your mates."

A roar of approval met his words, and he leaned down to kiss Laurel before they both sat down to dinner. Rowan joined their table, which was unusual, and after the room had settled, he leaned over to Laurel. "Your aunt is a most interesting woman. I hope she enjoyed her trip to Silver Moon. Have you heard from her?"

Laurel tried to keep her face passive but heard Shepherd snort beside her. She found his foot under the table and kicked him. "Lucy's great. She called to let me know she'd arrived home safely. She really enjoyed her visit and the town." She paused. Rowan had certainly been a thorn in her side at times, but she still cared for him and didn't want him to get his hopes up if there was an attachment to her aunt. "As much as she liked it here, I'd be surprised if she visited very often. She's attached to her land in Oregon. I was surprised she visited at all, to be candid with you."

Rowan nodded, "Yes, I can admire the love she has for her land."

She gave him a moment to see if he'd continue the conversation, but he didn't take the subject further. Laurel wanted to ask what their relationship was, but his line of questioning hadn't opened an opportunity. She sighed in frustration. Between Lucy and Rowan, it wasn't likely she would ever discover what happened between them.

Before long, Shepherd leaned over to ask if she was ready to head home. The way his voice tickled her ear sent shivers down her spine and she caught her breath before nodding and pushing her chair back. His loud voice boomed across the room, "Until tomorrow, warriors of the

Silver Moon pack!" Clapping, shouting, and howling sounded across the room. The buzz of anxious excitement was palpable in the room as they left through the double doors.

As soon as the elevator doors closed behind them, Shepherd pulled Laurel against him, wrapping his arms tightly around her waist. "I love you," he breathed into her hair. "More than anything else in the world. You're everything to me."

She leaned her head back against his shoulder as he pressed his hard rod into her backside. She moaned softly. "I feel the same, Shep."

He groaned and released her as the elevator opened on their floor. Before she could take a step, he swept her up bridal style and carried her into their apartment. Using his foot to kick the door closed, he carried her to their bed and gently set her down. He knelt before her and studied her face, using his fingers to gently trace her features as if he were memorizing them. Cupping her jaw, he leaned in and kissed her deeply, his tongue taking ownership of her mouth. He kissed her long and deeply, savoring the sensation. The feel of his hand on her face and his lips against hers were enough to create a pool of desire between her thighs and she pressed herself closer to him.

He understood and grabbed her gently by the waist, bringing her firmly onto the middle of the bed. He quickly shed his shirt and pants while she shimmied out of her sweater and jeans and tossed them to the side. Reaching behind her to unfasten her bra, he immediately lowered himself to suck her breasts, his teeth gently tugging at her nipples as she whined. Her core was throbbing for him, and she grabbed his hair to bring him back to her mouth. Lowering himself, he rubbed his shaft against her wet slit, coating it in her arousal and making her moan in anticipation. He tugged at her bottom lip as he watched her face in the throes of passion.

Pulling away, he traced her face down to his mark on her shoulder, across her taut nipples and down her hips, relishing the noises she made at his touch. He straddled her hips and flipped her onto her stomach, spreading wet kisses down her back to her hips as she moved against the sheets, waiting for him to enter her. He pulled her legs apart and

The Dream

positioned himself on her slit, slowly moving in as she raised her hips, wanting more of him. Laurel grasped the sheets as he stretched her. All her nerves were alive and tingling as he moved in and out of her, finally reaching above her to grasp the headboard for leverage to fuck her harder.

"You feel so good, Love. Your pussy was made for me."

His coarse voice sent tingles through her channel so that he could feel the vibrations of her arousal and moaned appreciatively. Every bit of her felt like it was on fire, and she begged him for more as her climax built into a heated frenzy. He thrust into her harder and faster, her cheeks clapping from the force of his movement, until they both climaxed. Shepherd rested slightly on top of her, putting most of his weight on one arm as the other arm wrapped around to massage her clit. Her body was still reeling from her orgasm and shook at his touch, but he didn't relent. His cock still filled her channel and he thrust slowly into her as he continued to flick and rub her clit. "Shepherd," she moaned. Her body felt heavy but the tremors from his touch on her sensitive bud sent jolts of pleasure throughout her body. She moved against him as he repositioned her, cradling her from the side. He draped her leg over his to give him more access to her clitoris as he continued to slowly thrust into her. Moving her hair to the side, he sensually kissed her mark. It didn't take long for her to come a second time, reaching behind her to grab his hair as she screamed his name. This time he rested, pulling her as tightly against him as was physically possible.

"Promise me you'll come back to me, Shepherd."

He held her so closely that she could hardly breathe. "I promise, my Love."

Chapter 14

When they awoke, it was still dark outside, and they were hesitant to leave the comfort of their beds. Instead, they held each other and talked quietly. Laurel rested against him as he lay on his back, caressing her hair as he stared at the ceiling.

"You know, growing up, I always imagined what my mate would be like. And Sunshine, I never could have imagined you. You have improved my life in every way. When I saw you that day on the street, your red hair glowing in the morning sun, those long legs that I wanted wrapped around me more than I've ever wanted anything before… it was all I could do not to drop to my knees right there in the middle of the street and thank the entire universe for you. But you're so much more than that. You're sharp as a whip, your nature is giving and nurturing, your words direct and clear. I couldn't have asked for a better mate. I just want to make sure you know how much I appreciate you accepting me and my pack. You've made us all better."

She leaned onto her elbow, letting his blonde hair run through her fingers. "I really do believe my dad gifted me that dream so that I'd recognize you and open my heart. I was always hesitant to give myself completely to anyone, but I couldn't possibly have given you anything less. The whole time you knew we belonged together, but you were so patient while I learned to trust myself. I've never felt more loved or protected than when I'm with you. It's a life I never could have imagined for myself, but I wouldn't give it up for anything." She paused her caresses and looked deeply into his forest green eyes. "I can't lose you, Shepherd."

He leaned up to kiss the tip of her nose. "I'll do everything in my power to ensure you don't."

Eventually, they couldn't put off the inevitable any longer. As they closed the door to their apartment, they saw Beck and Susu also leaving their apartment. Their expressions matched the grimness on Shepherd and Laurel's faces. They were silent as they got onto the elevator.

Just before the door closed, they heard Matty's voice. "Hold the door." They pressed the button and Charis and Matty climbed in. "Nice and cozy in here," Matty joked. "You assholes ready to rumble?"

Laurel couldn't help but smile.

Shepherd pushed Matty playfully on the shoulder, "Beck can ride with you. I can already see you're going to get on my nerves."

Beck shoved his other shoulder as he broke into a smile, "No way. You're not saddling me with Matty today. Put him with the new recruits."

"Hey, hey, hey brothers. Take it easy! No one appreciates me."

Charis snorted, "No, we just all know you!"

Matthius turned to her and gave her an evil eye as the doors opened onto the first floor, "You're supposed to be on my side," he grumbled.

She pinched his rear as they stepped out of the elevator. "You know I'm always Team Matthius."

Shaking his tush, he chided, "Hey, watch the rump. That's valued property."

Tables were set up with to-go breakfasts and lunches. Everyone gathered quickly and before Laurel had time to cry, they were gone. The remaining pack members stood outside and watched them drive away before silently going inside. They knew it would be a long day. The pack house was more crowded than usual since it now held most of the families and elderly as well. After breakfast, Laurel stood to announce the areas that were safe to go. They'd opened the event venue for more room and set up toys and play equipment for the kids. The training facility was closed but there was still the pool and gardens. The library brought books and hammocks were set up on the grounds closest to the pack house so there was plenty of room to relax. There were already pack members curled up in them, looking at their phones or reading.

The Dream

Laurel made her way to an empty table. She'd been thinking about what she wanted out of her relationship with Shepherd. Rowan had really gotten under her skin pressuring them to start a family. Shepherd quickly dismissed it, but Laurel had been turning it over in her mind ever since. At first, she wondered if it was her duty as Luna. She saw the hope in her pack's expressions when Rowan brought it up and she hated to deny them anything. But she knew those reasons were not enough motivation to bring a child into the world.

It had happened slowly once the idea had taken root. But this morning, when they were talking about their relationship and their future, she'd felt it. She wanted it all with Shepherd. It hadn't been the right time to tell him; she didn't want to distract him when he was about to be in more danger than she cared to imagine. But she was sure now. She wanted the babies that came from her and Shepherd's love. She smiled at the thought before bringing her phone out to call her aunt.

"Laurel! I'm so glad you called! How are you?"

Laurel leaned back and propped her feet in the opposite chair. "Hey Aunt Lucy. Just trying to distract myself and thought it would be a good time to call and chat."

"Distract yourself from what, honey? Are you and Shepherd doing okay?"

"Yeah, we're great. We've been having an issue for months with rogues crossing the borders and attacking the pack. They figured out where their headquarters are and went with a couple of neighboring packs to end it. They're confident they'll be successful, but I can't help worrying he'll be hurt…or worse. I hate this feeling."

"Why didn't you tell me there was an issue with rogues?"

"Well…I wasn't sure that you'd understand that most rogues aren't good since dad wasn't like that. And I didn't want you to worry."

Lucy sighed. "Laurel, I'm a big girl. You should've told me. It's my job to worry and I want to know if something is bothering you." She paused before continuing. "Is Rowan fighting?"

Laurel's eyes widened and she broke into an amused smile. She was thankful that Lucy didn't like video calls. "No, he's here. They left quite a few men behind to protect the pack." She could feel Lucy's relief over the phone and ventured a question. "Is there something going on between the two of you?"

The silence on the other end of the line seemed to stretch on forever. Laurel winced. She didn't want to be nosy. She knew her aunt was a private person. But her curiosity was overwhelming.

Lucy finally spoke. "I'm not sure. We got to know each other pretty well when I visited. He walked me to the hotel almost every night and we'd talk for longer and longer each night. I don't know. I like him. And he likes me. We'll see where it goes."

"So, does that mean you'll be visiting me more often?"

Lucy groaned, "It's possible. You know I don't like to leave home. I don't want you to mention it to anyone but he's coming to stay with me for a couple of weeks the end of the month."

Laurel was unable to hide her surprise. "Really?!"

"Don't sound so shocked, Laurel," she chided.

"It's just that I can't imagine it. But I'm excited for you. Both of you."

"Well, don't get too excited. We're taking it slow."

"I get it…and I won't say anything to him about it. But can I tell Shepherd? Please?"

Lucy sighed, "Yes, you can tell Shepherd. No one else. Especially not Charis. That's Rowan's call."

"I think Charis would love for her dad to find someone. But absolutely, that's his place. I won't say a word."

They shifted the conversation back to more mundane topics before ending the call. Laurel headed back to the pack house to check on everyone. Besides the children, everyone was quiet and distracted. She joined a group watching a movie, but she couldn't focus on it. Everyone had the same worried look on their faces. Shepherd promised to call when it was over, and Laurel found herself compulsively checking her phone. She was staring at the screen when Susu and Charis joined her on the couch, all but squishing her in the process.

The Dream

"How are you holding up, sister?" Charis whispered on the slim chance that anyone was paying attention to the movie.

Laurel shrugged.

"Me too," Charis said.

"Me three," Susu chimed in.

For the rest of the afternoon, they shifted from one activity to another, none of them holding their attention. Finally, Laurel's phone rang. Everyone in the common room froze and looked up at her with anxious expressions.

"It's Shepherd!" she announced as she put him on speaker. "Shepherd?!"

His voice was ragged but he managed to laugh. "Of course, it's me, Sunshine. And I'm all in one piece. It's over and we were successful. The rogue problem has been resolved."

Everyone let out a collective sigh of relief.

"Is everyone okay?"

"Our plan went flawlessly. We suffered no losses. There are injuries, some serious, and we're stabilizing them before we head back to our packs. But I think they'll all make it."

"What a relief!" she exclaimed as those around her hugged each other and high-fived.

"It'll be a while before we get back to the pack house. It will be tonight, but it'll be late. I didn't want you to worry."

"We're all just so thankful. I love you, Shepherd. I can't wait to see you."

"Same, Sunshine. I need to get back. Can you make sure everyone gets updated?"

"Absolutely!" She took him off speaker before lowering her voice, "I'll see you soon, Alpha." She heard his low growl over the phone.

"Can't wait," he responded before ending the call.

The atmosphere at the pack house immediately shifted. Laughter and conversation resumed, and the crowds thinned out as families returned to their dwellings. Laurel felt a nervous energy as she waited for Shepherd. She'd never feared for his life before. It gave her clarity on what she wanted. Though he'd never pressured her, she knew he wanted children. He'd been waiting for her for a long time before they met and had plenty of time to imagine their life together. But for her, Shepherd had been a whirlwind romance. Now she knew what she wanted. And she couldn't think of a better celebration of the pack's victory than to share that she was ready to start a family.

A few hours after dinner, a large group was waiting on the front porch when headlights appeared. They stood in anticipation as the cars pulled into the circle drive and stopped. Laurel ran forward to meet Shepherd as he stepped out of the car. He grasped her waist tightly, nuzzling his face into her neck. All around them, couples and friends were embracing. Shepherd pulled away but held onto her hand.

"I'm going to make an announcement in the dining hall if you all want to meet me there." As he led her up the steps, she took the moment to look him over. His clean clothes indicated he'd changed before coming home but she could still see deep gashes on his forearms. She reached up to touch them and he turned to smile softly at her. "I'm alright."

Once they were standing in the dining hall, Shepherd's strong, confident voice carried easily across the large space.

"Silver Moon pack, whether you're present or hearing me through the link, thank you for sending us off with your complete trust. It was because of you that we were victorious today. Our love for you and our desire to protect the beautiful community and relationships we have here drove us to fight harder than we've ever fought before. While we must always be diligent to protect our borders, today's triumph lifts the burden of the daily stress we've been under for the past few months. In groups of two or more, the border land can be enjoyed again. If peace continues, as we expect it to, we'll lift those restrictions as well. While we didn't lose any of our warriors, there were multiple injuries, some worse than others. We have quite a few warriors at the hospital. Please make sure you help in any way possible with the care of their homes and children while they recover." The pack respectively bared their necks to Shep as he took Laurel's hand to leave.

The Dream

Back in their apartment, Laurel stood on her tippy toes to give Shepherd a kiss.

"I need to take a shower, Laurel. We used a creek to wash off the blood, but I need soap before I hold you too closely."

Laurel nodded and followed him into the bathroom. She imagined battle was a bloody affair but when he'd returned in fresh clothes, she had allowed herself to accept a cleaner version of the day's events. She didn't like to imagine him killing others, although she knew this situation forced his hand. He grunted as he pulled off his shirt and Laurel gasped as she saw a deep cut, grossly stitched, across his abdomen.

"Shepherd, we need to have this looked at!"

He smiled down at her, "No, Love. There are worse injuries that need the doctor's attention. Besides, I'm a werewolf. I heal fast. This will barely leave a scar."

She lightly brushed her fingers near the area. "Did you stitch it yourself?"

He chuckled, "No. Matty did it. And he was pretty proud of himself so don't say anything to him."

He began to unbutton his pants, but she took over, "Let me. You don't need to bend over with this cut."

He shook his head but allowed her to remove his pants. As he turned to step into the shower, she saw his back littered with cuts and bruises. She tried to muffle a sob, but Shepherd heard.

"Alphas are always a target in battle, Sunshine. It's just part of the job. If the Alpha is killed, their pack is easier to defeat. I'm a strong fighter so you don't need to worry about me," he said with a wink.

Laurel took the soap and gently washed his body. She tried to shampoo his hair, but it was a reach. Kneeling in front of her, he took her hips in his hands and leaned his head against her stomach as she massaged his scalp. His head resting on the place where she hoped their future children would grow made her smile.

"Shepherd?" He raised his head to look up at her. "I've been thinking about starting a family ever since Rowan brought it up." He looked ready to interrupt but she placed her finger on his lips, silencing him. "And when you were in danger, everything became clear to me. For years, I let fear keep me from admitting I wanted to be a mother. I'm not afraid anymore. I trust you fully. Just because we may lose something isn't a reason not to have the beauty of the thing in the first place. I accepted before that our love was worth the risk of the mate bond keeping us together, even in death. But because of what happened to me as a child, I couldn't picture having a baby. But the thing is, all of life is precarious. That's why we should let love rule. Take risks. So that we can have a full life. I want it all. With you. I want to start a family."

A tear escaped Shepherd's eye as he stood, pulling her against him. "Are you sure? I'm in no hurry. You're enough for me."

She squeezed him in appreciation. "I'm sure. I've already thrown away my birth control pills."

He picked her up, trying to hide the grimace on his face from his injuries.

"Shepherd, put me down! You're hurt."

He broke into a grin. "I did forget about that for a minute. But now that you're here, nothing hurts. Kiss me, Laurel."

She let her hands run through his wet hair as she leaned down to kiss him. The water from his hair dripped down her nose as she tried to convey all the love that she had for him through the kiss. He deepened it and she instinctively grinded against his member as he moaned into her mouth, gripping her ass. Pressing her firmly against him, he carried her to the bed, and brought her down gently, never releasing her. The bed was wet from their shower and neither of them cared. They just needed each other. The warmth from their kiss spread throughout Laurel's body and she kept her legs wrapped around his hips as she moved against him. With one hand keeping his full weight off Laurel, he used his other hand to cup her face as he continued their kiss. It felt like they could never get enough of each other. She broke their kiss briefly.

"Shepherd, I want you now," she breathed as he kissed her chin before returning to her mouth.

His hand moved down to her breasts, kneading her nipples as she whimpered, pressing even harder against his shaft. His hand slid down

The Dream

to her sex, spreading her wetness along her slit before sliding a finger in to stretch her.

"Goddess, you're so wet."

"I'm ready for you, Shep. Please," she begged.

He plunged in two fingers, only moving a few times before using his fingers to coat his dick. He leaned back down, taking possession of her mouth again as he slid slowly into her. Her body flared to life as she felt him stretch her walls. Once she'd taken every inch of him, he pleasured her with steady strokes. She could feel the crown of his cock throbbing and it felt as if he was kneading her pussy with it. He wanted to be mindful of every moment, every sensation of her tight pussy pressing against his shaft, every time her nipples brushed against his chest as he penetrated her, the look of complete euphoria on her face that he knew was mirrored on his own. The ecstasy built between them, and he leaned in for a kiss, his strokes becoming more erratic as the molten heat in his core ignited. She moaned into his mouth, almost immediately breaking their kiss as she threw her head back, releasing her orgasm. Shepherd plunged into her, howling her name as he gave in to his completion.

He sighed and rested his forehead against hers before rolling over onto his back, bringing her to rest against his chest. They both lay, breathing heavily, and enjoying the blissful feeling. Before long, Laurel could tell by his breathing that Shepherd had fallen asleep. The wet sheets now felt cold, but she didn't want to wake him. She knew he was exhausted. She leaned to the edge of the bed and grabbed the blanket, covering them both as she laid back against his chest and sighed contentedly before closing her eyes.

She breathes in the smells of the forest as she walks down the path. The light filters through the trees and she feels a soft breeze rustle through the leaves and against her face. A deep peace rests within her and she stops, smiling as she takes in the scene around her. Suddenly, a squeal interrupts her meditations, and she turns to find the source. A small child is running toward her. Shepherd follows behind him with a little girl riding on his shoulders.

"Wait for us, Mommy! We want to hike, too!" she yells as Laurel kneels to embrace the boy who crashes into her arms.

Shepherd's voice cuts through gently but firmly, "James, you know Mommy can't pick you up."

"I know, I'm just giving her a bear hug, Dad."

His tiny hands release her, and she stands as Shepherd and the little girl approach her, Shepherd's hand reaching out to rub her belly. Her own hand comes to rest on top of his on her protruding stomach. "Be careful with our little one, Love. We don't want them coming early."

He releases her stomach and cups each side of her face as he leans in to kiss her. She feels the familiar tingling spread through her body as she relaxes into his touch.

"Ew, Daddy!"

Shepherd and Laurel laugh as they break their kiss and look over at the little boy, who appears restless and impatient at their show of affection. "Can we hike now?"

"I think it's nice. I want a man just like Daddy when I grow up," the little girl sighs.

"And that will be a long, long time, Millie Rose."

Laurel chuckles at his tone before grabbing his hand and turning back to the path.

"Alright! Let's go hiking."